THE ACTING PRESIDENT

THE HUNT SERIES BOOK 7

TIM HEATH

Copyright © 2020 by Tim Heath

All rights reserved.

No part of this book may be reproduced in any form or by any electronic or mechanical means, including information storage and retrieval systems, without written permission from the author, except for the use of brief quotations in a book review.

❦ Created with Vellum

ALSO AVAILABLE BY TIM HEATH

Novels:

Cherry Picking

The Last Prophet

The Tablet

The Shadow Man

The Prey (The Hunt #1)

The Pride (The Hunt #2)

The Poison (The Hunt #3)

The Machine (The Hunt #4)

The Menace (The Hunt #5)

The Meltdown (The Hunt #6)

The Song Birds

The Acting President (The Hunt #7)

The Black Dolphin (The Hunt #8)

The Last Tsar (The Hunt #9)

The 26th Protocol

The Penn Friends (Books 1 & 2)

A Boy Lost (Books 1 & 2)

Short Story Collection:

Those Geese, They Lied; He's Dead

PROLOGUE

Trial Verdict
Six Months From Now

The room was abuzz with whispers, rumours, comments. Heads turned with every opening of the door, though the Judge was still outside, the verdict still being discussed.

Most knew the defendant was guilty.

Journalists took all available seats high above, those with pencils in hand scribbling snatched sketches of the scene below them, the forlorn accused, stripped of former power, exposed for crimes few knew about, now surely about to pay for them. Other reporters made fast notes, taking in the atmosphere, jotting down thoughts for the following morning's front pages.

This story would be certain to lead the front pages of most newspapers across the country, and probably further still. The repercussions took it cross-border, at least.

On the dot of the hour at noon, the doors behind the bench opened once again, the Judge leading in the other officials, and the room fell silent, deathly still, as anticipation grew, the verdict decided.

Minutes later the defendant stood, those watching from the sides taking down the details––in written and artistic format––of what was surely the closing moments of a trial that had gripped the nation.

The fall from grace had been spectacular, losing all possessions––considerable wealth by anybody's standards––remarkable.

"Will the defendant please stand," the Judge ordered, total control of the courtroom, his word final as it had been all trial.

"I understand you wish to make a new plea?" the Judge enquired, head turned to the defendant, a low murmur beginning to circle the venue, as the anticipation of what might be about to happen moved between those watching.

"I do," came the reply, the tone sombre, possibly even repentant.

"And how do you plead to all these crimes they have presented you with?" the Judge beckoned.

"Guilty," came the instant reply, the eyes showing a flash of something––was that sadness, was that shame?––as a wave of noise spread around the courtroom like a wildfire through dry grass.

1

Last Year

Arkady closed the door behind him, the heat oppressive--he wasn't in Russia anymore--the food was different. He'd been two days in the country and knew the adjustment would take much longer.

His hotel was cheap, which suited him for the time being. At least it had air conditioning. The small table between two wooden chairs stood covered in papers, information Arkady had been working through before he'd gone to buy more cigarettes.

His army jacket hung in the wardrobe, the door ajar, the insignia visible--two red lines with three stars on them, two stars at the bottom, the third above and between the lines. *Colonel, Russian army*. He'd made that rank the previous year, twelve months before all hell had broken loose and he'd fled the Motherland.

He had not left empty-handed, however.

Arkady returned to the table, placing the packet of cigarettes on the edge of his bed, ignoring the photo framed on his dressing table of a truckload of soldiers smiling at him. His unit, a photo he couldn't look at any more, though it was something he took with him wherever he went. A reminder to him.

A needed wound.

He leafed through the paperwork, Kremlin letterheads aplenty, top secret memos flagged in printed Cyrillic warning all against leaking any of them. Arkady had no other intention.

He sat down, banging his elbow on the edge of the table, the pain of contact of wood to bone multiplied by the heavily bandaged burns on his arms which had yet to heal. He swore in his native language, the flow of words rich and vulgar, as he cradled his arm to his chest, the pain subsiding enough after half a minute to let go. He would leave the bandages in place for the moment, already aware he would carry the scars with him for life.

His one suitcase lay on the floor next to the door, his sole possessions when he arrived in the country, though he'd purchased a few clothes since. His uniform was merely a memento. He couldn't wear it, not this side of the ocean.

Arkady glanced up, looking across his bed towards the far wall–– a clock, window and the air-conditioning unit housed in proximity to each other. He took in the view: the Statue of Liberty, as clear as he'd ever seen it, a boat passing along the water underneath, the edges of part of the city visible beyond.

Inside that concrete jungle he would need to find someone. Somebody he trusted, somebody to whom he could pass on the information on his desk. Someone able to get it into the right hands, safe hands.

Locating such a person had to be his main priority now. He'd done the hard bit, the pain in his arm reminding him of his past once more, that picture of his unit ever before him, ever in his thoughts and dreams. It had to all matter, had to all be for a reason. He opened his phone and continued his search for the perfect contact.

Moscow City Court, Russia
Present Day

THERE WERE no camera bulbs flashing as she stepped from the car, Svetlana Volkov––she still carried her husband's name despite the split of four years ago––reaching the foyer and gracing the carpet leading into the building. It was no red carpet, however. Those days were long behind her now.

She was the President, the stand-in even if only for the time being. She wanted to become the first elected female President of Russia. The next week would see if they took that chance from her.

Rad's team flanked her on every side; he'd given the venue the once over the previous day. Radomir Pajari––Russia's best sniper for a generation––had been on her payroll to head up security from the day she took over. He was not present himself being at home with his wife.

"Ms Volkov," the man said, now inside the entrance to the Court of Moscow. She would get addressed by many titles on the five-minute walk into the court room, all polite, all variations. Not one of them using the word *President*.

She was just the substitute, the replacement for Filipov, who'd become the first assassinated sitting President of Russia. She knew all about that.

Except she was still there. She'd hung on for three years, acting out her boldest role yet, something that put even her Hollywood career into the shade. She was made for this. And she wanted to stand in her own right in an election, called early, perhaps even within months of the hearing.

As she walked the corridors––she was not under arrest, there were no charges, yet––she couldn't help feeling like a criminal. She'd done nothing wrong, nothing they could have found out about yet at any rate.

Her white fur coat trailed behind her as she walked, her pace confident, her shoulders relaxed. She carried an air of sophistication.

Yet they were threatening to take all this away from her.

The man she was following stopped in front of a pair of solid wooden doors, the inscription telling her this was where her fate would be decided. The man opened the door, stepping to one side, allowing Svetlana to enter first.

At the front of the room was a long bench, of a legal type. This was the Law Courts, though today this was the only chamber in session. Four men sat behind the bench, judges she knew about from the files, though she'd met none of them. Her team sat to the right, facing the bench of judges. On the other side of the central aisle, as Svetlana walked in from the doors and towards the front, sat the opposition. These men and women who wanted to expose Svetlana, to accuse her of something––anything would do, it seemed––and thus land something on her. Any criminal charge or indiscretion would be enough to remove her from the running. Nobody with a criminal conviction could stand for the Presidency. It was why nobody was speaking of Dmitry Kaminski anymore. He'd been in third place at the last election, the election Filipov had won.

Both he, and the runner-up were now in prison.

Svetlana didn't glance at the people on the left, instead gracefully taking her seat in the centre of the group which had been waiting for her. This was her show, despite the surrounding experience. She would not let these judges get the better of her.

All four judges were men. Despite her run in office, despite three years of championing the cause of women, of challenging the mindset in her homeland, there were still no senior female judges in Russia. She knew they could not make progress overnight, but if given the green light to stand, her team had Svetlana leading the polls comfortably. The fact there were more women in Russia than men helped in this matter.

"All rise," someone called, official procedure followed that week, despite this being a closed door hearing.

"Ms Volkov," the lead Judge said, his voice calm yet authoritative. "As you know this is a closed hearing. Everything we discuss in these four walls is subject to confidentiality and bound by the law of this nation we serve. You are not here as a criminal, though these are law courts. We have convened this hearing, together with my esteemed colleagues either side of me to bring before you several allegations which, should we find have weight, might in fact lead to a criminal prosecution." He paused for effect. They all knew why they were there. She couldn't help but detect a smugness on the face of the Judge at that last comment. He didn't like the thought of her being their next elected President. She already detested them all. It reminded her of her first big break in acting and what a similar lineup of men had made her do for it.

"I can assure you, I've done nothing that could disqualify me from standing at the next election."

A man from the group on the other side of the aisle choked on his tea. The four judges looked at one another, as everyone took their seats.

"Over the next few days," the Judge started, it still unclear to them all how long the hearing would last, "both sides will have the chance to have their voice heard." The other party had called the hearing, the Judge putting a lid on anything they might have leaked to the press so that the allegations would only get discussed behind closed doors for the time being. It would not look good for Russia if they proved these allegations true.

"I object, sir," said the head of Svetlana's legal team. "As we know this hearing is nothing but a ploy to stop our President from running at the upcoming election."

"I remind you, Counsel, we are not in a show trial. You need not object and interrupt, as you will all have your chance. And she is the *Acting President*, let us not forget. The country has not voted her into office, yet," he said, adding the last word after a short pause, as if offering her a little hope, though his eyes contradicted his words.

Svetlana motioned her lawyer to sit down and he obliged. The Judge continued, confirming much of what they already knew. There were no journalists in the building, nothing was to be reported to anyone.

The Judge opened the floor for the other side to speak. Svetlana had met the Prosecutor once before, a week before they called the hearing. He had come to the Kremlin on an arranged visit and stated that he knew all about her dark secrets and that he would expose her. She'd learnt all she could about him those last seven days.

"Your Honour, there are few people on this planet today who carry the grace and elegance of this woman. Few who light up a room merely by taking a step through the door. We all know of her glittering career as an actress, we've all been fans of her for a long time, I do not doubt. But I understand a darker side exists under this most beautiful exterior, a side to this woman that I am shocked to discover. In public she shows one side of her nature. I'm here today to question and expose the side we do not see, the side that I believe we need to see, need to know exists, need to know if it is true. Because if it is, your Honour, I believe she is a very dangerous woman, mixing with the most dangerous and vilest of people."

He stopped there and the Judge was silent for so long that it was another of the judges who spoke next.

"And? What are these allegations you bring?"

A quick glance at his notes and then the Prosecutor spoke. "Your Honour, I want to question Ms Volkov about her connection to Yuri Lagounov."

The four men behind the bench glanced at Svetlana as the name was mentioned, trying to read any signs that she recognised the name. There seemed none.

"Who?" she asked, right on cue.

2

The Cage––Outskirts of Moscow
Two Months After Filipov's Assassination

Yuri Lagounov's men watched him drive away. This wasn't something he would let them even see. This was his thing, and he was getting good at it.

The two cars parked outside the warehouse told Yuri that his guests were already there. Two oligarchs now waited for him inside. This gave Yuri a sense of power. He pulled into his space, getting out of the car and glancing around, making sure there were no prying eyes looking in his direction. They had dealt with the police, the FSB too––each oligarch pulling strings where they had the opportunity. He was sure not even the masses at the Kremlin knew anything about what was happening.

Yuri went in through the one door not boarded up, his appearance initially startling the men.

"Who are you?" Russia's eightieth richest man asked as the middle-aged former boxer walked in.

"This, gentlemen, is my show. I'm why you are here."

"You're Lagounov?" came the reply, the realisation setting in seconds after, the oligarch smiling at the thought as he took in the scars and the tattoo-laden arms.

"In the flesh," Yuri said, walking to the side of the cage that stood where the ring had once been. He'd converted the place a few months before, and held Russia's most recent official World Championship Fighting event there not long after, but had taken it off the market following the assassination of President Filipov. He'd spent a lot on the place, money suddenly free-flowing. No-one questioned where it came from. With a man like Yuri, it could have been any criminal activity.

It was, however, a recently discovered nearly endless pot of cash. He wouldn't tell anyone about it, not even the oligarchs present. He was in their league now, financially anyway, not that they would ever believe him.

The money had given Yuri an idea. He'd heard the rumours about the Games that his country's oligarchs played. Now he would go one better.

Both oligarchs had already put up the cash––their stakes in the game, something that made it a risk, and therefore a thrill. They'd selected their man––sometimes it was women who would fight, this time it was men––and agreed with this fighter his fee for performing. His fee for winning. Only one of the pair would win the prize, the loser––if he even could walk from the cage––left with nothing. The money that oligarch had put up for his losing fighter then going to the winning oligarch.

The twist, as there always had to be, was the winning fighter could select any amount he wanted from the computer, the transaction electronic and instant. They should select the amount agreed with the oligarch before the fight, using the stakes already put forward. The winning oligarch would receive the stakes from the losing oligarch, coming away from the successful event millions up. Only that losing Russian billionaire would have a financial hit.

That was unless the winning fighter got greedy. Told they could type in any amount––and nobody would take less than promised them––it was then a game to see if they would settle for what they agreed on. Should the winning fighter take more--these were still early days of these fights, this just the third one--then the winning oligarch's stake stood forfeit; he would have to pay double the difference to the losing oligarch who also got to keep his stake.

So the art was finding both a fighter who could win--because winning was always the goal--while finding someone who was also honest enough to stick to their prearranged agreement.

The first two fights had focused too much on getting an honest competitor. It led to a boring contest where nothing happened.

Yuri already sensed today was different. There was an edge between both oligarchs, a pairing he'd been keen to put against each other, Yuri well aware there was a history between the two men. Neither would want to lose this one.

"Have your fighters enter the arena," Yuri said, the instructions passed through moments later, and his face lit up as he saw the first of the two beasts leave his changing room.

Eddy Frank was six-five, one-twenty kilograms and built like a rhino. At forty-three, he was ten years older than his opponent, but what he might lack in youthfulness, he more than countered with experience. A former soldier turned streetfighter, Eddy was a New Yorker born and raised, and he'd agreed to come to Russia to fight for seven million dollars. It was an offer he couldn't refuse.

Baxter Bone emerged seconds later from the other side of the building, a towel draped over his shoulders, a swagger that spoke of confidence and arrogance. He'd lived in London his whole life, been inside various prisons for ten of his fifteen adult years, and had always mixed with the wrong crowd. He'd flown to Moscow via several cities to compete for five and a half million pounds which, with the crashing British currency, was worth about the same as his opponent. Neither knew the other man's amount, nor the fighter before him. They'd been kept apart until that very moment, and there was a visible show of strength from both men as they first clapped eyes on the other, like two lions sizing the other up.

Eddy had the muscle advantage, but Baxter hadn't survived the gangs of East London by dodging a fight. They had raised him on them.

They came to a standstill all but nose to nose, neither breaking eye contact with the other, Yuri himself stepping forward before anything might be about to kick off. He had a good feeling about this encounter.

"Gentlemen," Yuri addressed the men, switching to English, his accent strong––he sounded like every Russian villain in every American film. "You know the rules. You will enter the cage together, after which I will lock you both inside. I will then switch on the computer at the back of the cage. You merely need to be the first man able to enter the winning amount on the transaction page and I will send you the money. You remember what amount you are fighting for?"

Both men nodded, not breaking eye contact with their opponent. They couldn't forget such an amount easily.

"Very well, in you go," Yuri ordered, both men moving in through each of the doors, Yuri closing both behind them as the two oligarchs moved in closer, faces pressed against the wire for one final word to their fighter.

"Remember what you are fighting for, the amount we agreed upon. Keep that in mind," the Russian said, Eddy giving no response, his mind on the contest, his focus absolute.

Yuri moved to the other side of the cage, activating the screen for the computer, the keyboard reached through a small opening in the metal wire.

Eddy charged at Baxter without hesitation. His elbow smashed into the man's face, the nose spraying blood immediately. Drops splashed onto the oligarch, still close to the cage and he stepped back, surprised by the ferocity. It knocked Baxter to the ground, but this wasn't the first time someone had hit him like that, and he rolled away before Eddy's knee came crashing to the floor, the fight very much on.

Both oligarchs had taken three steps back, fear and excitement etched on their faces, Yuri switching his gaze from the two fighters to the Russians momentarily, thrilled always to see such wealthy men feeling genuine fear. He knew that look, knew what they were going through. Neither oligarch wanted to lose. Could they trust their fighter to deliver?

Over the next five minutes, the two men continued to attack each other. There were no time-outs in this contest, no respite. There were no rules. The only instruction was the first man who got to the computer and typed, got the money.

Both knew they had to down the other fighter before they could manage that.

The previous two fights had been lame affairs, the loser surrendering each time. Yuri knew neither man in the ring now would surrender. The oligarchs knew that too. This one might get nasty.

The crack was loud and clear, Baxter jumping two legged into the side of the American's leg, the bone snapping instantly. Eddy let out a cry, but his drive to continue kicked in moments later, his arms grabbing the Londoner, fingers gouging the eyes. Both oligarchs turned away, the fight now close, on the floor, hand to hand. Eddy wouldn't be able to stand, and when the adrenaline stopped, would need some serious help with that leg.

Yuri pressed his face ever closer to the cage. This fight was reaching its climax, and he still didn't know which way it would go.

London
Twelve Years Ago

CLIFTON NILES LEFT *the office before five that Friday night, nothing at all unusual with that. It'd been a long week, another seventy hours clocked up at the firm he owned, a firm he ran with his partner. She had run her own Venture Capital firm, as he had. Their coming together had been good for both brands and once both firms were in bed together—as were their owners by that stage—the merged business had seen massive growth. Niles & Spence was now one of the go-to firms in the City. They specialised in ultra-high risk, their terms harsh, their wealth vast.*

They understood what they were doing and as a couple, as a business empire, there seemed no stopping them.

That all changed with the women.

Soon the thrill of the business wasn't enough. It started with one affair, which was over before it got started, yet Clifton couldn't stop there. He was wealthy and successful, and everyone knew his name. Soon he was away as much as he was at home—a golf trip here, a business conference there, his partner Adele Spence left to run home base, that being the business. They had no children, no official plans to marry. Business was too good for such distractions.

Adele followed Clifton out of the building that Friday. She had just taken a call from one of his oldest friends, his golfing buddy, Clifton off to play yet another game. He'd become obsessed, it seemed overnight, with the sport. She loathed the game, but if it kept him happy and focused, she didn't mind. It hadn't detracted from what he did for the business. In fact, she saw it helped.

Taking the call, she assumed the friend was running late, or perhaps needing to call off that week's game. Yet he was calling from the Bahamas, his house undergoing major renovations. He'd been there for the last month, soaking up the sunshine, helping the build.

He'd not played golf with Clifton in over a month.

She was out of the door in seconds, Clifton only just leaving the building at street level and she reached the ground floor just in time to see him jumping into a taxi. She raced out, thankful to flag down another cab soon after, and in true Hollywood style, directed the driver to follow the vehicle in front.

Thirty minutes later they were on the edge of London, the council areas giving way to private homes, an area common with City workers because of the quick train connection from the nearby station. Adele paid the cabbie, generously tipping him and was just in time to see Clifton entering a large detached house. She was too late to see who had opened the front door and it had been shut by the time she was near enough to see anything.

She sat on a bench in the park opposite, waiting for his return. She knew there was another woman inside, sensed it in her gut as one does when going back to the doctor after a biopsy and fearing the worst.

An hour later they appeared at the door, the woman—barely that by the look of her—in a dressing gown. They kissed on the doorstep, something lingering between a quick peck and a longer kiss, and she watched Clifton walk down the front path with a spring in his step.

The bastard.

A week later he snuck out of the office again, once more supposedly playing golf with his Bahama-based buddy. It was late and Adele stayed on in her executive office alone, the office quiet, their roughly one hundred staff off enjoying the start to the weekend. The cleaning team would soon arrive, the security men on the doors until nine, but she would be out before they locked the building. Gone were the days when the pair would fool around the office after dark, the last to leave, roaming the corridors of their five thousand square-foot office as if it were the Garden of Eden.

Now temptation had come, a slippery serpent–bitch come to rain on her parade. Adele vowed that Clifton's fall would be catastrophic.

In the first of many late night sessions, she made financial transfers, made calls, pulled in clients to her own portfolio, a portfolio set up separately, unconnected to the current business, a portfolio that would remain hers when the inevitable happened.

And it would happen. She would pull the rug from under him if it was the last thing she did.

3

Moscow City Court, Russia
Present Day

"I've never heard of Yuri Lagounov," Svetlana confirmed, a member of her own team writing the name down as instructed. If someone was working outside their President's control, that was news to them and troubling at the same time.

The prosecution merely nodded. They'd expected the denial.

Svetlana sat there calmly now, her face relaxed.

"You do not know of a man by this name carrying out covert events around Moscow?"

She shrugged her shoulders. *Enough said, tell me what you think you know already.*

"Your Honour, Lagounov is a violent man, a man who has an evil desire for blood and pain. A man who puts on a show for the fun of it, who delights in aggression and violence."

"And what in god's name does he have to do with me?" Svetlana asked, on her feet suddenly now, her face flushed. She was angry the hearing was even taking place, let alone connecting her to whoever they believed Lagounov was and whatever they believed he was up to.

"I'll get to that in a moment," the Prosecutor merely said, before carrying on with what he had prepared that morning. "Someone has informed me that this criminal has been gathering together certain oligarchs, many of whom frequently attend Kremlin events, where foreign men and women get forced to fight against each other, the winner walking away with millions."

"Again, what does this have to do with Ms Volkov?" her lawyer asked.

"It involves State money, we believe."

"State money? Impossible. Nothing passes the treasury without approval by the President."

"*Acting* President," the Prosecutor corrected, "and that's my point. You must know something about it?"

"Well, you are mistaken," Svetlana said, taking her seat again, serene once more from her outburst of seconds before.

"And I second that," said another man, there because he headed up the state treasury. "While the President signs off everything we do, I'm personally fully aware of all our financial dealings, as you know." They did. He'd served under three Presidents already. "And I assure you I've never come across the name of Yuri," and he looked down at his notes before concluding, "Lagounov." It was true.

"Perhaps you need to check your sources?" the Judge proposed to the prosecutor.

"Your Honour, my source is legitimate," but he left it at that, looking across to Svetlana with delight in his eyes. He saw the flicker of hesitation that this caused the Acting President, the knowledge that someone might have spoken, someone she'd been working with, someone perhaps still working for her, yet willing to talk.

Still, this present situation made no sense to anyone there. Was there more they thought they had on her, or was it merely this one claim?

"If the money is not from the State, it's therefore from Ms Volkov's personal fortune." Everyone knew she was worth about two billion, before she'd taken office.

"Believe me, the money's tied up in other things," she said, dismissing the comment out of hand.

"Maybe I'm talking about another source," he said, his eyes boring into her. Panic filled Svetlana for a moment, the man's mouth moving, words flowing which took the conversation on, but she'd not heard anything. *Does he know about the money?*

The Judge stopped the man mid-flow, however, soon after.

"Do you have a firm connection between Yuri Lagounov and Ms Volkov?"

The Prosecutor paused for a moment, his mind heading down one track, before refocusing on what the Judge had asked.

"Your Honour, I'll get to that right away." He reached into his briefcase and took out copies of a paper giving one to each of the judges and dropping the final one in front of Svetlana's lawyer. "This is the arrest warrant issued a year ago for Yuri Lagounov. The man has since vanished, and they have made no arrest. You'll see at the bottom of the warrant that Svetlana Volkov signed it," the name circled on each sheet as if they could have missed it. It wasn't unusual for a President to sign such a warrant.

"This is what you are bringing against her?" the man to Svetlana's left countered.

"She claimed not to have heard the name before."

"You think she remembers the countless warrants she's signed over the last three years?" he asked, almost mockingly. He pulled a few sheets from his own briefcase. "There have been seven hundred and twenty-seven state legislations signed since President Volkov took office, forty-six treaties with other nations, countless resolutions with regional governments right across this country, and over four hundred arrest warrants, the criminals mostly captured already. Do you really think in her capacity as President of this vast nation we expect her to remember the exact details, and a name in this case, of every single one?" He threw his hands in the air for good measure, taking his seat in exaggerated exasperation, as if the whole idea had taken every ounce of energy from him. It was a splendid performance, something Svetlana would have been proud of herself.

The Prosecutor continued as if unperturbed. "They issued the warrant following two years of extensive surveillance. The CIA had contacted the FSB about concerns they had over an American citizen who had flown to Moscow. The man never returned. Naturally, the Security Service took the information seriously. Yet after all that work, and three days before that very arrest warrant was signed by Volkov," and he raised the copy in the air, pointing it towards the Acting President as he spoke, "a memo originating from the Kremlin itself was sent to Lagounov, warning him about the arrest. It appears he fled Moscow that very night, the warrant issued days after the man had vanished."

He passed the four judges a copy of the memo, this time not giving one to Svetlana's team, the four men taking in the information, which didn't have any name on it, save for the fact it purported to be from the Kremlin.

"Is this one of yours?" the Judge asked, holding up the memo, one of Svetlana's team standing up and going to collect it. He took it to Svetlana without saying a word, who with one glance saw it was one of hers, but nothing her team had ever known about.

"It's nothing I'm aware of, nor does it look like something my office would have sent," she said, calmly, her heart racing. There had to have been someone speaking to them, perhaps someone still in place at that moment. The thought sat badly in the pit of her stomach.

"Is that so?" the Prosecutor smirked, doubt painted as plain as day across his face.

"Where did you claim this came from again?" Svetlana asked, her effort to make the question sound casual, as if she didn't care about the answer, not lost on the Prosecutor.

"It's not only a where, but a who. We have a whistleblower."

New York City, USA
One Year Ago

Jeff McKay cleared the security check shortly after nine that morning. He was in the only Federal building he knew about, and though not the CIA themselves––their whereabouts in the city somewhat of a mystery––there were rumours they had a unit there. He was sure before the day was out, his information would get to them, regardless.

Located just a few blocks from his office, he'd slipped in there on his way to work that morning, nothing but a call to his secretary telling her he was first running an errand. Some errand. He didn't even know why he was there.

Contacted the week before, from someone he suspected to be in the USA, possibly also New York given their reference once to seeing the Statue of Liberty from their bed, he'd started to gather the information he was being sent.

Jeff was a freelance journalist who had travelled the world in his prime, though basing himself only in the US for the last decade. He still covered Russia, his stories covering their former Cold War counterpart. It was why he suspected they had chosen him, that and his likely proximity to where the whistleblower was hiding. Jeff was sure the Americans knew nothing about this mystery Russian––Jeff knew the nationality, knew the role the person claimed to have had, even if he didn't know the sex of the informant––but the information had checked out, his journalistic instinct telling him this was the real thing.

Someone had dirt on Svetlana Volkov and was prepared to share it with him.

Once he had shared it with the CIA, he was free to publish it. And he would, though he had to have the government on his side before he did.

They told Jeff to sit down, his request passed on that he wanted to speak to someone about highly confidential information. It was five minutes before they ushered him into another room, two men in suits waiting for him, names given but no sign which department they worked for, nothing.

They had to be CIA.

"Show us what you've got, Mr McKay," the lead officer said.

"Please, call me Jeff. A week ago an informant contacted me. He's Russian, claiming to have a lot of dirt on the Acting President, Svetlana Volkov," he said, adding her name as if they needed it. Everyone knew that the former actress now ran Russia.

"And this source is local?"

"Yes," Jeff said, after a brief pause.

"You've met with them personally?"

"No, everything gets handled electronically," and he left it at that. He wasn't about to tell them how and when, for fear of losing his exclusive access to his source. That would risk the information vanishing altogether. This person had seen the need to find him specifically. Jeff had to assume it was personal, because of his journalistic history, not just random. It had to be genuine.

"And they check out?"

"Yes," Jeff confirmed. If this was the CIA he was speaking to, and if the informant was local, it would be clear the CIA would check their records for all arrivals from Russia in the last few months. That would narrow down the search to a shortlist before long. Jeff didn't have the resources or reach to do anything himself and didn't want to risk his connection. He was happy to be on the inside of what could be one of the biggest stories of his long career.

"What do you have?" the officer said, now through the preliminaries. They had done this kind of thing a dozen times.

Jeff handed them a copy of the only piece of real information his source had sent him so far. The source claimed it was the reason he started gathering evidence at all.

"An American citizen, New Yorker at that, flew to Moscow nearly two years ago. Recruited by a local Russian group here in Manhattan, his visa was fast-tracked and he flew on a private jet owned by this man," and Jeff passed across another sheet, the oligarch's photo and a little information displayed at the top. The source had sent all this information to him.

"And?"

"He never returned."

"I see. Do we know what happened to him?"

"My source says they took him to an event organised by this man," and Jeff passed over another piece of paper, Yuri Lagounov's name and details given at the top, though there was no photo this time. The two agents looked knowingly at each other as soon as they saw the sheet, Jeff noticing immediately. He followed that thought with a question.

"You know this name?" he said, voiced in a way that suggested to them they had better not lie. He'd seen.

"Yes, we know the name. He reportedly did some unthinkable things in Chechnya under Putin. We've never been able to confirm anything. The Kremlin always denied all knowledge."

They sat in silence for a while.

"Well, now they can't stay silent. There is more to come, I'm certain of it. Like I said, it was this incident which caused my source to turn, and they started gathering information before leaving while they still had the chance. I believe they arrived here recently."

That gave the CIA a likely timeframe, closing the net considerably. They would go away and do their research, finally collecting a short list of five names of people with Russian heritage who had arrived into JFK airport the previous month. They would monitor these people, two agents put on each of them. They hoped to intercept the information ahead of Jeff. It worked better for them that way, no longer the last to know.

"I take it you'll publish this?"

Jeff paused, not because he didn't know the answer, but because he knew they might not like what he had to say. "Yes, but I wanted you to know first. You'll know everything when I know it. Anything too sensitive, I'll hold back from reporting."

"I see," the officer said.

Jeff didn't add that the source had given him another name, that of a hard-hitting Moscow Prosecutor who Jeff was to send the information on to.

They exchanged business cards.

"You can call us next time," the officer said, the three men now standing at the door. "It's secure, you need not come all the way here." It hadn't been that far, but Jeff preferred calling them rather than making too many return visits. It also confirmed his suspicions that this was the CIA as hoped. They shook hands, the two agents going back the way they'd come, Jeff safely returned to the entrance foyer. He pressed out onto the busy streets and jumped in a cab, despite his office being a matter of minutes away.

4

London
Eleven Years Ago

Adele Spence sat at their breakfast table that Saturday morning. Clifton had not come home the previous night, not the first time business had kept him away. Except, for the entire year, she knew exactly what type of business he got up to.

Across the table were photos, printed out and covering the entire surface of the wooden table, something that had served them over the years, countless meals shared at that very spot. Now it only displayed his sins, the women he'd been seeing, the lies he had been telling.

She was seething.

However, she wasn't going silently. Another business now existed and registered in her name, the client list carved from their current firm already building nicely. She'd drained the assets as best she could, the existing firm's future on a knife edge, an area Clifton had no direct interest in.

He soon would.

His car pulled up outside, the gravel telling of his return. Adele took one final gulp of the vodka, emptying the glass, the kick she needed. The door would soon open. This fraud of a man would soon walk in through their front door, a home they had shared for many years. Then it would kick off.

She heard the key first, the squeak of the hinges as the sturdy front door opened in on itself, the silhouette of Clifton, bunch of flowers in hand, case pulled behind him as he stepped in through the door. He called before seeing her in the kitchen, a glass in hand, her face reddened. She was drinking.

"I got these for you," he said, holding out the flowers. Still she didn't move, her eyes murderous, her gaze fixed. "You okay?" he asked, taking one step into the room, then another, his eyes spotting the photos: the evidence, his many affairs.

She swore at him, the glass thrown—not at him, thankfully—smashing on the granite worktop by the hob.

He stood there stone-faced, as if he'd done nothing wrong. She had caught him, what could he say?

"Well?" She sounded indignant. He wasn't even denying it.

"Well, what? You've had someone following me."

"Someone following you? You think I would let anyone in on this? You think I would trust someone enough for them not to gossip to the media?"

She wouldn't, she had to do it herself. He should have known.

"You caught me," he said, all too easily, a shrug of the shoulders as if dismissing the matter. So what?

"That's your defence? That's all you will say: you caught me?"

"What do you bloody want me to say, Adele?" He went over to the drinks cabinet now, a glass in hand. "Where is it?" he said, once he'd opened the cabinet, his bottle of thirty-year-old whisky empty.

She smirked. "Gone," was all she said.

The row that followed would have the neighbours calling the police, an officer arriving midmorning, the pair ignoring him until he appeared at the kitchen window, knocking on the glass. Neither of them had become physical, at least. Clifton was not the violent type, but they had let their tongues loose, their language enough to shock even the hardened policeman.

THREE DAYS later both sets of legal teams were already on the attack. When they discovered that she had largely stripped the accounts, he was up in arms. She'd done it legally, however, an equal partner. They pointed out all they could offer Clifton was that in the separation—it wasn't a divorce, never having got married—they could factor in the money she'd taken into the arrangement. She would not benefit very much from it, though it did significantly limit how much spare cash he had available.

The fight was mostly over what happened to the company, the press already picking up on the split—they'd rowed at the office just the once, but in that industry, once was enough. The merged firm was without question stronger because of their connection, their two smaller firms reputable, but the joint business was one of the top ten venture capital firms in the country. The clients were now the hot ticket, and calls had started almost immediately—not too dissimilar from the scene in Jerry Maguire, when Maguire first walks away from SMI and frantically starts calling his clients trying to get them to sign for his new company.

It enraged Clifton to discover she had already started that process months ago.

The lawyers knew they were in this one for the long haul, teams already in place to handle the litigation. Both sides looked to cause as much damage and expense to the other as possible, matching blow for blow the efforts of the other side in a process that would end up taking twenty months to conclude, costing over nine million in legal fees alone.

The Cage––Outskirts of Moscow
Two Months After Filipov's Assassination

DESPITE HIS BROKEN LEG, Eddy hadn't let go, blinding Baxter in one eye, the two grappling the last of their strength from each other for ten agonising minutes.

Eddy had Baxter against the edge of the cage, his face smashed against the metal again and again, flesh cutting away, as neither man gave up their grip on the other. It was clear the stronger of the two would prevail, however.

Both oligarchs stood in stunned silence, fear present for sure, but glued to the spot. This was fresh, vivid and as real as they'd known. It captivated them despite often not being able to look. They edged closer as blood poured from Baxter's face; the man going unconscious, something missed by Eddy until the oligarch shouted.

"He's down! Go for the money for god's sake." He'd seen enough.

Baxter didn't move.

"Help him," the other oligarch called, looking up at Yuri, whose grin hadn't left his face for the entire ordeal.

"Not until the fight is over," Yuri countered.

"It is over!" he said, looking at his man, a pool of blood gathering on the floor underneath his face.

"The fight ends when the victor has claimed his prize," Yuri pointed out, the statement enough to refocus Eddy who still needed to get across the cage, somehow hold himself up so he could reach the computer keyboard, and be conscious enough to type out the agreed amount.

Eddy pulled himself free of his opponent, his own body bloodied, his hands covered in red, and gave out a yelp of pain as his leg reminded him of its condition.

"He'll never even make it across the cage!" the losing oligarch exclaimed, only losing if the other man claimed the prize. His own fighter might be dead before that happened. He didn't want that on his conscience.

"It's what you both agreed to," Yuri snapped, putting the man back in his place, a look fixed on his face that neither oligarch had seen in him until now.

Over the next twenty minutes, Eddy clawed his way around the edge of the cage, using the metal to drag himself, saving as much energy as he could. He knew he couldn't walk, knew Baxter broke his leg, the pain threatening to overpower him but the closer he got, the more his adrenaline raced. He needed enough left in him to stand at the computer, and if not stand, to be close enough to claim his prize.

Yuri moved back around to the rear of the cage, leaving the oligarchs at the front, the losing fighter bleeding out long before

Eddy was even close to finishing. Still, the fight was only over when the prize got claimed.

"You must reach the computer Eddy," Yuri said, the American now within two metres of the base of the cage from where the keyboard rested, some three feet off the ground. "Remember, whatever you type in the computer will be the prize you receive."

Yuri looked across at the two oligarchs, Eddy's Host not looking at all impressed with the choice of wording, as if begging his victor to claim another amount, to take more than the seven million dollars they had agreed between them, and if doing that, to cost the oligarch his victory.

"A little more effort and you'll be seven million richer. Just as we agreed," the oligarch called as if to remind his fighter of the deal. The Russian had never told him it would be this brutal, this bloody, that he would have needed to kill or otherwise die himself. Eddy had not once looked back at his opponent. He knew he wasn't coming after him, the fight very much over. He already suspected the man was dead.

His leg screamed pain at him again.

Eddy took several deep breaths, drawing in as much oxygen to fuel the muscles that still had something to give. He would have to get to one leg, his good leg, there was no other way. And it would hurt.

The scream that went up as he pulled himself into the initial position was enough to send shivers down the Russian spines, but it didn't deter Eddy, who steadied himself before leaning against the cage, his left leg rooted and weight bearing, his broken right hanging.

"Remember what we agreed," his oligarch cautioned.

"Screw that, did he say you wouldn't walk again when he signed you up?" the losing oligarch shouted, victory still possible if he could get Eddy to up the prize money. He had five and a half million pounds riding on this.

"Ignore him, Eddy, it's a simple break," his rival retorted, but that seemed to irritate Eddy all the more at that moment.

"A simple break? What do you bloody know about pain, about getting your hands dirty? I've killed a man for you!"

"For me?" The Russian laughed at that. "I didn't tell you to kill anyone, just to win at whatever cost it took. You're the one who wins the seven million."

"It could be much more than that, Eddy."

"Shut up!" the oligarch snapped at his compatriot, feeling the vulnerability of his position, the win and those millions slipping away from him as fast as the fight had ended.

"You didn't tell me I would break my leg!" Eddy screamed, pain written across his beaten face.

"That was your fault. Now get this finished and claim the money. Remember, anything different to what we agreed and we have an issue, do you understand?"

"Screw you!" he swore. "This leg; that fight. It's got to be worth over seven million." There was recklessness in his eyes now.

"That's right, even double that!" shouted the other oligarch, suddenly in a winning position. The bigger the difference, the more he would get paid.

Eddy's oligarch turned on the Russian, grabbing him by the neck, his face inches from the other.

"Enough!" Yuri bellowed, which caused both men to take a step back. "This cannot get physical between the two of you. The fight is over. It's now only the spoils in play. I will remind you, gentlemen, that I will not accept any such aggression from either of you again!" He'd spoken to them in Russian, the exchange heated, but lost on Eddy, who'd put his fingers to the keyboard while they'd been confronting each other, while Yuri had been speaking, his index finger hovering over the digit seven.

"Just type the prize and we can all get out of here!" his oligarch said.

"I want more," Eddy replied. They couldn't change the amount now, the Russian had been clear to him. Seven million dollars was enough, even if he had needed to kill a man to get it.

"You can't have more!"

"You can take as much as you think you're worth," the other oligarch said. It didn't matter how different the amount was, anything but seven million and he would walk away from there with his stake returned to him, the difference paid to him, and his own fighter dead on the cage floor. The latter mattered little right now. Victory was in his grasp.

Eddy's finger moved to the number eight key, then the number nine.

"It's got to be worth another couple of mil," he said, as if this were a negotiation. "I know you're good for it." He was; the money not the issue for him at all.

"You do that and you won't leave this cage," the Russian stormed back.

Eddy looked over at him, nothing but contempt showing on his face now. The Russian might be wealthy, but he was no hard man. He was no match for him.

"He's bluffing," egged on the other oligarch, enjoying the occasion more and more, seeing his rival squirm those last five minutes.

"I can type any amount?" Eddy asked, this time to Yuri, who was standing behind the computer, mere inches away from the American on the other side of the cage.

"Yes," he confirmed, an air of caution in his voice this time, however. "But changing the amount you agreed beforehand will have significant connotations for your Host," he added. Yuri looked over at the oligarch, whose face remained calm, pleased that balance was being added.

"Bollocks," Eddy laughed, pain cutting him off as his leg reminded him just how broken it was. His fingers typed out the amount. Nine and a half million. He pressed send, the screen confirming the amount as transferred. Eddy swore to himself.

Once he had removed the computer Yuri came back around to the front of the cage, addressing the two oligarchs. To the oligarch whose man had died in the cage, he said; "Congratulations. I will return your stake to you, and you will receive from your counterpart five million dollars within the week." Double the difference. It was what both men had needed to agree to before being allowed to appear. Yuri turned to the other oligarch, a man now fourteen and a half million down all because his own fighter had become greedy at the end.

"You'll pay him before the week is out," Yuri stated, no room for movement allowed. "My men will deal with the Brit," he said, waving at the body. "I hope you found this entertaining," he ended, turning from them both, heading back out through the main door.

The winning oligarch chuckled. It had been like nothing he'd ever experienced. The other Russian, who'd been a part of the Games before, was less than thrilled. No-one liked to lose, especially when he'd seen his man win. The winning oligarch, glancing back once towards the cage, turned, and saying nothing more, left the building.

The Russian approached the cage. Eddy had lowered himself to the floor again, almost the forgotten man in the room at that moment, but his oligarch had not forgotten. The Russian opened the cage, stepping in through the gap, careful to avoid the blood of the fallen challenger.

"You did a very foolish thing," the Russian said, stepping forward, gun pulled from his suit pocket, shooting the American twice in the head without waiting for a reply. The money now gone, that much was clear. But he could never allow the American to enjoy it. The oligarch pocketed his weapon, turned and headed out the building.

It had cost him many millions. He'd had worse days, but not since the weeks of *The Games*. He said nothing as his driver pulled away from the area.

5

Moscow City Court, Russia
Present Day

They came back from lunch on that first day a few minutes late; the Judge and prosecution waiting, three people sent out to bring back the entourage. They'd had a lot to talk about over snatched bites of food. Svetlana looked rattled.

Once everyone settled into their places again, Svetlana's lawyer stood up to speak.

"Your Honour, I motion to dismiss this whole hearing under Presidential Command with immediate effect," a proposal expected by both the Prosecutor and the panel of judges, none of whom seemed to react. Volkov's team lunch meeting had involved no food at all; they'd run out of time. The revelation that someone was talking had put panic in them all, Svetlana more than most. There were things even her team around her might not have known. She had only told them so much. She was adamant that they could not allow a traitor speaking lies wrapped in half-truths access to that tribunal, the motion decided upon in the last few minutes of their time together.

It was the Prosecutor who stood up and spoke first.

"Might I remind you she is not an elected President of this fine country, and therefore in legal terms, has not earned the right of a Presidential Command, just yet."

Svetlana's man when silent for a moment, mouth open, the Acting President giving his leg a tap under the table after a few seconds. *Say something, you blithering idiot!*

"Your Honour, ever since Svetlana got invited to step into this most esteemed role, she has come across the same prejudices that we see in this courtroom today."

"And what might those be, if you don't mind enlightening us all?" the Judge asked, to the amusement of the Prosecutor across the aisle.

"That our President is a woman. Sir, it is no mystery that a woman has never run this country before, no hidden fact that Russia's record in this matter is woeful. Politics, it seems and for far too long, has been the haunt of the wealthy, the influential and, let me underline, the men in our great nation. Yet, let me remind you," and he was pointing at Svetlana again now, "there are few people in this nation today that the population have more respect for, more admiration for than Svetlana Volkov, coupled with the strong belief that she does so much for this nation. She is both wealthy and influential, and we all know it was only her support at the last minute three years ago that saw Matvey Filipov ascend into power."

The Judge held up his hand; the speech had gone on long enough already. Standing now, the Prosecutor took the chance to address the room.

"And this is an important point, and something I for one do not dispute. It was only because of Ms Volkov's endorsement that Filipov won the vote. A vote which was taken by the people of this nation, in a free and fair election. *El-ec-tion*," he said, pronouncing every syllable for dramatic effect. "This is the reason we are here today. We know you are pushing through legislation which would make an autumn election, four years after the previous one, a real possibility. So we are here to look at the conduct of Ms Volkov, looking dutifully over these last three years, to see if she is, in fact, fit to run in the election. To determine if, in fact, she is eligible." He paused there.

She could only be ineligible if she had a criminal record, which she didn't. They clearly thought that might change before the week was out.

The defence lawyer stood again. "If it's her record since being asked to take on this role we are discussing, then let me start with her efforts for equal rights," and he pulled out a hefty document, designed to show them all that Svetlana meant business in this area.

"Her work in Samara is a prime example," he began.

Samara, Russia
One Year Ago

SHE'D TAKEN the ninety-minute flight from Moscow, heading east and landing in Samara shortly before lunch. It was her third visit in the last two years, and this one for the inaugural regional conference she'd put together.

Samara had been the test case. Close enough to the capital, but small enough to see progress. Her team had been working hard to enable, and give greater opportunities to, more women in business and owners of businesses at that. They had made finance available, this coming from Svetlana's own foundation, something she'd set up especially. She would not do this with State funds. This had to have her name all over it.

They set programmes up, Samara focused on extensively. This conference, and the expected gathering of nearly one thousand women-in-business, was the culmination of the previous two years of breaking the ground.

Now the crop was showing.

Svetlana Volkov was introduced as the President of Russia and this was met with huge applause––the programme had been the making of most of the women in that auditorium, taking them from the edges of poverty to independent businesswomen. It took a full five minutes to get everyone quiet enough for Svetlana to go to the microphone, have everyone take their seats and begin her address.

"Dear friends," she started, the signature of her time in power. She was Svetlana to those around her, friends to the people, one of them, although she was far removed from nearly every aspect of life these people experienced. She'd once been like them. She knew what it was to be downtrodden and abused, to have men, in positions of power, misuse that power and make you do things you didn't want to do. Now that had all changed, and she could do as she pleased.

"I stand before you today a humbled woman," she said, pulling off yet another fine performance, her eyes moist on cue. "Humbled by the success stories here before me, humbled by the hard work and results so many of you have seen, all of you in fact, given that you are here today." A generous round of applause continued for a minute before she ushered this one to a close. "Gone are the days when women in our nation had to stand back and watch others lead the country forward. Our proud homeland has sent women into space many times, but the heights of political and business orbits seemed, until recently, one step too far. How is it we can circle the globe and yet not run the country?" Another round of applause, Svetlana taking her time to open a bottle of water, pouring it slowly into the glass, all the while allowing the applause to continue.

"That changed when I became President," and the noise became deafening, the one-thousand-seater arena packed, the women on their feet once again. In these contexts, she never referred to herself as the Acting President.

"Two years ago I first launched the ЖвБ," she said, sounding out the letters in Russian. WiB. *Women in Business*. "In that first intake there were thirty-three of you, all of whom I believe are here today," and there was a roar from the front rows on the righthand side of the venue to prove the point. Svetlana smiled; she'd met many of these women in the early days, though now others ran the programme. There were too many for her to get involved with personally now. Such a conference as she now addressed was the only way of addressing them all. "That first group was such a success that we quickly multiplied. And look what we have today!" she said, her arms in front of her and sweeping the auditorium from left to right. The fruit of her efforts.

"What you've started here in Samara we will take to every region of Russia!" Another deafening boom went up, the audience now abandoning their seats, most remaining standing for the rest of the speech. "I'm delighted to announce the national rollout of WiB, starting in the capital next month, with another twelve cities, and plans for every major city to have its own programme running before the year is out. Mark my words: this is a new day for women and their rights in our nation. Yes, we will raise families, yes we might marry, but god damn us first if we don't also lead successful careers, make money, grow businesses and empower others to do the same!"

The crowd didn't go silent for ten minutes, Svetlana giving up eventually––her speech was over anyway, she'd got the required reaction––and she stepped back from the microphone, waving to the crowd, to her crowd, her audience, her voter base.

It was simple maths. Aged eighteen and over, there were over eleven million more women than men in Russia, twenty percent more in fact. *Voters.* Win the female vote, win the election. She was the female vote. She had instructed her team to focus on dominating that demographic. Given the applause still ringing out as she went backstage in Samara, she knew she had made her mark in that city.

Moscow City Court, Russia
Present Day

"As you might already know, after she successfully trialled the programme in Samara, it is now running in all twelve cities with a population of over one million people. Of the two hundred and one cities with a population between one hundred thousand and one million, WiB operates in ninety-four locations, with plans for the rest to be in place within three years. As you might expect, the growth and success of this programme has been unparalleled in Russia. There are also fourteen projects in smaller cities, these coming about via connections within the programme, businesswomen taking the initiative and running workshops in their own birth cities, something we don't yet have the resources to do centrally." He perused his notes again, though much of this information most knew. It had been a real success. "As of today, forty-thousand, four hundred and ten women across one hundred and twenty cities and towns in Russia are part of her course. Twenty-thousand of these women represent businesses that did not even exist before the programme started. For the twenty-thousand who did, there has been a documented twelve percent average increase in wealth in each company. This represents billions of dollars, spread right around this country, firms paying taxes which help both the local and national economy, boosting employment, and as a direct result," another glance down at his notes, but this number he had printed on his memory, "giving sixty-five thousand, nine hundred and eighteen people work who, one year ago, did not have a job. And this number will only increase in the weeks and months to come, as the businesses we are working with continue to grow, as new cities and new programs start, and as word continues to spread."

"That's all very well, and congratulations on that success," the Prosecutor cut in, bored already with the rattling off of statistics they all knew well already. "But what I'm keen to understand from Ms Volkov, is where Isabelle Fairburn and Esther Waters fit within this programme?"

Svetlana's mouth went dry.

6

The Cage--Outskirts of Moscow
One Year After Filipov's Assassination

Snow covered the ground, the building icy, adding another edge, another factor to what was promising to be a fascinating afternoon. Security was heavy outside, Yuri having employed more men as the months progressed, the fights continuing. This wasn't for the authorities to know about.

Each oligarch had his own team in place. No billionaire wanted to be seen in the venue at such an event.

Yuri joined the two billionaires beside the cage, his presence known to them both, this being each oligarch's third contest. With three wins between the pair, they were getting a taste for it.

Today would be the first time either man had brought a female into the arena.

Isabelle Fairburn was English, sourced and flown across from the same country her oligarch Host lived in, one of the few Russians who still lived in the UK. She was thirty, had wealthy parents but drugs and alcohol had taken her away from them, crime becoming her means of income. The authorities had never caught her.

She'd never cheated an honest person, targeting the greedy, the crooked, anyone with a secret to hide. It's what had drawn her to her Host. She seemed the perfect pick, particularly for an event which required the unusual pairing of both raw aggression––you had to win the fight to claim the prize, and there were no rules once inside that cage––with honesty, a virtue it seemed so few, when it came down to it, possessed.

She was ready for a clean start, knew she couldn't continue as she was, knew she would end up behind bars before too long, and the offer had come at the perfect time.

Twelve million pounds for one fight, providing she won. The oligarch had thrown the money at her, paid for training, hired her a coach. The offer was the highest yet, his belief that such a figure made double-crossing him at the end of the contest less of an appeal. He levelled with her, told her that if she cheated him, it would have dire consequences for her parents.

She swore to him the money was plenty. She had already booked herself into a rehab centre the day after she was to return from Moscow. The place didn't come cheap.

And six months later she was ready, leaner than ever, a mix of multiple fighting disciplines studied, some mastered, enough to give her an edge in the cage. Her Host had high hopes.

Yuri moved between the oligarchs.

"Are your girls ready?" he asked, with too much glee in his eyes for what would be a brutal affair. Both Russians nodded.

Esther Waters was the first to leave the changing room, and she couldn't have been shorter than six feet two. French, and not yet twenty-eight, she had a considerable size advantage on her opponent, who emerged from her own door seconds later, the two women setting eyes on each other for the first time. Neither showed any sign of fear.

The frenchwoman's Host had recruited her in Brussels, Esther working in several gyms in the city. He'd offered her six million to come and fight, unknown to her therefore half the fee that her opponent would receive if she won.

The two women faced each other, Isabelle level only with her opponent's chest, but she'd fought many her size before, some even bigger. Skill didn't need size, if you knew what you were doing.

The fight lasted only ten minutes, the blows savage, the blood flowing.

Isabelle would emerge from the cage twelve million richer, the desire to cheat her host negligible, if even there, the fight an honest one. Face covered in blood, her hands too; she walked from the cage. After washing up at the sink, there was not a gash on her. It was not her blood.

Her Host walked out soon after, six million the richer himself, a good day's business and exactly the result he had hoped for.

Isabelle would spend the rest of the day in her hotel room, resting and checking her account, but the money was already there, and wasn't going anywhere else. She smiled. If she did things properly she would enjoy herself that night, using the hotel's ground floor bar enthusiastically, before flying to London the following day and checking into rehab straight from the airport, likely still inebriated.

London
Eight Years Ago

THE MESSAGE on her phone merely said Congratulations on the first year!

And what a year it had been. Adele smiled at the message, walking in through the main doors of an office she'd taken ownership of three hundred and sixty-five days earlier. The sender was her longest standing client, going back over a decade with the old business, one of the first to move with her when the dust had finally settled.

It had been a profitable year.

Clifton Niles and Adele Spence had formally moved free of each other the previous summer, twenty bitter months of lawsuits finally over. Even for the two plaintiffs, it had become too much. Neither side had held back in the battle over those key clients, those even more lucrative patents that their old firm owned. Now they were in play, and the fists were flying.

Neither law firm had ever dealt in a split that was as acrimonious as the Niles/Spence case had turned out to be. Training lawyers would study this case for decades to come.

Following a behind-closed-doors meeting between the lawyers leading either side, it was the legal teams who finally got their clients to back down, give up the fight, and look to walk away with something.

Adele and Clifton would have fought until there was nothing left, the legal fees eating up the capital quicker than even the hungriest of hungry caterpillars.

A referee would have called a boxing match sooner, the fight deemed a draw. Yet, in business, in partnership, there could be no draw, no way of keeping the pair working together. Finally, they signed an agreement, dividing the business in half, dissolving what was there, establishing two new firms, each partner with their sole name on the new enterprise, and able to piece the rest together from there.

Niles & Spence, one of the most lucrative VC firms in the city, and now easily the most high profile, was disbanded and made into two companies at the immediate conclusion to the case. Clifton Niles didn't like it, neither did Adele Spence. But they had run smaller firms before, not using their names, yet the coming together had propelled both the business and themselves into all the right places.

Now the entire City knew who they were.

Spence Capital officially came into existence the day after they agreed the settlement.

The location had been a final hurdle that appeared to be one too many for them to navigate. In the City's heart—venture capital heaven—there was no obvious space for another firm, let alone two, which everyone knew, needed keeping apart. Nobody wanted the couple or the employees passing the enemy in the lifts each day.

The solution presented itself somewhat as a saviour coming from the heavens. A large firm of stockbrokers, long established in the same area, had grown over time, finding a similar issue a few years back when they were looking to expand, instead setting up a parallel office in another high-rise two blocks away. The offices could see each other, the people in constant contact, but it was the best they could do.

Discussions were rapid, the stockbroking firm proposing they move into the Niles & Spence building, which was easily big enough, allowing even more room for expansion in time, and the two new firms could each take one of their identical offices.

Thankfully the pair agreed, and even more astonishingly, when individually shown the options, they independently opted for a different building. That was one nightmare conflict both sides gave silent thanks for avoiding.

Adele had opened the doors of Spence Capital the following morning, three hundred people coming with her from the old firm—they allowed these people to choose, the split mostly equal—and she made no small noise about it.

She stood that first day in her top floor office, looking across at the other side, Clifton Niles in the identical space, a glass of something in his hand, raised in a mock salute towards her while his other hand raised its middle finger.

Goal number one was to get up to speed. All the clients knew by that stage who they were working with, but once the firms were legal they knew they were fair game for poaching. It's what businesses like theirs did. It was why they were so successful, why they could afford such offices, such lifestyles, such employees.

"Everybody," Adele called, that first day, champagne flowing freely. "We know what we have to do. Any way we can close them down, let's do it."

Nobody had any doubt who she was talking about. This was war.

A year on from that day, she couldn't have been prouder. She loved running the company, loved arriving at the building each day—the one negative the need to walk past Niles Ventures on her way in each morning—loved getting one over on those bastards whenever it happened. And it had. They'd stolen more clients from them than from anywhere else. They'd equally had more poached by them than any other firm.

What she was looking for was the knockout punch. Given the opportunity, she would love to take them over, put them out of business, ransack *their client base. She dreamed of the day when Niles would discover she had purchased the controlling stake, or forced him to file for bankruptcy. It became her sole passion, her single pursuit.*

The trouble was, Clifton Niles had exactly the same obsession. The one issue for both businesses; they were equally strong, equally matched. Like two wrestlers paired against each other, neither party could get a firm grip to flip the other and win the contest.

Little did either know that within five years, that very opportunity would present itself, and not through anything they could manage. Unrelated to them, events were unfolding in Zurich, Siberia and ultimately Moscow which would, in time, lead them both onto someone's radar, someone with the means and the motivation to get involved in a situation few would have risked.

For one of the pair, it would be a game changer. For the other, their very existence was suddenly under threat.

7

New York City, USA
One Year Ago

Jeff dropped the documents back onto his table. They'd arrived the night before, the courier with no clue when quizzed who had ordered the delivery. He was just doing his job, told Jeff to call the office if he needed to know anything more.

Jeff wouldn't bother to do that. It was clear this whistleblower knew what they were doing.

Jeff felt tired. Ever since first being contacted, ever since first going to the CIA, he couldn't help but fear he was now being followed, possibly by the Russian, probably by his own government. Why did these things always seem to involve him?

Now, what equated to a small manuscript-sized wad of information had arrived, marked for the attention of the British this time and not his own country's Security Service. He'd read into the early hours, falling asleep on the sofa somewhere around four, and woke at nine with a stiff neck and a gut sense that this would only get worse.

Given what he'd just received, he was clear there would be more.

It detailed the life of an English woman, a millionaire in fact. It showed her connections to a Russian oligarch--no scandal there. Couldn't billionaires buy any woman they wanted, she a fine example? It suggested she had had little money until a trip to Moscow changed that, the name Yuri coming up once more.

It spelt out the source's suspicion--it was clear he was himself no longer in Russia--and went into detail about what could have happened. There were details of her stay in the hotel, her departure the following day, and following three months in the one-thousand-pounds-a-night rehab centre, she was a new woman, riches and all.

The report then detailed who he needed to send it to at MI6, Anissa's name and details listed, a summary of the history she had tracking these Russians.

Jeff was yet to work out a way of getting anything to the British, sure that even an attempt would violate some unknown, unwritten rule somewhere deep inside the Pentagon.

He needed air, needed to stretch. His back couldn't cope with too many nights on the couch, the previous one far from the only time that had happened.

Slipping on a pair of jogging bottoms, he tied the laces on his trainers, locked the front door and took a slow jog through Central Park, lost in the surrounding crowds. He mulled over the information. There was no doubt his source had more information which could lead to the exposure or even the impeachment of those in power, and Svetlana Volkov herself. He'd not got to that yet, his source testing him, watching him, to see if he could trust him. So far Jeff had done everything the Russian had instructed him to do.

Was he being followed as he jogged along each path at that moment? He had nothing to hide and knew nothing more than those to whom he'd passed the information. Only that latest batch might cause an issue between himself and the CIA. He couldn't let them discover what he had to do, that was all.

An hour later he was home again, showered and making a fresh batch of coffee, the day not early anymore, a full day's work ahead of him, but he'd already told his secretary to hold all calls. He would work from home that day. He called his brother.

"Can we meet? I know you're seeing the folks later. It won't take long."

The idea had come to him as he finished his run. There was no way he would risk sending anything from the city, sure the Feds or someone would monitor his actions. His brother was going west later, flying three states to where their parents now lived. Jeff had said he was unable to go this time.

The brothers met at eleven, Jeff placing his backpack on the chair to his left, the two men facing each other at the four-person table.

"I need you to take something with you," he whispered, having scoured their immediate area, happy they were not being watched at that moment.

"Is everything okay?" His brother seemed concerned.

"It's fine," Jeff said, dismissing the matter out of hand. "I'm not sure who's here, and this needs to reach the right person."

"What does?"

"There is a package in my bag, nothing but paperwork. It's addressed and in a box. Take it with you to Chicago and send it by Fed Ex from there. I'll cover the cost once you're back."

His brother didn't follow up with another question, accepting of the matter. He trusted Jeff and was happy to help though he was concerned at the hint of a threat to his brother's safety.

"I don't think anyone has followed me, but I will not take any chances. We'll take a coffee together," his brother already checking the time, but his flight wasn't for three hours, "and then I'll leave. The bag will remain here. When you go, take it with you. Don't stop for anyone."

"You're starting to scare me," he said.

"Don't fret," Jeff smiled, "it's not that important, but I'm being overcautious."

They spent twenty minutes catching up, their conversation louder now, their coffee enjoyed, before Jeff got up to leave with little fanfare. His brother watched him go then looked around the place but nobody seemed bothered by his presence there. Once Jeff was clear through the door, he stood, dropping the backpack over one shoulder, a handful of dollars left on the table, and he too headed for the door, his eyes on the mirror by the entrance for anyone moving behind him. There was nobody.

Three hours later he was on the flight. He'd popped home, opened the backpack and removed the only item inside it, a cardboard box that weighed about the same as a half ream of paper. Jeff had addressed it to Anissa Edison, a location in London. He slipped the box into his own carry-on bag and took a cab to LaGuardia Airport.

Forest Dacha, Russia
Present Day

THE ALARM SOUNDED on his smart watch before six and Rad got out of bed quietly, careful not to wake Nastya, though still she stirred, ever the light sleeper. She checked her clock, a wedding present from her uncle and aunt.

"It's not even six, darling," she said, sitting up as Rad dressed, a week of construction work ahead of him in what was his first decent time-off away from work in a long while. With Svetlana in Moscow all week, the Law Courts checked and cleared by him a few days before and his team capable of managing things from there on, he took the chance to head out of Moscow. Nastya's uncle––he would have to stop calling him that soon, he knew, as he had no family himself; these were his uncle and aunt now––had promised to help him break ground that week on what would be their future home. They couldn't stay in their current dacha for much longer––snug for his needs as they were but inadequate for a married couple, and heaven forbid they had a family, as the aunt had said more than once––though he had turned down the offer to stay with them. Married now, they needed their own space, needed time together.

Both her relatives understood that, happy that Nastya was still only a few kilometres away, dense forest all that stood between them. Kostya and Olya hoped that constructing a proper home for the couple would encourage them to spend more time there. They both liked Rad very much, delighted at his connection to Nastya, someone they looked after as if she were their own daughter. They'd never been able to have children themselves.

"I'll put the water on," Rad countered, dressed now, smiling at his wife, a term he still wasn't familiar using, though married for more than a year already. He still couldn't believe his fortune. She was too good for him, and he spoiled her rotten.

Nastya couldn't have been happier.

Spring had come early that year, the snow largely melted by mid-April, the ground thawing not long after. That made the prospect of digging the foundations in that first week of May all the more motivating. Five solid months of good weather were approaching, with nights getting ever shorter, the light of day lasting that bit longer, though the covering of trees reduced the impact somewhat. Still, there was time. Rad had the energy and strength for the challenge, though without the oversight of the uncle, he wouldn't have known where to start. Kostya had built his own home, the one where Rad had first met Nastya, and knew what he was doing.

At eight both men were outside, Rad embracing the only male figure he had in his life, someone now related by marriage. He might as well have been his father. The State had raised Rad in an orphanage, a system harsh to a boy with few friends. After he had been helped to escape, he had spent most of his childhood years in the wild, in forests like those around them now, honing his hunting skills, training his eye. It was the making of Russia's most decorated soldier, the top marksmen in the army before he'd reached twenty.

"Olya will be over in a while," Kostya said, directed at his niece, who'd come out with a fresh pot of tea for them both.

The two men surveyed the plot, Rad not knowing what he was looking for, but mirroring Kostya's actions, anyway.

They'd marked out the square with string the day before, within

Rad's plot of land, not that there were fences or markers to show where private land finished and open forest started. They all knew Rad worked for Svetlana Volkov, the older couple knowing not much else than that––they knew not to probe––Nastya understanding a little more, though not everything. There were things he'd yet to share with her, wanting to broach the subject but not having any idea how. Part of him wondered if he should keep some of his history, some of his actions, from her. He was a soldier, soldiers did some difficult things. Every male in Russia had been a soldier once, national service requiring they serve for at least a year when they turned eighteen. Kostya would have served. Rad had never once spoken with the man about what he'd done or where he'd been.

It was how it went.

Kostya passed Rad a spade, the older man happy to have Rad volunteer for the heavy lifting work if he told him what to do.

"Let's clear back this area, get all the greenery out. That pile of rocks can move and then we need a metre deep hole at each corner."

Rad got to work, Kostya doing what he could as well to speed things along.

By eleven, Olya had joined Nastya, the two women sitting on wooden chairs––there wasn't anywhere else for them to be, which highlighted the need for a home––and the plot was at least looking a little more prepared. Rad was finishing the final hole, waist deep in the ground, shovelling soil into a pile outside the squared-off area.

Kostya took in the progress moments later, a fresh cup of tea in his hand, himself covered in mud. Rad climbed from the hole and joined him after a minute.

"You work fast," the older man said.

"I'm used to following orders," Rad joked.

Rad took Nastya by the hand, the Russian laughing as he pulled her to the line marked out with string.

"Okay, imagine with me for a moment," he said, stepping over the string. "Follow me," and she did. "We're inside the front door. There's the lounge in there, the kitchen here," he said, motioning with his hands, his mind running through the plan. He rattled off the rest––

the bedroom, bathroom, spare room. He didn't call it the nursery, but that's how the women heard it. "In the roof there'll be a place where I can work, and space for another room if we needed it."

They walked to the far side of the area, the bit that looked down towards the river, though trees obstructed their view at that moment. "We'll have a deck out here, it might wrap around the whole building in fact, but we'll sit here and grow old together," he said, kissing her on the lips, the two then standing on the spot, in the mud, transported to a time from then when they'd finished, when they would be alone and this would be home.

"It's stunning," she said, both the image and the hope, and she kissed him again.

Kostya coughed. "Too much of that and we'll get nowhere," he said, a smile breaking out on his face.

"Can I help?" Nastya asked, but Rad had heard the women's conversation from a few minutes before, Olya mentioning several jobs that needed doing at home.

"There is plenty you'll get to do. You're designing the interior, remember," he winked, knowing she had a flare and ability for design. He hadn't mentioned the plans to convert his old dacha, once the home was built, into a workshop for her, where she could pursue her love of fashion. "But why don't you help Olya, we'll be okay here for the day," he said, indicating he'd heard them both talking earlier. She smiled at him, always her considerate gentleman, and turned to her aunt.

"I'll drive," she said, and three minutes later, Rad watched them disappear around the bend, the sound of the quad bike lingering for another minute before that too faded.

"Let's get this foundation-post set then, shall we," Kostya said, the rest of the day spent mixing concrete and pouring it into the corners.

8

Moscow City Court, Russia
Present Day

That day of the hearing had come to a close, Svetlana still locked in with her lawyer Abram, who'd been standing alongside her all day, facing what was to him fresh allegations. He'd known at once that the President had recognised the two names. The last sixty minutes of proceedings had been brutal, the close eventually called, Abram's only hope by that point to run down time, get the session over with, and then understand what the hell they were handling.

"We need to find out the name of the man who is talking to them," she demanded, pushing aside his question about what she'd known or knew about Isabelle Fairburn. Svetlana knew now it had to be a man leaking to the prosecution, despite her team being by far the most gender-balanced political group Russia had ever known; the women on her team would divulge nothing.

Plus, given what the whistleblower knew, it had to be a man. She'd never let her female staff in on such things.

"Is there any truth in it?" There was an edge to the question, Svetlana stunned for a moment. She didn't know what part of the day's mud he was asking about. Perhaps he thought it all true?

"No, Abram, there is no truth in what is being said, just twisted information, from a disreputable source whom I fear will sling a lot more mud before the week is out." This was just the start, they had been told to be available until at least Friday, perhaps the weekend. Both sides had already given the judges access to their information. No doubt the judges already knew what lay ahead for her. She couldn't help but feel exposed, vulnerable; not a position she ever expected to be in again.

And she was not even officially President yet. All the power and protection that came with the Presidency was still waiting. Within reach, but still unavailable. Winning an election, it showed, was in fact the only way. And they planned on calling one, two years early. The country had gone through enough uncertainty. An interim President could only remain interim for so long. It could never be a permanent arrangement.

The dust had truly settled on Filipov's short time in office. Many waves had been caused during the campaign; two rounds of voting had been required and still it had gone to the wire.

Svetlana had had nearly three years of press conferences, delegations and political speeches––not to mention the half dozen projects she'd established, all aimed at women, all with money thrown at them––the changeover period had run its course. Money didn't matter. *Get me results, make them fantastic, I don't care how much it costs.* Now the country needed fresh elections, she needed them too. Her country ready to rubber-stamp what Svetlana and her team knew to be a foregone conclusion. Her investment in the female population was no accident.

But an election had to happen. Then she would have the power, then she would gain the protection.

"And is there anything I need to know about?" Abram asked carefully. Both knew there was.

"We can't let them take this away from us," she said, a change of tone, a different response to what he had hoped from her.

"We won't. I won't," he added. He'd not let her down yet.

"I fear it will get more difficult before the week is out," she said, the first sign of emotion threatening to get the better of her. Few now saw her this vulnerable. It was a first for Abram.

"Accusations don't hold water unless they are true," he paused, adding, "and if there is proof." He was sure there was plenty of which she might be guilty. You didn't represent billionaires without knowing you went very close to crossing the line with nearly every case.

"And what if they have that?" Until a month ago, when she'd first raised the idea about an early election and when exactly it should happen, it seemed to them all plain sailing. She was the most popular politician in the country for a long time, or so her team of pollsters reported. "We know they've charged people in the past with criminal cases, moves done with the sole purpose of removing them from contention." It was true Russia had a history of that, particularly in recent years with outspoken voices against Putin. Abram wasn't sure if she meant someone specifically or the judicial system.

"Svetlana, I need to know if there is anything criminal that they might have on you. I can't be in that room tomorrow or the next day, caught unprepared, while they lay evidence after evidence before those four judges, before us, and have you expect me to find a way out of it. You can't put me in that situation. So tell me plainly: is there something I need to know?"

"No!" she said immediately, "There isn't," she added, less forcefully, with less conviction as if as an afterthought.

"Good," he said, genuinely. He wanted to believe it, anyway. "And this British woman, this Isabelle?"

"Her name crossed my desk, on an operation linked to the investigation of Yuri Lagounov. This was months after she'd left the country."

"And the money? She returned to the UK, it would seem, a different woman."

"Yes," Svetlana said, puzzled. "That I never understood."

Abram coughed briefly, clearing his throat as if assessing how to word his next question appropriately. "And this Lagounov? What is it you discovered he does?"

She paused for a moment, in thought it would seem.

"That we never found out, though I'll have my team reopen the investigation," she started. Everything got put on hold once she issued the arrest warrant, and once it was clear the Russian had fled Moscow. "He seemed to mix with several very wealthy men, known oligarchs too and not only based in Moscow, either."

"Was he a threat?"

"I don't think so, and it appears wherever he is now, it isn't here," she said, meaning Moscow.

"Might he be the source?"

She pondered that thought.

"I don't think so. It could be his way of cutting a deal, but these women, the American man who went missing. It only puts him in the firing line if something criminal had taken place. I think we can cross him off the list," she said, Abram not aware there was a list yet. She stood up, her lawyer following her to the door. She was free to leave the Law Courts, free to go back to her home, which was the Senate building, within the Kremlin complex. Previous Presidents had built their own homes within Moscow, kept by them once their time in office was over. Putin's still sat empty, the former President behind bars, entirely thanks to Svetlana.

She would make do with the eighteenth century construction, highly secure, already within the most secretive location in Moscow. She knew nobody would watch her there.

That night, she sat alone, curtains drawn, drinks cabinet drained. She would spend another night asleep on the sofa, drinking herself to sleep eventually after 1 am.

9

London, Moscow, Alicante
One Year Ago

Adele Spence sat at the table for two sipping a glass of wine that came at three hundred pounds a bottle. It was a pleasant vintage, a taste she had grown to appreciate over the last few years. Across from her, in the exclusive London restaurant, sat her first client, their history long and colourful.

"To five years," he said, congratulating her not for the first time on what was another milestone to savour. She'd made the man three million in the last year alone, netting nearly as much herself in salary, the company's breadth of clients and ready cash the perfect combination. Risk had always been her specialty, offering her clients the same challenge she faced herself, but pushing through for the result, regardless. And there had been plenty of both––stunning financial gains and spectacular losses. Overall, they were well ahead as a firm, that year's three million pound personal bonus for Adele by far the best in the five years since establishing her new firm. Things would only get better.

"And to many more," Adele added, their glasses clinking, their eyes locked together. Twenty years ago, when she was still young and climbing the ladder, she would have assumed he was interested in her. She might have played along with it, knowing anything she did would prove good for business. Now it was only the money. She enjoyed being around successful people, enjoyed the spotlight herself.

"Do you ever hear from Clifton?" the man ventured, the one client who could ask her something like that, their history firmly established.

"No," she said, which was true. They hadn't spoken to each other directly since the trial, though both often spoke freely in the press, in the boardroom, in front of clients about the other, and it was never polite.

Her client smiled. He could recognise hatred when he saw it.

"Still that bad?"

"Worse." As much success as she had seen, the enemy––as that firm had become from day one––had done equally well, the two firms growing at the same rate it seemed. She saw estimates putting her chief competitor at a value of one hundred and ninety million. About the same as her business too. The theft of clients from each other had continued. There seemed no lengths either side would not go to score one over on the other.

Some clients refused to work with either, in fact, despite the money on offer. They didn't want to take sides, didn't want to step into something seen as the unforgivable move by the other firm.

Most enjoyed the contest from the inside, however. The animosity had only raised both firms' profiles, ultimately sending more business their way. There seemed no stopping either firm, yet if it cost her half her own fortune, Adele vowed to use it to ruin Niles Ventures if it was the last thing she could do.

"He even tried to get a stake in my firm," Adele spat, Clifton's scheme eventually spotted and actions taken. "Tried to cajole one of the firms I deal with to sell their stakes. All done in secret, naturally. It wouldn't have given him much control, but perhaps a thorn in my side."

"What did you do?" He'd known of the move. Clifton had approached him for the one hundred thousand shares he owned, a five percent stake in the firm, something Adele had offered him to sweeten the deal when he moved. Clifton had even offered to pay fifty percent more than they were worth. He seemed desperate. The client had refused and never told Adele of the attempt.

"Figuratively kicked him in the balls," she said. It was plain that given the chance, she would do it literally without a second's hesitation.

"Ouch," the man said, a smile on his face.

"Exactly," and she finished her wine, enjoying the last sip as it slipped down her throat.

"Gentlemen, it is thrilling to have you gathered together in the same room." The group had not always been together in the past, the oligarchs previously divided between two groups in the Games, based on their value. They'd also never met in Moscow, the events mostly taking place in St Petersburg, at Svetlana's mansion.

The Acting President stood and looked at each of the men. Roman Ivanov was the wealthiest man in the room now. He had been cautious. A lot had changed in Russia in the last few years. Svetlana had reached out to him two months before, inviting him to the meeting, inviting him to once more be part of something special.

He had lost a lot in the final event of the Games and had never trusted Filipov after that. He wasn't entirely sure Filipov's successor had what it took, either. She had run the Games, that was one thing. But run the country?

Still, he was there, alongside the familiar faces of Popov, Budny, Markovic and Utkin. While they had been in separate groups in the Games, they knew of each other from the world of business, often meeting at the various conferences. Few oligarchs ever went against another in business, especially those involved with the Games. It was an unwritten rule. During the events themselves, all bets were off—who might come out on top, who would leave broken?

"If you will indulge me with a little more of your time, I have some homework for you, and a request that we gather next week on the Costa Blanca for what I assure you will be the most fascinating thing you've ever been part of," she said, leaving it at that. The Games had involved some edgy events in their time, memories that would take some topping. Three of the group, something they wouldn't confess to Svetlana, had got their taste for risk from the now on-the-run Yuri Lagounov, the cage fighter of Moscow.

She handed out two documents to each man present, both files about ten to fifteen pages thick.

"I want you to read up on these two people," she said, holding up her own copy of the information she had just distributed, "and do whatever research of your own that you want. But nobody goes directly to either of them. No-one is to do business with them. Learn what you can," she said with a smile, adding "I'm sure you'll see much to exploit."

Roman Ivanov flicked open the first page, neither the name Clifton Niles nor the man's picture ringing any bells with him as he continued to listen to Svetlana speaking from the front of the room.

"One of the pair will holiday in Spain next week, and I have a proposition they cannot refuse. As always, you'll be watching. Bet against each other, work together for all I care. Find ways of exploiting the situation. Gamble on the outcome," she added, the group aware that she had not explained what the task would involve. "The payout for one of these two will be huge, offering them all they've ever wanted. For the loser, it'll destroy them. You'll see. Bet carefully, and bet shrewdly. And I'll see you in Alicante next week, gentlemen!"

THE WEATHER WAS STUNNING; the marina packed with boats, winter months still a long time away even if the heat of summer had already passed. In the distance Svetlana could see the Santa Barbara castle, high on the Alicante coastline, looking down on the city from above.

She'd been in Madrid the previous couple of days, the first visit by a Russian leader, albeit the Acting President, in a long time.

Her visit to the east coast was, officially, purely personal. She travelled light, Rad with her although he had only got married the month before. Work came first, as she always reminded him.

Still, he had the day off now, the building secure, Rad off in search of the beach and a little vitamin D.

On the flight down from Moscow, after preparing for the summit in Madrid with the Spanish government, she had completed her plans for what was to come in Alicante. She was greatly looking forward to these days on the Mediterranean coast.

She had updated herself with the latest reports on Clifton Niles, the man they were there to test, and if he passed, potentially reward with vast amounts of money. She still wasn't sure how she felt about that last part––she wasn't sure he needed any more outside funding. But then again, what she was offering would not be small. It would be game-changing money, a figure picked out so precisely that she was sure he would understand its significance immediately. If he didn't, she had over-estimated the man.

Regardless of the outcome, she had made her mind up about the businessman a long time ago. She was looking forward to seeing what the gathering oligarchs would make of it all. She couldn't wait, in fact, feeling like a child on New Year's Eve, Grandfather Frost soon to appear, presents in tow. Present-laden childhood nights represented very few of her New Years, however. These were hard memories. Her father worked three jobs just to make ends meet. There wasn't much to go around. She had left home still a teenager, still very much a child. The real world had been a harsh wake up call, a brutal learning curve. It had shaped her to who she was today––talented, streetwise, wealthy, and with an axe to grind.

She finally had everything she needed, money no issue thanks to Filipov and his deep secrets. That only left fun to pursue. She hoped that for the five oligarchs, by the weekend, they would see something in her they might not have known was there. She hoped to kill two birds with one stone.

She drove herself up to the castle, the venue she'd chosen for the meeting. There were tourists still around, but enough private parking, and rooms away from the public, to allow six high-profile Russians to meet together without drawing a crowd. As she stepped into the building, it pleased her to see the five men already waiting for her, most standing at the windows, looking down onto the city below, the beach and the sea not far beyond.

"Thank you for all getting here," she said. They didn't really think they had a choice, although the idea had interested them all from the beginning. Having an inside track with the current President, seeing what she could really do was never bad for business.

"We are here to target one man," she said, the start of what she hoped would be a contest like they had never seen before. She pulled out his photograph from her bag, though they'd seen it in the report she'd handed them all. "This is Clifton Niles, and he's forty-eight. He's British," she added, the arrogance clear on his face, the suit suggesting he knew he was king. *If only.* "And he's here this week on one of his gallivants," she added, without elaborating. Roman Ivanov could sense bitterness there, but didn't know why.

"There are five of you here with me today, and each of you is to come up with your own challenge for Niles to face. I want the action here because first, it restricts your time to prepare and doesn't allow you to call on local Russian assets that you might have if we were back home. Second, it's less likely to arouse suspicion in someone like Niles if the action comes to him rather than if we'd tried to get him to Russia. And third, he'll be so high on drugs by now that he'll most likely accept anything you throw at him."

She paused for effect, the men drawn in, taking in the fact they would have to set a challenge, but still not entirely convinced where the edge was. The Games always had an edge, that was the appeal. Offer a poor soul the chance to claim millions on the lottery and watch them try to scramble back to the country of the winning ticket in time to claim it. That they could understand, manipulate where they wanted to hold someone up, turn blind eyes where they wanted someone to succeed. The oligarchs ultimately played against each other, the Contestants merely little pawns in the games of the rich and powerful.

However, Clifton Niles was no poor sucker. True, he was nowhere in their league financially. Even Utkin, the least wealthy of the five oligarchs present with a value of $2 billion, was thirty times richer than Niles. However, the Brit was a millionaire, with a growing business and a shady reputation, and while little of his equity was liquid, he lived a wealthy lifestyle. A wild lifestyle it seemed from all accounts. Someone like that, at the top of their relatively small tree, took convincing. Men like that never wanted to play second fiddle. Svetlana had just upped the stakes.

Svetlana pulled another pile of sheets from her bag, something prepared and planned. Each of the five pieces of card, when she laid them out, had a word written on it. *Character, Honesty, Strength, Bravery, Courage.*

"Gentlemen, you will each be randomly assigned one of these cards," she began, "and will come back here in two days with your challenge. Your challenge has to focus on the trait listed, aimed to test Niles in that area primarily. Choose wisely, however. Too simple, and he will pass your test and make you look a fool." That comment brought a reaction, as she knew it would. She had learned how to speak to billionaires. Learned how to speak to men. They were game.

"However, choose something extreme enough and perhaps Niles will bolt. If he fails your challenge, whichever one of you manages that will collect the prize himself."

"The prize?" Budny asked, the third richest there, worth $9.6 billion and therefore wealthy enough to not need anything from anyone.

"If Niles passes all five challenges, I will award him one hundred and ninety million British pounds."

Even for the men present, they blew their cheeks out. It was a considerable sum of money and for a man like Clifton, provided enough of an incentive to run with the idea.

"But we aren't all on a level playing field," Utkin pointed out. Roman Ivanov was worth seven times what Utkin was. Svetlana smiled at that, already having thought it through.

"No-one can win because of their resources. Any challenge that you set has a maximum cost limit of ten million pounds. Anything you spend comes out of your own pocket. But I strongly encourage you to use all your means to make that figure much less. If, for example, you get him to walk away without spending a fortune yourself, you'll earn the respect of everyone here, not to mention the one hundred and ninety million paid directly into the account of your choosing."

"So we merely have to think of something that he won't do?" Markovic said, the fourth richest of the oligarchs present, and silent up to that point. His face had given the least away over the last five minutes, Svetlana seeing scepticism there. She would have to focus on him before the week was out.

"Yes, in a nutshell. A line he might not cross, but in walking away, he'll be turning his back on the prize."

"So he'll know the amount on offer?" Markovic replied.

"Yes," Svetlana smiled, the men nodding in appreciation. It made the challenge that much more real. "However," she added, the tone and timing causing a sudden silence of the murmurs that had crept in. They knew there had to be a twist. "I'll set the order in which these challenges are to take place, based on their complexity and any other factors that come to light. If you set an impossible challenge, you will go last."

"So Niles might have given up before he even gets to ours?" Roman asked.

"Yes. So you are playing not only against Niles himself, but against those in this very room. Ten million is your limit, so that keeps everyone on the same page. The easier you set your task, the earlier your challenge gets presented to Niles. Too easy, and he completes it without issue, moving one step closer in the process to the prize and eliminating you from contention. But pose a hard challenge and you risk not getting the chance altogether. The decision on that is yours."

She moved back to the cards on the table, the five traits she wanted each to focus their challenge on.

"Now to who gets which of these," she said. "These I will assign randomly. It seems only fair." She reached for the card with *Character* printed on it. She pushed her other hand into the bag, drawing out one of the five plastic balls it held, each with a name of an oligarch written across it. "Markovic," she said, handing him the card. She picked up *Honesty* and handed it to Popov, the second name pulled from the bag. She reached for the word *Strength*, her hand into the bag, feeling the three balls that remained. "Budny," she said, once she had read the name. "Two left," she said, reaching for *Bravery*. She moved the balls around in the bag between her fingers for a while before selecting one at random, both the remaining oligarchs stepping a little closer, clear they each wanted this one. "Utkin," she said, turning the ball around as if this were a World Cup draw and the cameras were watching. Utkin took the card when she handed it to him, a smile on his face. "That leaves *Courage* for you, Ivanov," and she passed him the cardboard, while producing the final ball from the bag, showing him his name was the last one there.

"You have forty-eight hours. Niles is in the city for at least another week, which gives us five days to complete each challenge. When you leave this building, you may go anywhere, meet anyone. I do not permit you to contact Clifton Niles or anyone connected to him directly. Believe me, I will know." She didn't give them any more than that, but they would play by the rules, mostly. "You will each be back here in precisely two days and will present to me, privately, your proposed challenges for him. I will inform you together the order the challenges will take place. And remember, the first challenge will be the same day, so bear that in mind. That will be all," she said, picking up her bag, turning before any of them might have asked her a question, and she left the room. A few seconds later they heard a car pull away.

"Okay, friends," Roman Ivanov said, though the men were merely acquaintances. Oligarchs had few friends, especially among the ultra rich. "We know what we need to do. And I'll say this for her. She sure knows how to put on a show. Have fun, everyone," and with that Roman mirrored Svetlana's action of seconds ago, heading out of the room, the other oligarchs doing likewise, each man already working through their ideas. Pitching it at the right level would be the challenge, none of the men able to second guess the others.

10

Hampstead Cemetery, North London
One Year Ago

Anissa stood in the same spot she always stood, three feet back, her husband's grave in front of her, her two sons' graves positioned either side of that one.

The family gathering.

The grass in the spot she stood had died months ago, the grieving widow's visits increasing, hoping each time the tears would finally fall, yet all she continued to feel was darkness. *Cold. Angry. Loveless.*

It was three years to the day since their murder, three years to the day when Anissa's nightmare happened. She'd not been at the funeral, not out of hospital herself until a month after the bodies were in the ground.

They hadn't been sure she would recover. Her parents had wanted to bury the dead. Anissa had also now not spoken to her parents in almost a year. A year ago, they'd been there together, as they had for the first anniversary. Now she was alone.

She didn't even know how things stood with her and Sasha; the pair having moved in with each other following her release from hospital, the setup purely practical. She'd needed somewhere to live, not wanting to return to the family home. She had since sold that. The sale proceeds still sat in her bank account.

Anissa had also needed help as she was not able to manage physically on her own, at least initially. Sasha had been insistent he helped. The Russian was recently single himself, living in Alex Tolbert's London apartment, but his flatmate and colleague had not been seen or heard from in years. The one thing known was that Alex had survived, that he was most likely in prison somewhere in Russia.

That was little use to either of them. Sasha couldn't easily return to hunt for his friend, having escaped Russia himself the year before, previously working for the FSB in St Petersburg. Russia had banned Anissa from travelling to their country for five years. There were still two years to run on that, not that she had the slightest inclination to jump on a plane at the first opportunity, save for finding Alex. She deeply missed him. They both did.

Anissa had manufactured the relationship with Sasha, something part of her needed physically at the time––she was beside herself with grief––but it was more than that, and she knew it. She'd used him, the perfect alibi for when she'd exacted her revenge on the traitor who'd given her up. They found Bethany May dead at her London home. They had found nobody responsible; the trail going cold with the assassination of Filipov in Moscow. Before his death, popular suspicion had Filipov behind the murder of May, for turning against him by offering secretive information she had on the Russian.

His death had a natural way of closing the difficult and tenuous link––it was easier to throw her murder into his file and have them all sent to storage now the man was dead.

Except Anissa had killed her.

She wrapped her scarf around her neck, the wind picking up and blowing across the cemetery, enough to send a shiver down her spine. She'd always hated graveyards, but since the killings, since that moment, she'd found solace here. This was where her story had started and this is where it ended. Six feet under, between those three coffins.

Life had no meaning anymore.

The rich kept getting richer, their crimes unpunished, their deeds unexposed. Despite chasing the Russians for years, despite all the information and inroads they had, they were always too far away, too far behind. It didn't help that both of the previous two DDGs had actively tried to curtail them, Price because of his connection to Dmitry Kaminski, May as a mole for Filipov.

At least somebody had got to Filipov. The official story was that Putin had pulled the trigger. Few questioned that story anyway, the man sent to prison, the Russian actress swept to power overnight. Anissa would have been happy for her, happy for the change had Svetlana Volkov not featured so heavily on that now doomed wall of evidence. Svetlana had been the lynchpin behind the whole movement, the ringmaster at that grandest of spectacles. How Anissa had so initially misread the always glamorous, always charming movie megastar. Now she was the Acting President of the largest national land-mass on the planet. That role intrigued Anissa the most.

Her mobile rang. It was Sasha.

"Hi," she said, answering the call, her eyes taking in the words engraved on her husband's gravestone as she listened.

"I'm here," he said, "I'll wait by the gates. There's something you need to see in the office."

She thanked him. He was a nice guy, but she couldn't help fear she was losing him. Was that what she wanted? Was it what she needed?

She'd moved out of Alex's apartment two days before, the third anniversary approaching, her long-term colleague still missing, her live-in lover not as open as he had been. She needed space, needed time. Nothing was easy for her anymore.

Sasha stood at the gates. He knew where the graves were as he had been at the burial but he couldn't see Anissa from where he stood.

He lent against a post, playing a game on his phone, the post not as strong as he thought, as it moved an inch. He glanced at the post, Sasha standing upright for fear it might collapse. Graffiti covered the post as it did most surfaces in the vicinity. Stickers of various ages, some years old, littered the circular metal in various forms of completeness. He looked up at the post, which wasn't as tall as he had expected, not the street light he had assumed. It housed a camera, a CCTV lens the like of which covered much of London. It covered the gates.

Suddenly something clicked in his mind.

Stuttgart, Germany
One Year Ago

ANASTASIA KAMINSKI STOOD behind the draped curtains of her cousin's house, a home she'd been staying at for the last two years. A similar age, they'd grown closer than ever since she moved to Germany, her break from England and separation from her imprisoned husband swift and final.

Yet standing there, spying out through the thick curtains onto the street she had not ventured onto for two days, she knew the men following her were her husband's doing.

She'd first noticed something five days before, a stranger's glance lingering too long and terror ran through her. She had carried on her tasks, going about life as usual––she didn't know how long they'd been on her tail, but wasn't worrying her enough to make her change her routine––but soon picked up the signs that there were others.

She started seeing repeats, men from a day or two before cropping up again. It realised her worst fears; they'd found where she was hiding.

However, she had nothing to hide––besides the guilt of turning her husband in, a final attempt to get closure on a marriage that had hit the rails long before she'd started an affair with the MI6 agent. She had ultimately done it for Alex, turning in the man who had once been her lover, but someone she had now seen through, seen the same dangers MI6 had seen. But it was too late. Alex had already fled, believing that she still loved her former husband, Dmitry, despite her best efforts to have him understand.

Alex had gone off to Russia, and she'd never heard from him again.

Anastasia had fled to relatives in Germany, who she knew would take her in. It didn't surprise her, now these men were watching, that Dmitry had sent people to investigate. She only hoped they wouldn't hurt anyone, especially her cousin. They didn't deserve exposure to that side of her life, as much as she had already sucked them in. This was Germany, this was separate from all the mess that had swamped her in London.

Yet, here they were.

They had to know she was onto them now, given her actions those last two days. Perhaps they thought she was ill? While she tried to stay away from the window, it was possible they could see her--watching her watch them. She didn't care anymore. They could all go to hell. She toyed with merely confronting them, walking out the front door in broad daylight, when the street was busy and calling to them. *Here I am, what is it you want with me? What message might you carry from Dmitry?*

She'd not yet plucked up enough courage to do that, however.

Anastasia stepped back from the window, her cousin moving around in the kitchen. She was sure her host had picked up the change in her behaviour, but had said nothing about it, to her credit. Did she know that they were being watched? Would those men move in the next time it was just Anastasia home alone? Is that why they were waiting? Should she tell her cousin? But that would lead to the police being involved, and she hadn't come to Germany to file more police reports, to appear in any more papers.

She sat on the sofa, pulling her phone from her pocket. It was a new device, as was nearly everything she now owned. A local number, new handset to go with her entire wardrobe of new outfits. She'd fled, needed a clean break. She had sold the family home in London; the contents sent to charity--someone, somewhere, had got themselves some very nice furniture––and everything handled by the legal firm dealing with the divorce.

How Dmitry had got the word out, she didn't know. Or what he was after. She was certain he sent them to get the agent. Perhaps they didn't buy the story that Alex was missing? Perhaps they were waiting, watching for the stranger arriving in the night, the man on the doorstep quickly allowed inside, embraced, kissed?

That had been her dream years ago, Alex arriving when the dust had settled on everything, the couple free to continue their relationship, and this time openly, in public, around others. They could be free. No more hiding in hotel rooms, no more sneaking off to his apartment.

She scrolled through the contacts, only a few copied over from her old handset, only a few numbers now needed. She stopped on the one contact she knew she could speak with, the one number that might make any difference. She didn't know who else to approach. Pressing the call button, she put the handset to her ear. It was a while before the female voice answered, presumably wondering who the mystery caller was, for it was a number few people had. It wasn't on any public record, so no chance of a misdial, and Anastasia had figured that seeing a German number appear on the screen, the agent would soon work out who it was.

"Hello?"

"Anissa, it's me, I didn't know who else to call." Anastasia would avoid saying her name––she realised after the call that made no sense, as the men already knew where she was, camped outside her house.

"Why are you calling me?" Anissa asked, fast and not quite her usual self. It'd been a tough day already. Too many reminders of years gone by reaching out and wanting connection.

"I don't have anyone else to speak with, not about this," she said, fear in her voice.

"What is it you think I can do, Anastasia?"

"They're here," she said, her voice breaking off, the emotion, raw and fierce if not yet overpowering, stopping her from speaking.

"Dmitry's men?" Anissa probed to no response. "Are they with you now?"

"They are watching," Anastasia replied, after an awkward silence. "They've been following for days, possibly longer. I only noticed something on Monday." It was Friday.

"But nobody has approached you?" Anissa asked.

"No. I've not gone out since Wednesday. They must assume I'm onto them now."

Anissa took a long, slow breath, audible even on the call, before speaking next. "I'm not sure what you think I can do."

"I'm scared," she said, tears coming now, her voice wobbling.

Anissa gave the woman time.

"You need to go to the police. You need to be calling the German authorities, not someone working in London."

"I came here for a quiet life, came here to wait for Alex," she said, Anissa not at all sure of what that had to do with what she'd just mentioned. "I came here to get away from the camera, get away from the attention. If I go to the police, then it'll all become known, they'll know I'm here, the papers will follow me, Dmitry will know my every move."

"He already knows where you are, if those are his men, Anastasia. I don't understand."

Anissa could hear the Belarusian weeping now.

"If the police move me, if they hide me from these men, Alex would never find me," she finally managed, the effort and words now too much for her, the dam breaking, emotion flooding out.

Anissa understood it at last, understood that feeling of hope against all odds, the one in a million viewpoint where anything could happen. Anastasia still loved Alex, Anissa had learnt that from their last conversations in London. The Belarusian had ultimately done it all for Alex, but he'd gone. Gone before he found out. Germany was the only place he knew to look for her, the relatives the only connection she had to that country.

Anissa knew the stupidity of such hopes, the last few years teaching her nothing else if not that.

"He's not coming back, Anastasia," she said, coldly, though regretted her tone once she heard it. "I believe he is alive, however."

"What?" Anissa had mentioned that to her in the past, but it was nothing concrete. She'd taken it as false hope.

"Someone on the inside. Someone in Russia said they arrested Alex. It had been the intention to take him alive. I believe he's possibly still being held somewhere. Perhaps the Kremlin is waiting for a time to reveal him. Perhaps they will demand a prisoner swap?" Her choice of example maybe wasn't the best, Anastasia jumping on that last bit as if Dmitry might come out of prison.

"You mean they might demand Dmitry's release?"

"Hardly, given it was Filipov who wanted the man exposed. Svetlana Volkov won't want such a rival on Russian soil, either."

Both women remained silent for a few seconds, Anastasia pondering what Anissa had just said and seeing the logic. Dmitry would not be coming out of prison for a long time, she knew that. She reminded herself of it. Yet his fingers and reach could still go beyond the bars. She knew those had to be his men outside.

"Is there anywhere else you could go?"

"Aside from my relatives here, there is only Belarus. It would be ten times worse there, I would have no privacy."

Anissa couldn't help think *that's what you get for marrying an oligarch and being worth millions, perhaps even a billion.* She resisted speaking her mind.

"Look," Anissa said, her tone indicative of what was to come, "you have the means to go anywhere, to vanish. Keep your number or ditch it if you think they are onto you. If I ever hear from Alex, I'll contact you. If you change your number, message me. Don't use a name," Anissa said, thinking for a moment. A nature program she'd watched from the night before came to mind. "Use the codename *Tern*. An Artic Tern flies ninety-thousand kilometres a year. It's always on the move. So use that name. If you change your number, need to lose your phone or anything, update me when you can. I'll store your number. If I ever hear anything, I'll let you know."

"Thank you," she said, glad that her hunch to call Anissa had paid off.

"Stay safe."

"I will. Goodbye," and Anastasia ended the call. It was time she made her own migration. She had the funds, had the freedom and now the drive to go. Anissa was her connection to Alex, she didn't need to stay in Germany. She could travel, see new places. She refused to consider the thought of looking over her shoulder the whole time. These men were not there to grab her. They were waiting for Alex to arrive, as she was, ironically. Even if they caught up with her, she doubted they would do anything. She wouldn't let them find her, and whenever she got suspicious, whenever something or someone didn't fit, even if only the slightest hunch that something was up, she would move. She would become a master at it. Living life, free and tethered to nowhere.

She would switch phones often, she decided. Pay in cash, leave no trail. Once she memorised Anissa's private number, it didn't matter what telephone number she had, what country she was in. She would merely update and move on.

She knew she would need to plan her escape carefully. It was better she were long gone before they realised the fact. She would travel constantly for days, before picking a final destination. It didn't matter where right now. She had time. She felt freedom now like nothing she'd known before. Tomorrow she would leave Germany, perhaps for good. She went to tell her cousin. The news would likely make her sad, but she would understand. They all would. Saying goodbye would not be easy. But she knew it was for the best.

11

Moscow City Court, Russia
Present Day

It was the morning before the second day of the hearing, her team in early, Svetlana standing before the group, ever the leader.

"Show me the numbers," she said, the question directed towards her pollster who had been ordered to join them especially that morning. She had been running fresh opinion polls across the twelve largest cities, and in a selection of smaller towns. Noticeably all locations where Svetlana's projects operated.

"If the election were tomorrow, you'd win in the first round," the pollster confirmed, the numbers showing a slight increase in the lead over the previous month. They were heading in the right direction.

"Thank you," Svetlana said, the numbers good. Something Putin always found to his advantage was that it wasn't the biggest cities which won you the election, but the rural votes that counted. Putin had regularly lost St Petersburg and Moscow, yet carried on in power. The female majority population in the rural areas was even higher than the cities––Volkov carried a number in the high seventy percent range when polling these areas. It appears the babushkas across the country didn't mind Svetlana one bit. They'd stopped running polls in these rural areas after the fourth consecutive one came back as another landslide in her favour.

"All that remains now is to keep myself in contention," she said, as if that week's hearing was a mere time-trial in some competition, a hurdle easily cleared before reaching the main competition. Yet equally these four judges might hand Svetlana a criminal charge, eliminating her from a contest which was already hers to lose. She didn't seem to show any nervousness, which brought reassurance to those around her, buoyed themselves by the self confidence on display. They all trusted she knew what she was doing.

"What about the male vote?" she asked, happy to number crunch a little further, time still available, minutes that her lawyer Abram would have preferred using to discuss any last-minute hearing matters, but he remained silent, Svetlana in control.

"That's harder to say. There is no rival yet, no clear candidate who could stand against you. If an oligarch were to challenge, you might lose the male vote," which didn't matter, as long as she kept hold of the *golden goose*, which in this case was that female vote. "You have a following amongst the mid-aged groups," the results showing between thirty- and forty-year-olds, a decent double digit percentage would back her, regardless. This age range matched the profile of the demographics her films aimed to reach. They had probably been fans of hers for years, growing up as young men with posters of her on their walls. Now she was President. For the current youngest voters, the numbers were inconclusive. Perhaps they already deemed her too old to be a sex symbol anymore, a person their parents might have admired, but someone now only associated with politics?

"Let's speak to the television stations," she said. "Encourage them to show a batch of my films over the coming months, remind these men what I once did." She smiled at the thought, the team noting down the comment. Whether it would work, they didn't know. It didn't seem like it could do any harm. She still was an exquisite woman. If a twenty-year-old could connect with the twenty-year-old actress version, swim suits and all, they could easily get on board with the current version. A woman who held political power now to go with her unblemished looks. The makeup took longer to put on, the process requiring more skill, but the public face showed few signs of change from that young starlet who first graced Hollywood. She had to play to her strengths.

"Focus on the cities, though," she said. The scheduling for the national stations, given the many time zones across the country, meant the same channel had local control over the broadcast. They streamed live events as they happened, naturally, the news updates as well going out live on the hour. But films and soaps got shown prime-time locally. "Start with St Petersburg and Moscow." There were proportionally more men in these cities than in the more rural areas. She already had the rural vote, the old women perhaps less enthusiastic if they covered their screens with half naked images of their President. But a boost in the male vote in the centres of power couldn't hurt.

She dismissed her pollster, turning to her lawyer once the woman had closed the door behind her.

"Anything we need to address?" she asked him, the room quiet. There were two minutes before they would call them through. What could he possibly say?

"No," he replied, standing up as Svetlana took a step towards the door, the others following suit. A few minutes later they sat in the courtroom, the prosecution arriving moments later, the judges not long after that. They were sure the day would be another interesting one, and so it turned out.

12

Alicante, Spain
One Year Ago

Svetlana was the first to arrive at the castle that morning, the sunshine as pleasant as ever, no need for the iconic fur coat. She'd left it in Moscow. She didn't need that image in Spain. She didn't want any attention, either, in Alicante.

She'd booked two rooms for the entire day just to be sure. They had arranged refreshments in the main room, the one she'd met them all in the other day. The views were spectacular and the men would spend time together. In the smaller room, Svetlana would hold her one-on-one meetings, hearing the men out, understanding the challenge each oligarch was proposing. Then she would need to rank them. The thought that later in the day, only hours from then in fact, they would carry out the first challenge, sent an extra burst of energy through her. She was back. This was happening. This was now. Three years she had waited, three years she had given press conferences, met with governments and politicians. For the first of those years, she'd been in Filipov's shadow, the last two just her.

However, these oligarchs were ultimately the one crowd she had longed to be around the most. She loved to put on a show, loved seeing these men squirm and suffer, loved the thrill of the chase, the fear of a loss.

Twenty minutes after she first arrived, the others began to show up, each of the five men there before eleven.

"Please help yourself to the food and drinks on offer," she said. "I don't know how long this next process will take, but I'm sure we'll wrap up before lunch. That said, I would like to begin the process immediately, so I won't keep you any longer." She glanced at Markovic. "Follow me, Arseni," she said, no hint it was a suggestion. The other four waited for the door to close before moving over to the drinks, Svetlana taking a seat on the sofa, Markovic pouring himself a coffee from the refreshments in the smaller room before joining her on the opposite sofa.

"Congratulations on everything you've managed up to now," he said, though there was an edge to his words. Her reply took him by surprise.

"We both know that in this context, none of you is impressed by me getting women into business, giving them a voice. If this coming week fails to impress, if I'm unable to put on a show worthy of your time, money and efforts, I'm as good as finished."

"I wasn't implying..." but she cut him off.

"Yes, you were," she said, smiling. "And it's perfectly natural. We've had little time to talk business, you and me, since I took office. I know many of your kind are wary of a woman as President." It wasn't clear what she meant by *his kind*. Did she mean oligarchs, or men? Possibly both. At least the five there that day had a shared history with Svetlana, a secret one they hoped few knew about. That didn't make her a shoo-in for the top job, however. That role came with vast responsibility, vast power too. Not to mention opportunities. "So I want to show you exactly what I can do," she said, leaving that thought there. He soon realised she was talking about the five days before them, the challenge she had set them. "Tell me what idea you have come up with?"

Markovic produced a British lottery ticket, the sort used previously in the Games. The ticket was only a few days old, however.

"I want to go first, so I've kept it simple. There is no better test of character than an easy out."

"I see," she said. "How much is it worth?"

His luck had been in, the idea coming to him immediately, calls made to his old team, the ticket secured that very night.

"It's nine point three. Sterling." That much had been luck, the fact there was a ticket won by such an amount at the time he needed to find something. "Present him the chance of nine point three million pounds upfront to walk away, or he burns the ticket and risks moving on."

"You'll let him burn the ticket?"

"He'll have a copy, but yes, it'll be what he thinks he has done."

Svetlana smiled. The idea was simple, that much was clear. She wrote some notes down, looking up from behind the pad thirty-seconds later.

"Let me make sure I've got everything. Your challenge is to present him a ticket for a guaranteed nine point three million pounds if he walks away and claims the winnings now. Or he burns the ticket and moves on?"

"Yes."

"You are assuming I'll put this challenge first. What makes you that confident? If this is the last challenge, there is no contest."

Markovic knew that, but he also knew his fellow oligarchs. From the people some of these men had been watching, he knew they planned to up the stakes.

"I'm gambling a little that they will present much harder tasks than mine," he said, his eyes suggesting he knew it was not much of a gamble. She knew they would all be watching each other, seeing what they could learn from their rivals in this task.

"Very good," she said, putting down the pad. "You may rejoin the other four, but please send in Popov next." Markovic stood, turned slowly while securing the lottery ticket back in his jacket pocket and opened the door. Popov appeared through the still open door ten-seconds later and closed it gently behind, a glass of orange juice in his hand.

"Please, take a seat," she said, the oligarch doing just that.

"He seemed rather pleased with himself," he said, a nod towards the door showing he was talking about Markovic. "Thinks he's come up with a winner, does he?"

"That remains to be seen," Svetlana said, her expression cool, the slightest smile breaking out as she continued. She couldn't disguise the fact she was already thoroughly enjoying it all. "If you will please tell me what you've come up with?" and she picked up the pad, very much the examiner placing her subject under scrutiny.

"I had Honesty," he said, placing the word-bearing card on the table in front of them both as if she needed reminding. "You are offering this man a vast prize of one hundred and ninety million if he completes all five challenges. I want to see if he'll kill someone for that money."

Svetlana sat back. She had wondered if it would get to this: breaking the law had stopped no-one in the past, but she also had more to lose now.

"I see," she said. The oligarch had taken her at her word, producing almost the opposite from Markovic, who'd spent nearly all his limit in buying that lottery ticket. This would cost Popov nothing. "And the target?" She was sure Popov would have someone in mind, perhaps a rival of his own. That said, Niles would only have the one day to complete the task, whenever it fell in the week. That ruled out something happening in Russia.

Popov dropped a photo onto the table. It showed a young man, shaven head, minders around him. "He's mafia, a real nasty piece of work around here, nothing like his father I'm told. His father is the Don, head of a power family in this region. A fair man, mostly. The son is trying to break away, getting into drug smuggling and people trafficking. He's bringing shame on the family. However, for the task, this information stays between us," he said, a smile on his face.

"Niles isn't to know anything about the man?" she asked, already catching on to where Popov was going.

"Exactly. Is he prepared to kill a complete stranger for no given reason so he could claim those millions? I don't know a better test of the man's character than that."

She wrote some notes for a minute, Popov collecting the photo, finishing his juice, while looking down at the view from the window.

"If he walks away," he added as if as an afterthought, "from what I've learnt of this street rat," he said, waving the photo, "I might even pull the trigger myself." He laughed at his own words. Svetlana looked up from her pad.

"If you can send in Budny next, please," she said, Popov already at the door, leaving the room, the other oligarch soon appearing, an eagerness in him she'd not seen in the other two. He sat down before she could even offer him a seat.

"Well, let me have it," she said with a smile.

"I had Strength for my challenge, so it got me thinking. This Brit is no bodybuilder from what I've seen. His fights are verbal, in business, in risk. So I want to focus on strength––an actual fight, I mean––but it'll overlap in some other areas. Is that okay?"

"Tell me what you have in mind," was all she replied.

Budny dropped a three-page document on the table, the photo from the first page catching her eye. It was of a young Spanish-looking guy tied up to a chair in a room, and on the floor underneath the man, the cardboard sign she had given him two days before, with the word Strength written on it.

"This man raped a woman two nights ago. The woman is too scared to go to the police. It's also far from the first time he's done this."

"I see. And you caught him how?"

"Does that matter?" He had a point, and she shrugged her shoulders at that.

"Go on," she said, asking him to elaborate somewhat.

"It's simple, really. I have a plane booked for a pleasure flight, but the pilots are mine. We will list Niles as the only passenger. Before they take off, they will tell Niles that the other guy is a rapist. He must sit opposite him, wondering what's about to happen. He's not to know anything until after takeoff. Then, at twenty-thousand feet, above the mountains, somewhere remote, the pilots will open the door and jump from the plane. Before they jump, they'll toss the one remaining parachute onto the space between the two men. Then they'll jump."

"Leaving only Niles and this rapist on board?"

"Exactly. The plane will most likely crash unless they can fly the thing. I'm not aware either of them know how. Is Niles prepared to fight for that parachute? Is he strong enough to win a fight?"

"If he isn't, Niles is dead, either in the fight, or when the plane crashes."

Budny nodded as he spoke. "If they do this, either this rapist dies, or Niles dies, yes."

She sat back. It was easily the best she'd heard yet, once again pushing what they were doing so far past the line of legality that they couldn't even see it anymore. However, that had never stopped them. And she hated all rapists. She picked up the report, looking more closely at the photo. If the Spaniard Budny had in custody was too strong, it would make the fight uneven, risk losing Niles altogether. However, the guy in the photo, bound by ropes with a gag in his mouth, looked weak and pathetic. Strong enough to overpower a smaller female, but not a man himself.

She spent two minutes carefully writing some notes.

"Very well," she said finally, looking up with a smile. "It's a good challenge, and you have hit the brief."

Budny thanked her, standing up from the sofa. "Utkin in next, I guess?" he asked, sure that the order she'd given the cards out was in fact the order she was calling them in. She smiled and nodded, no need for a voiced response.

A minute later Utkin was on the sofa, a fresh black coffee cupped in his hands. He'd done a lot of research online about Clifton, learning more than the outline Svetlana had given them, seeing the newspaper coverage the separating pair had attracted at the height of the breakup. It had been the images leaked by Adele, a naked Clifton in bed with yet another woman and splashed across the tabloids, that had piqued his interest. Clifton's reaction had been telling. For a man who seemed desperate to get naked behind closed doors––the accounts of his cheating were astounding––he didn't like everyone seeing him that way. Two days ago, Svetlana had handed him the word Bravery.

"My challenge is simple," he said. He hoped not too simple, though he didn't mind going first if that was the case. "We are in the city's heart, the most visited tourist spot there is." They had seen that to be the case, the surrounding buildings of the castle, all open as usual, with a steady mass of people walking through and around the area. The views alone were worth the fifty-minute climb in the day's heat. "It takes just under an hour at a good walking pace to get from the top of this castle to the marina at the water's edge. That is the time limit my challenge will have. One hour. If he fails, I win the bet."

She'd not considered there being time limits allowed. The other oligarchs might well object, feeling he was unfairly making a move for the money. But an hour was enough time for Niles to get there, so she resisted speaking, for now.

"And he gets dropped at the upper level of this castle, naked on the dot of midday, and has sixty minutes to get to a designated spot in the marina, or he fails." Utkin sat back, trying to read the expression that had grown upon Svetlana's face. She smiled at his proposal.

"Naked," she said, echoing his word from a moment before.

"Completely," Utkin smiled back. "Is he brave enough to take up the challenge? Is his modesty worth more to him than one hundred and ninety million? And I know why you chose that amount," he said, his eyes all-knowing.

"Do you now," she sighed. It was likely one of them might at least have worked it out. "I would appreciate you keeping that from the others." They seemed to have an understanding. He enjoyed having one up on the group.

She wrote more notes. There were no crimes involved in this challenge, though what Niles might do would be on him. She liked the challenge very much.

"Very good," she concluded. "Please send Ivanov in, and then I shall need a little time to think." Utkin left the room, Ivanov coming in a minute later, a little conversation shared between the group in the brief moment the five oligarchs were all together.

Ivanov took a seat on the sofa, placing his piece of card bearing the word *Courage* on the table between them. He'd spent most of his time those last two days watching the other four oligarchs. He had a fair idea what most of them were planning.

"You didn't say we couldn't ask you questions first," he began. Svetlana picked up the pad but closed it carefully when his eyes darted towards it, before inviting him to share his challenge with her.

"What is it you want to ask?" she said, aware she'd given no such rule, but not assuming until that moment that any oligarch would need to ask anything.

"I would like to go last," he said, not a question, merely a statement, and something she'd already said was not for them to request. She would choose the order. "Hear me out," he added, aware that given her response, she was about to cut him off, reminding him of his place. She closed her mouth, indicating that he should continue. "Done correctly, it'll give us all a follow-on, something to monitor and watch once the challenge is over. Assuming Niles makes it to the end."

"You would have to convince me a little better than that. You haven't mentioned your question yet, nor what your challenge is."

"I know Popov is interested in the Don's son, and that Budny has a rapist in his hotel suite."

She seemed genuinely shocked that they knew each other's plans, which was stupid, she realised immediately. The wealthiest oligarchs always watched the others.

"Is either of these challenges to kill someone?"

She sat back, thought a little about what to say, but wanted to see where he was going.

"Yes, both are."

Ivanov smiled at that, his own thoughts falling into place. He had decided not to come up with a fixed plan until he was in with her. As the last man handed his card, and the wealthiest there, he'd gambled that he would be the final man in to see her, Svetlana therefore already aware of the four other challenges. He would use that to his advantage.

"Popov's challenge, is it that Niles has to kill the son?"

"It is," she confirmed, still eager to see where this was going, the eagerness overriding her sense that she shouldn't be telling him what another oligarch had planned.

He smiled all the more.

"Okay, then this is my challenge, and something I hope you'll hear me out on why it should be the final task, but I hope you'll see that already."

She was hesitant at that thought. The last time she had allowed one oligarch to dictate how she did things, it had been the downfall of the Games.

"Go on," she eventually encouraged.

"If my challenge comes after Popov's, and Niles has killed the mafia kid, then to complete my challenge, Niles will have to confront the Don face-to-face and confess to the crime."

She got it. Did he have the courage to do that, knowing if he walked away, especially if this were the last challenge, he was turning his back on the prize? But if he went through with it…

"You want this to be the last challenge because they might just kill him?"

"If that happens, I won't get the money," Ivanov countered, ever the shrewd negotiator.

"Oh," Svetlana said, taken aback by that last comment.

"No, that'll be too simple. The meeting will be somewhere public. It's no secret that this kid is the bane of the Don's life. However, he is family, and you don't kill a family member. I propose we arrange a safe way to have Niles meet with the Don. If Niles wins the prize, he'll have money to protect himself."

"Because you know the Don will go after him," and she got it perfectly. There would be no riding off into the sunset with the cash, not with the mafia on his tail.

"Exactly. And Niles is a Venture Capitalist. He'll see the risk element immediately. He's thrived on risk, but when it's his life on the line, we'll see exactly how far he's prepared to go."

She liked the idea immensely and didn't mind that showing. All five men had come up with such different challenges, such unique approaches. She already had a fair idea where most of them ranked, just a couple she needed to think through.

"Very well, I'll grant you the request, as I don't want the mafia getting wind of what we are doing, which is what would happen if yours was the third or fourth challenge. Please don't tell the others, however. I will be out in the next ten minutes. I'll let you all know then."

Ivanov stood, not saying another word, taking the smile off his face as he got to the door––it wouldn't help him if the others knew he was so delighted––and he left Svetlana alone, closing the door behind him as he rejoined the men.

13

Forest Dacha, Russia
Present Day

The meat now cooked slowly over the fire, the two men washing themselves in the banya while the women chopped spring onions. Progress with the new house had been good, though there was still a long way to go. Rad wondered if they would even get to the walls before the week was out.

With the four corners now firmly cemented in place, beams lay on the edges expectantly, the level perfect. They hoped to get the base down mostly tomorrow, giving them a firm foundation to build upon.

Rad sat in the banya for a final minute, surrounded by steam, water poured on the coals for one last blast. He felt clean at last, his pores giving up the dirt and grime that had accumulated during the long day. He showered himself down one final time, put a towel around his waist and, slipping on a pair of shoes, walked over to the dacha to dress. Nastya watched him from beside the fire, blowing him a kiss as he went in through the door. The smell of the meat was incredible. He hadn't felt that hungry in a long time.

Twenty minutes later they were sitting around in a circle, the fire ablaze, the meat cooked. The night had drawn in. The brightness of the fire made anything over twenty metres away vanish into the darkness. They were safe, the fire enough to keep hunting animals away, even if the smell of the delicious meat might have drawn them in.

Nastya had put her rifle on the table and Rad's weapon was out too; Kostya weighed it in his hands, impressed.

"What is it you say you did for the President?" he asked, a topic they hadn't overly discussed. The conversation always had a tendency to move on to something else when raised, or a sudden silence might ensue. Nastya looked up at her uncle from behind the piece of meat she was eating, her eyes speaking volumes even if her mouth was full.

"Security," Rad confirmed, once he'd swallowed what he was eating.

"But this?" Kostya said, eyes on the weapon, appreciation plain to see. Rad got it. That was no standard issue weapon, no real use in a security capacity.

"That's when I go hunting," he said. Kostya knew it was no hunting rifle, far too powerful, far too specialist to be only that. Rad had meant nothing about hunting animals, however.

They chatted a bit, Rad answering a few more questions than Nastya thought he would, the food enjoyed, as darkness crept in. Soon the last of the logs sat on the fire, the older couple eating as much meat as they could manage. They needed to head home; the journey done somewhat more easily in the light that remained than in total darkness. Nastya lent them her rifle, saying they could never be too sure, and kissed them both goodbye. Kostya promised to be back early the next morning, not specifying a time. Rad would be ready.

They watched them leave, Rad and Nastya returning to the seat they were now sharing, Nastya on his lap, the last pieces of meat picked at as they chatted.

"You know, there is so much I still don't know about what you do for Svetlana," she started. "So much I don't know about what you did before, either."

"That's because you know I don't like to talk about work around here," he joked, but she could see there was more to it than that. *Don't like and can't talk about work,* she wondered.

"I'm serious though. You know everything about me," which was only partly true, but of the pair, she had always been the more open, the one with the most to share, the least to hide.

He went silent for a little while, the last of the meat played with between his fingers before he ate it, chewing on it slowly, deliberately.

"I've wanted to tell you," he said after an eternal silence, Nastya just sitting there, patiently waiting. "There's so much, and I'm not sure what I can share. Not sure you would want to know."

"Why wouldn't I want to know?" she said automatically, initially surprised, as if he thought she wasn't interested, that she didn't in fact care about what he did. Then she got it. She might not like what she found out.

"You were in the army, right?" she said, which was safe ground. She knew he was, most men had served, still had to serve. He nodded. "Look, I need not know the specifics."

"I was a specialist," he said.

"A sniper," she confirmed, aware he had a brilliant eye for a target, the weapon not anything a common soldier would have or need, nor be able to use.

"Yes," is all he said. The outworking of such a role was plain to her. She didn't need to ask if he had killed before, didn't need to know how many. That was soldier Radomir, a different time, a different man. Not her Rad, not the man she had married.

"So how does a specialist in the Russian army go from there to become head of security for the President?"

He smiled at that thought; the job kept him in Russia, kept him close to Nastya. It gave him the chance of a normal life, a way out, when only a few years before, he assumed he would die in battle. Someone would have got lucky, an enemy able to outfox him or a bomb exploding on him. It was the inevitable end to most snipers.

"It was Filipov who pulled me in, in fact," something he'd never told her. Filipov had been President when they had first met, first fallen in love. Rad had told her he'd done a writing job in recruitment during those months. The President was dead before they married.

"Were you in charge of security for Filipov?" she asked fearfully. If that had been his job then he had failed––Filipov had been assassinated––but if that had not been his role then what had he been employed to do?

"No, I've only done that for Svetlana. She saw what I could do, who I was, and insisted I stay close." He held Nastya tighter now. "I had met you by this point anyway, my beautiful distraction. The President's offer was everything I thought I would never get, everything I needed to stay close to you."

"So what did you do for Filipov?"

He broke eye contact after a few seconds, his green eyes moist. He remained silent.

Vauxhall House, MI6 HQ, London
Ten Months Ago

"It's confirmed," Gordon announced, his team checking with their cousins across the pond. "The CIA has him on record codenamed *Gremlin*."

The package sat on the desk before them, Anissa and Sasha joined by Gordon Peacock, who headed up the technical side of things at MI6 and had been a longtime help to the agents.

"Gremlin?" Anissa quizzed.

"Apparently, someone selected it for its similarity to *Kremlin* and the dirty little monsters lurking in the shadows. They report they've never met him. The information passes through a freelance journalist with a long history of work in the region. It's known that Gremlin is stateside, probably in New York, the Americans confirming they are following several persons of interest, but can't give us a name."

"But the person is Russian?" Sasha asked.

"Yes, that is what the journalist said."

The package had arrived the day before, initially carefully screened, nothing of danger reported. Inside the box, which had a Chicago postmark and was addressed to Anissa, there were only papers. Lots of them, and the information looked interesting.

"They want to know why we are asking," Gordon said, referring to the CIA, which both agents understood.

"Tell them we had a sniff of something." Until they knew what they were up against, it didn't help to offer too much truth, not at that stage.

The report that someone had sent to Anissa went into great detail about an Englishwoman named Isabelle Fairburn, the name meaning nothing to her. But the more she read, the more it all set alarm bells ringing, the similarity too obvious to all those Contestants they had been hunting for many years. Were the Russians up to their old tricks again?

Yet Ms Fairburn hadn't claimed a lottery win, that much was clear. The reports didn't show this, but a check by Gordon for all dates over the previous year for all the big winners had shown there had been no unusual results, no tickets claimed at the very last minute. That was how it had always worked within the Games, oligarchs securing a winning ticket ahead of time, paying off the winner in cash, yet keeping the ticket unclaimed and running down the clock. Then a day or two before the time was up, they would present the ticket to a stranger, usually someone they had flown to Russia for another reason. The challenge had always been to see if this person could get back in time, especially if hampered. The group of ten oligarchs would then go up against each other, some backing the Contestant, others openly opposing them. It was their way of flexing their financial and influential muscles. No billionaire ever wanted to lose. People had died as a direct result.

Now, suddenly, some years on, a woman heads off to Russia, comes back days later, and announces herself a millionaire overnight.

Anissa knew this was no coincidence. She pulled her chair in closer to the table, sitting up straighter now.

Svetlana Volkov had always ultimately been behind these gatherings, the events most often taking place at her St Petersburg mansion. Anissa had been watching the building once; there was no way to penetrate without raising the alarm.

Now this woman was President. And these millionaires had started appearing again.

"Are there any more people like this?" Anissa asked, Gordon writing a note.

"I'll look," he said, having seen a change in Anissa the longer the day had continued, a glimpse, if only a small one, of the old Anissa returning. He had sorely missed that.

"And see what you have on this Yuri Lagounov," she added. That had been a new name. The Moscow-based man wasn't an oligarch, she knew that much. She'd learnt most of these names by heart during her years of investigating them.

"I'll also see what I can find out," Sasha added, the only Russian based at MI6. Though his access to the old systems was no longer there, he had ways and means to discover things often faster than even the tech guys at Six. He didn't recognise the name Lagounov either, though being based in St Petersburg when he served in the FSB didn't help.

Gordon left to get on with the task, Sasha swinging his chair around and back to his computer, working his own angles. Anissa remained at the table, flicking through the sheets of paper. Her mind raced through the possibilities. Though she didn't have any proof that this involved the President, she couldn't help but assume it all did.

At the time Anissa had seriously wondered about a change of career––she'd lost the love for the job after the death of her family, seemed resigned to losing Sasha as a lover, and couldn't stand not knowing where Alex was––this had landed on her desk. It offered a way of getting back at Svetlana, whether she was involved or not.

The wall of evidence might have gone––though an official investigation had never been sanctioned by MI6––but Anissa had it all memorised. They could probably use very little in court, even if a trial was ever a credible option. No, the bombing had changed that.

This had been warfare for a while now. While Filipov had ordered the kill, the question which sat heavy and had demanded an answer for far too long was whether Svetlana had known about the order to blow up her family and done nothing about it. Could she have stopped it? Could she have warned them? Did she, in fact, approve it? Was it her advice even, the aide to the President, his closest adviser?

If there was any dirt to find, Anissa vowed afresh that day, she would find it.

14

Alicante, Spain
One Year Ago

Svetlana stood before the five oligarchs, the contest about to start.

"I thank each of you for the time and thought put into creating your challenge. I will not tell Niles what each challenge is until the day on which he is to complete it. If he walks away at any point, the event is over, and I will give the victor the prize for having stumped our Contestant. You may gamble between yourselves. That is up to you. I ask, and the challenges alone speak for themselves, that in no way do any of you interfere in any task. If there is a time limit in place, you cannot help or hinder Niles. We will observe, and we will process, but nobody will involve themselves once the Hunt begins."

She'd used that word for the first time, a word so connected to those original Games, when Contestants hunted the tickets, hunted routes out of the country, hunted ways of claiming their millions. The oligarchs hunted their prey too, keen to stop these people claiming the money and in the process winning millions from their fellow Hosts. This was different now, but it was compelling.

"I will now announce the order and the nature of each challenge proposed. The first will start this afternoon. Markovic, that will be you. We will present Niles with a lottery ticket worth nine point three million. His choice is to either accept it and walk away from the remaining challenges, or burn it and proceed." Markovic looked chuffed with himself, the other men looking somewhat unimpressed. They didn't feel there was much risk of Niles taking that, though they could see how burning the ticket would force the issue. "The second challenge belongs to Utkin. That will take place at midday starting from the top of this castle. We will release Niles naked, nothing with him, and he has one hour to make it to the marina. If he manages that within the time allowed, he will have finished task two. If he does not make it in time, the challenge will be over."

The other four looked at Utkin who looked happy, but nobody said anything to him.

"Day three, should we get there, belongs to Popov's challenge," and she paused, which only added tension to the room. "Is Niles prepared to kill a stranger for this prize?"

Both Utkin and Markovic, neither of whom had contemplated anything illegal, looked at their fellow oligarch with a little suspicion. It was Svetlana who clarified.

"The target is a nasty piece of work and whose father heads up a large mafia family."

That comment brought a few smiles around the room.

"If Niles managed to kill this specific stranger––he will not know who the man is, that information is only for us to know––in the time permitted, he will have passed that challenge and can move on to day four." She paused, silence absolute around the room.

"Challenge four belongs to Budny. We will load Niles onto a plane, informing him before the flight takes off that the man opposite him is a mass-rapist. During the flight, the two pilots will open the doors, and before jumping out themselves, will throw the remaining parachute between the two men. Our cameras will then watch what happens next," she added with glee, the plane already being fitted out by her team, though there were no guarantees they would make it that far. "If Niles is strong enough to overpower his opponent, and assuming he survives the jump, he will have completed the fourth challenge and will move to the final day."

The four men turned to Roman Ivanov, the only oligarch left, his task the fifth and final one.

"And yes, Ivanov is last. If Niles makes it that far, for the one hundred and ninety million pounds, Niles will need to confront the Don whose son he had just killed, and confess to the murder. The location will be a public place, the meeting only between the Don and Niles. If the Don kills Niles on the spot, Roman has agreed that this loses him the challenge. If he walks away from that, Niles will claim the prize."

"With the mafia on his back," Popov added, a thought the entire room had come to at the same point.

"Very much so," Roman said, with a smile.

"Gentlemen, we have our challenges, and we have our order. This afternoon, we will present Niles with his first task and see what he does with it."

Vauxhall House, MI6 HQ, London
Nine Months Ago

IT HAD BEEN a month since Anissa received the package from Chicago, from the whistleblower. Most assumed it was a man, though nothing confirmed that. They knew they were Russian.

Perhaps only the CIA and, because of them MI6, knew the person lived in New York.

One or two pieces were making the news, the information apparently being carefully managed. Someone was waiting for the right moment, biding their time. Most of them thought there was much more to come. All assumed the closer they got to the election in

Russia, mooted as imminent but not announced, the more damning the information and revelations would become.

Many papers had already coined this source as *the Snowden of Russia*. The American President, particularly, watched with glee, serving the final few months before he was kicked out of office himself following a series of leaks.

Anissa had looked into Isabelle Fairburn. Her parents were wealthy, somewhat influential, though not politically. The family had money, had done for decades. What fascinated the agent was the news of the strained parent/daughter relationship which had predated the new wealth by years. There had been no improvement since, in fact. The money had not come from the parents. Anissa was thankful to cross that option off the list.

It had to have originated in Russia.

Anissa set up an investigation into money laundering with New Scotland Yard, overseeing the police unit tasked with carrying out surveillance. Two weeks into that, they had little to go on, the warrant for access to the bank account not yet granted. Gordon said it probably wouldn't tell them much, anyway. The money could have come into the account via several offshore banks. It would be nearly impossible to trace back if it were the Russians.

Sasha had been distant with Anissa for the previous month, Anissa aware she had asked for space. But he seemed happy with the arrangement. At work, they had not discussed their relationship. They kept everything professional. They shared an office, worked together constantly. Neither wanted to break that up, but the longer it all went on, the longer this silence over the one thing they needed to discuss, the increasingly awkward it became between them both.

Sasha knew she was cooling to him, and though he'd seen it coming weeks before she said she was moving out, it had still hurt. He'd thrown himself into the relationship as it was all he knew to do. She needed someone, needed him. He felt sorry for her, more pity than he had ever felt. Yet two years in, it remained a relationship of pity, not love.

Now she was in her own place, Sasha had assessed what he

wanted. He didn't want a physical relationship with Anissa anymore. They worked together. They had a deep history, a deep connection, but that was it. In fact, living together, as convenient and nice as it was, only complicated matters.

He felt relieved when she went, though he would never admit that.

"Look," Sasha said, lunch time approaching although it was still too early to eat, "we need to talk properly about us," he said. "Want to grab a coffee in the canteen?" He left the room without waiting for a reply.

Now he's wanting to do this? She locked her computer and went after him.

Thankfully, the canteen was still empty, the staff behind the counter preparing the dishes for the rush that would come in three quarters of an hour. Sasha got two coffees from the machine, joining Anissa at the table they had chosen, and placing the beverage in front of her.

"So?" she said, as if a game of chess was about to start, inviting Sasha to make the first move.

"I know we've never properly talked about us, Anissa, and it bothers me," he said, avoiding eye contact at that moment.

She'd not known when or if this conversation would happen, and she had not worked out what she would say. Still the words felt absent. Why wasn't she prepared?

"You think the staff canteen on a Tuesday morning not long before lunch is the place to do this?"

He looked up at her. She seemed only half serious, though he looked around at the empty tables.

"Seems as good a place as any," he said, not sure what the real issue was.

"Fine," she said dismissively. "Are you breaking up with me?"

That question caught him cold. She was the one who had moved out, she the one wanting distance. Why was this on him? Why did she seem to care so much, why so bothered?

"I thought you had already made that decision?"

She laughed at that. "Sasha, I moved out to have time to think. We couldn't stay in Alex's apartment forever. I needed my own space. Perhaps somewhere we would live together again someday." That was news to him, but he let that thought drop. He couldn't help but pick up a desperation in her that hadn't been there before. When they were together, still living in the same place, it were as if she didn't seem to bother much about him. She'd shown passion in the early days, the first weeks intense. When he had fallen for her, she'd eased off. Then she moved out. Now, it seemed, at the thought of losing him, she was reverting to that desperate soul, that passionate soul, the one who wanted him close.

"But you never told me that," he said.

She looked at his puppy dog eyes, the emotion raw, the pain clear.

"Don't even think you have the monopoly in the hurt department," she snapped, the fierce side once more on show, something he'd seen her try to subdue those last three years.

"Anissa, this isn't you," he said.

"What do you even know about who I am?" she snapped, standing abruptly, before storming out of the canteen. Sasha remained seated, open-mouthed, unsure of what had just happened. Had he gravely misread the situation? Had he taken what he thought was coolness and distance and been wrong? Did she love him? Did she want to spend the rest of her life with him?

Even if she did, did he? The fact he couldn't answer that immediately told him all he needed to know. He didn't love her, not in the way she deserved, not in the way he needed, either. He felt sad for her, felt deep pity for what had happened. He liked her very much, admired her as a woman, as a colleague, but he didn't love her. Not that way. And he thought she felt the same.

Her reaction appeared to suggest he could be wrong.

THE LUNCH CROWD had thinned somewhat, Sasha still in his seat, two coffee cups empty. Gordon Peacock sat opposite him in the seat

Anissa had occupied an hour and a half earlier, the technician having spotted Sasha, and joined him for lunch. Yet the Russian had eaten nothing.

They had talked, Gordon aware his colleague needed a listening ear, Sasha happy to sound off. He had no-one else to talk with besides Anissa, who had not returned his calls over the last hour, or Alex, who he'd not seen in three years.

Gordon had known the pair were together, Anissa having told him once that she was living with Sasha in more than just a practical way. He had been happy for the connection, the two agents lonely. It seemed a good match. Gordon had said nothing to anyone in the office. The relationship offered no risk to national security, there were no checks to run on the new partner. *Leave them to it.*

Sasha glanced around the room, Gordon picking up an increasing agitation growing in the Russian over the previous five minutes, something pressing inside, but unsure if the Russian could say it.

"Do you remember when I asked you to check MI6 records to make sure Bethany May's details were not in the system?" Sasha asked, a question he had put to Gordon around the time somebody had killed the DDG.

"I do," Gordon said, sensing for the first time there was more to his suspicions than Sasha had ever let on.

"You said there was nothing," Sasha confirmed.

"Yes. It is standard procedure. May betrayed people here. They moved her records elsewhere."

"Is there any way Anissa might have been able to find them?"

Gordon looked confused, not liking where the conversation might go, nor what the accusation could become.

"No, not under her name. But I searched all references. There were no details to find," he said, pausing before asking the one question now pressing. "What is it, Sasha? Do you think Anissa had anything to do with the murder?" He almost hated himself for asking, sure that Sasha would spit back in his face, disgusted that a colleague could suggest such a thing, telling him how out of line he was.

Sasha merely blew out his lips, silence the preferred option for the moment.

"I don't know," he said, taking the final sip from his cup before throwing it, basketball style, into the bin across the room. *Three points.*

Gordon sat back in his seat. He didn't know what to think now, didn't know if he wanted to discuss it, didn't know if he should.

"The morning that they murdered May, the probable time of death recorded by the coroner, Anissa had been out of the house."

Gordon looked a little puzzled. He didn't know the details but knew MI6 had an alibi on record for her. That was because Sasha had agreed to vouch for her.

"She made me say she was home," Sasha said. He wouldn't add that they'd slept together for the first time the previous night, in the early hours in fact, though Anissa had vanished before he woke.

"She'd said she needed to go to the graves, needed to seek permission from her husband about me," Sasha said, not elaborating, Gordon able to work out the meaning, regardless.

"I see," he said.

"She might have been out for a few hours, I don't know. When I woke up, she wasn't home. She came back about an hour later."

"It's not too unlikely that she went to the graves, though?"

"You're right," he said, nodding his head as if that thought were sound, "but when the murder came to light, when we knew the time of death and day it happened, she made me swear to confirm that she was home. She said it would look weak, she didn't want MI6 knowing she had been out, didn't want them knowing she'd been to the graves."

"Sasha, that doesn't make her a killer," Gordon said.

The Russian paused for a moment.

"The thing she said that bothers me wasn't how weak it made her look, but the fact she couldn't prove she was at the cemetery. She asked me to say she was home. Made me be her alibi."

"It still doesn't mean she did anything."

"It's just this," Sasha said, another glance around the room, the tables nearest them both still empty as they had been at the start of the conversation. "I'd never noticed before, I don't know why. I've been there a few times."

"Been where?" Gordon said, somewhat confused.

"The cemetery. I was there the other month. It was the third anniversary of the murders. She asked me to pick her up at four. I arrived a little early, called her to let her know I was there, but waited at the gates. There was a camera there, the post rusting and weak. It must have been there for years. It wasn't new. The camera points to the entrance, Gordon. She didn't need me to be her alibi, she could have proved she was there."

"And?"

"Well, she either knew the camera wasn't working––but how would she know that? Or..." and he paused, as if the words were too hard to let them pass through his lips lightly. "Or she wasn't at the cemetery at all."

15

Moscow City Court, Russia
Present Day

S vetlana remained lost to her thoughts over lunch, her team in the next room, the Acting President at the table, salmon roll untouched.

Her thoughts had wandered to the years gone by, when served the same sandwich––it was where she first got a taste for it––in a Hollywood studio. Then she would have been in her trailer, a vast and luxurious space afforded to only the biggest stars.

She was every bit that. She was surrounded by crew members, always with people there to help her, but despite that she spent most of her time alone, even with her husband being on these trips with her. She'd only ever flown solo once, the last time when the marriage was already publicly over.

Privately, it had never been a marriage, merely a convenience, for both of them. She ate alone, slept alone in Hollywood, always. She didn't even know where Sergei went.

The contrast to those times on set couldn't have been more extreme. Make-up, costume, agent, manager, sound, camera, director, cast, plus a dozen roles she didn't even know the names for, usually kids not much older than eighteen. All surrounding her, in the background mostly but there to help.

Lunch was alone, prime cut of salmon in a sesame seed roll for one, in her trailer. She hadn't tasted that type of sub in years, and though the Russian variation wasn't the same, sitting there that lunchtime in the Law Courts, the morning still a blur––there were people crowding around, not all there to help her this time––she was once more on her own. She pushed the plate away.

The prosecution had asked about relationships. Apparently being Acting President meant such matters had to be discussed. Then lunch was called. She knew they had raised the subject like that to make her ponder for the next hour what they might ask.

She had been around plenty of influential Russians for the previous three years, but this had always been the case. She had married one and to the outside world they were a happy and successful couple, even if just for the cameras. It was also great for business. Now she was single. Now she was in charge. She was certain the other side would make much of her singleness, making out it was a liability. Some man might see becoming the President's partner as a golden ticket or she might fall in love with a third world dictator, or a first world monster.

She would be ready.

What she wouldn't give the time of day to, was talk about her ex-husband. She doubted they would ask, clear that it would be painful, but then again, that might merely incentivise them. She had prepared her answer, however. Her own personal life was a difficult chapter that didn't concern the court and wasn't something she would talk about.

How wrong that assumption would be.

"CAN you tell me where your husband is at the moment, Ms Volkov?"

The tension had been building for the last ten minutes, the Prosecutor taking no time since the resumption of the hearing to continue the path he had started prior to lunch. He had worked up to the point of asking the latest question, Svetlana expecting it to come from his mouth at any moment.

"How would I know?" she merely said, as if that were enough for him. He hadn't been her husband for several years already but she brushed the Prosecutor's choice of wording aside as nothing more than a cheap jab.

"You deny knowing his whereabouts?"

"We aren't together, in case you are the only person in the country who missed that piece of news."

The comment brought a laugh from her own defence team, though the other side seemed less than impressed. A smile grew across his face. None of the judges reacted to her response, either, two of them making notes as they always did.

"So you are telling me, that despite holding the office of President, despite being in office for nearly three years, despite having the FSB under your direct control, in all this time, you haven't once asked them to enquire or find out where your husband is?"

"My ex-husband!" she snapped, "and no, I haven't."

"I see," he said, looking through a sheet he picked up from the table as was his practice now when he had something meaty to reveal, his prompt to the judges that he had once again trapped Svetlana in her words.

"Is that because you knew he was already dead, killed in the last months of Filipov's presidency, by direct order of the President himself?" He looked up at Svetlana, his face all knowing, his smugness visible.

Svetlana's lawyer rose to speak into her ear, unaware of whether there was any truth in what they had said, not knowing it himself.

"Is that true?" he whispered, his mind working through the next questions the prosecution might ask if it were. She ignored him for the time being, a hand movement telling him to sit back down, which he did.

The Prosecutor merely looked at her, raising one eyebrow as if to invite a response. *Well?*

She said nothing.

"Your Honour," the Prosecutor started, stepping from his table as was now common and passing yet more sheets of information to the four judges, "our source was there. These leaked Kremlin reports show that men under Filipov's direction were ordered to a remote location in Siberia. They did not record exactly what happened, but you'll see from the second page, it reports that these Russian soldiers killed both Sergei Volkov and Lev Kaminski. You'll also note the initials of the man who led the mission, a man reported to be the same soldier now heading up Ms Volkov's personal security, no less."

The judges took their time looking through the documents, Svetlana turning to her lawyer enraged––it had to be true then––and mouthed to him *find me the name of this source and I mean yesterday.*

"It's very convenient, isn't it," Svetlana started, defiance growing with every word. She would not answer the question if she could help it. "You claim to have some magic source, someone supposed to have been there, knowing all these things. The paperwork is convincing, but Your Honour you need to know who this man is. For all we know, these are fabrications cobbled together by my opponents who will stop at nothing to disqualify me from this race. Yet I've done nothing wrong, and even if these reports are genuine, they relate to a time before I was the President, carried out by a man who always acted alone, who didn't tell his team what he planned to do, a man more secretive than any of you realise. Make them produce this source, have him stand before you and let us see what he knows."

"You're suggesting that Filipov would have done such a mission, with such a target, and not even told you, his closest aide, a woman, and I'll quote you, *who was in on every major decision, with him all the time.* You are telling this court that this time, he kept you in the dark?" the Prosecutor said, picking up on one aspect of what she'd just said, ignoring the bit about producing the source as if she'd never voiced it. There was no way they would do that, nor did they have the source.

Her justification for stepping into the Presidency had been that very line of reasoning; that she had been around everything Filipov did. She knew distancing herself too much now would only walk her into another problem area.

"This wasn't a decision about which he involved anyone," she said, which was true. Though she knew about it, she was on the outside, couldn't have intervened even if she had wanted to.

"And was Radomir Pajari on that mission?"

She took the piece of paper from her lawyer, looking at the information for the first time herself.

"*RP* are hardly uncommon initials now, are they?" she said, wanting to sound as if the connection were merely coincidental. She had known Rad had been in Siberia. She had heard the man debrief the President.

"Yet we know *they pulled RP* from Syria the day after Filipov won the election," the Prosecutor said, passing around another sheet, the man having used the initials, but this time the sniper's full name appeared. Svetlana turned to her team as the judges were reaching forward for the latest offering.

"Find me a dead soldier killed within the last two years who could have led that mission, and who shares these initials," she whispered. If she could place another there, someone who couldn't answer questions, it might keep Rad from the Law Courts, keep him from being cross-examined as she was. Her lawyer made a note, something he would pass to his team at the next break. The quicker they provided a name, the better.

"Tell me, Ms Volkov, did you have a happy marriage?"

The change in the line of questioning was dramatic, one judge looking up from the information, perhaps considering intervening though that wasn't his role.

"I don't see that as any of your business," Svetlana snapped, happy to speak for herself where her lawyer might have been better placed to stand up and object. He might have suppressed the question.

"Naturally," the Prosecutor smiled, not at all perturbed, his careful line of questioning leading to his next blow. "Well, let us assume, as you both regularly reported over the decades in all the papers, that you were a happy couple," and his smirk at her at that moment suggested he believed nothing of the sort. "All I'm saying is that not two minutes ago you apparently learned, for the first time and from my mouth, that your husband was in fact dead, and yet there has been no reaction. In fact, you are arguing about the source, about these initials. You seemed unaffected by the news, however. The news that your husband is dead."

"My ex-husband!" she snapped again.

"I'll beg to differ there. If the timing is correct, you were both still legally married at that point, the divorce had not gone through."

She'd walked into that one without knowing, so ready to fight the lies she'd forgotten to react. The news should have been a shock, if she knew nothing about it, if this were the first she'd heard about it in three years, perhaps wondering why Sergei was silent, why he'd not appeared anywhere in thirty-six months. She should have done something, but to feign sorrow now would not have been the answer, even for an actress of her renown.

"Your Honour, obviously this news would have been hard for my client, and I ask that she have some time to collect her thoughts," her lawyer said, standing up, motioning his client to say nothing more.

They granted the request, the Prosecutor smiling as he left the room, fully aware he had her on the ropes. There was plenty more coming her way before the week was out. He would give her the respite, knowing she needed it for what was to come next.

16

Alicante, Spain
One Year Ago

The villa Clifton Niles had hired for the two-week stay was all you would have expected from a City hotshot from London who thought he was everything. Someone had called the police to the gates twice already the previous week, the parties loud, the women a plenty, the drugs free flowing. Niles was a casual user of most recreational drugs, something he reserved for his holidays and down times. Not something he allowed to follow him back to London.

The meeting was to be between only Svetlana and Clifton; the oligarchs would have to make do with the video replay, a camera in her bag. The Brit knew precisely who the Russian was, her request to see him highly unusual, and somewhat alarming at first. However, when she arrived, her car was buzzed through the security gates and there was no-one besides Niles standing there to greet her when she exited the vehicle.

He could hardly believe his eyes. In person, she was every bit as glamorous as he had seen on television, and few women alive could compete with her for natural beauty. It made his own country's history of female leaders look remarkably second rate.

She walked in through the still open door to his villa without saying a word.

"So, are you going to tell me what this offer is?" he started, the Russian placing her bag carefully on the kitchen surface before taking off a summer jacket, not that anyone needed anything like that in the heat. He recalled she usually wore a white fur coat. She probably felt the cold more than others.

She'd led him to believe the meeting was something about business. The appointment had to happen behind closed doors, naturally, just the two of them, but she guaranteed he would want to hear her proposal. He said he was all ears and agreed to the visit that same day.

"What I'm about to offer you is something you can never talk about, is that clear?"

He'd had these types of conversations before, usually in his top floor London office, but never with a political leader. Least often with a woman.

"I know how it goes. Tell me what you want. This was a holiday."

"I'm not here today to discuss business with you, don't worry."

"I thought…" he started to protest, Svetlana raising a hand and cutting him off, regardless.

"Not business of your usual kind, but there is a lot of money available. In fact, you could walk away with one hundred and ninety million pounds by the end of this week, paid directly and tax free."

He took in the amount, toying over its significance.

"One hundred and ninety mil?" he repeated, questioned. Pleaded.

"I thought that would get your attention," she grinned, wondering what the five watching oligarchs made of the Brit at that moment.

"What's the catch?"

She smiled. He was game for it, she could tell. "Five oligarchs have presented to me five different challenges. Five hurdles you have to jump, if you will."

"Five challenges?" The prospect that there were Russian oligarchs involved concerned him somewhat. He knew them by reputation only.

"Each potentially more difficult than the last. Some will allow you to walk away with something, but each stage would only be a fraction of the whole pot. If you want the full prize, you must complete all five challenges."

"What are they?"

"Not so fast," she cautioned, knowing he was interested. "You'll only know the next challenge ahead of you. If you decide you cannot complete or do not want to attempt any of the challenges, then your claim on the money is over."

"I only get the one-ninety if I finish all five tasks?"

"Yes," she confirmed. He was smiling. That was a lot of money, enough for him to achieve his goal. Enough for a lot more earning potential after that too. How hard could it be?

"Who's involved, besides you?"

"Does it matter?" she shot back, just as quickly. He thought about that for a moment. It didn't matter, actually.

"How do I know I can trust you?"

She laughed at that, a joyless laugh.

"You know who I am?" He nodded. "And I came to you, for what? For the fun of it?" That was true, but was not the point she wanted him to understand. "I'm good for my word," she confirmed, when he said nothing.

"You'll give me one hundred and ninety million, just like that?" He shook his head. "There's a catch, I know there is."

"The only hurdles are these unknown challenges, that is all, I can assure you." He wanted to believe her, though he didn't know her, didn't trust her either.

"Nobody turns up to a random stranger and offers him this kind of money."

"Clifton, I can assure you, you are no random stranger."

He seemed both pleased with that and equally concerned at the same time.

"You picked me?" he asked.

"Yes, I picked you," she confirmed. "As of this week, Niles Ventures is worth one hundred and eighty-nine million, and Spence Securities is worth one ninety." He didn't need the salt rubbed into the wound to know that much. Both firms had started with the same finance, both grown at basically the same rate, even if Adele's firm––his former partner and lover––had nosed themselves in front one month ago. Neither firm was strong enough to take the other over, the fight too evenly matched, the hatred too.

"You want me to take them over?" His nostrils flared at the mention of the enemy, yet his eyes danced with delight at the prospect.

"No, you want to shut her down, that is no secret. I'm merely offering you a prize. What you do with it is your decision."

One hundred and ninety million pounds. It would be enough to buy a controlling stake, enough to pull the company from underneath her, and when they were closed, there would then be hundreds of clients waiting to be snatched up, dozens of patents too.

"You want me to do this," he repeated, firmly, as if he'd not heard the previous answer, or chosen not to believe a word. "Why?"

"I have nothing against your ex-partner, Clifton, believe me."

"Yet, you'll give me the money to ruin her?" He scoffed at the idea. He wanted the money, he knew that, and he wanted to put that bitch out of business. But though he thrived on risk, he never took a gift for granted. Especially coming from a group of wealthy Russians, presented to him by the Acting President herself.

"I'll let you into a little secret," she said, drawing in a little closer as if someone might overhear them, although they were alone and had been the entire time. His senses came alive to her perfume, rich and overpowering, entirely enticing. "This isn't the first time we've done something like this. When you own the amount these oligarchs do, having fun moves to a new level."

She stepped back, resuming her previous position, her delightful fragrance still lingering.

"It's all for fun, you mean?"

"Entirely, but the incentive has to be real. Has to be something you really want. Let's cut to the chase, Clifton," she said, her tone suddenly switching from friendly and tempting, to direct and businesslike. She knew she had him, had for a while. "I know you want this money. I wouldn't be here if I thought that wasn't the case."

He remained silent for the time being, the camera relaying the image of a man pondering his predicament. The five oligarchs were transfixed and the room they were watching from silent.

"And I can walk away at any moment?"

"Yes," she said. She needed to reiterate the caveat. She wanted him to see the challenge through completely. "You'll only hear each challenge one at a time. There are no guarantees that any challenge offers you a cash reward for quitting," she said, emphasising the last word, gaining a measure of pleasure from the grimace it caused. "Only if you complete all five challenges as set before you by each oligarch will I hand you my personal computer, the transaction details completed, all ready for you to press enter."

"And that sends me the money, just like that?"

"It sends the money out, yes," she confirmed, coolly.

"Yeah, okay, I'm in," he said, his eyes flashing with excitement, his fingers tapping his left knee constantly––a clear tell if this were a game of poker––suggesting he might not be as confident as he was making out.

The room of oligarchs let out a roar of satisfaction at Clifton's acceptance of the challenge. Another fine performance they had witnessed, the country's best actress still able to play a role perfectly.

"Very good. I will give you the first challenge immediately. You'll have the rest of the day to decide, but I won't leave until you have." He seemed both flustered and encouraged by that prospect. "And remember, by my estimation, the challenges get harder with each level." She pulled an envelope from her bag, the perfect copy of the lottery ticket given to Svetlana by Markovic earlier. She placed a cigarette lighter on the table.

"Your first challenge is this. Inside this envelope is a winning lottery ticket, claimable in the UK. They purchased the ticket last week in London. It includes the exact details. The ticket is worth nine point three million pounds. Your challenge is very simple. Take the ticket and walk away, but if you do that, you will have failed the overall challenge. There will be no prize on offer apart from the winning ticket. Or," and she paused, Clifton expecting the caveat even as he reached for the envelope which he now left unopened between his fingers. "Or you take that lighter and burn the ticket, completing the first challenge and advancing to the next task which will happen tomorrow."

"Bloody hell," he said, his London accent coming out stronger than earlier. "Can I see the ticket?"

"Check it for yourself. I assure you it is the real deal."

He opened the envelope, proceeding to do the same thing that every single Contestant did first in the Games. He reached for his phone, tapped away a few times, eventually getting to the Lottery HQ page and whistling at the confirmation of that week's winning numbers. He checked the date of the ticket again, looked back at his phone. One winning ticket existed for the rollover jackpot of nine million, three-hundred thousand pounds.

"It's a hell of a lot of money," he said, sure only five minutes before that he could handle whatever a bunch of wealthy old Russians might throw at him, and yet here, at the first fence, he might fall.

"It is for so many people. I'm sure it is for you, too. But it's not enough, is it?"

He knew Svetlana meant it not being enough to put Adele Spence out of business. The woman who had humiliated him, driven him to others, stolen from him and forced the closure of their market-leading business.

Markovic watched on, the keenest man in the room at that moment, as the camera in Svetlana's bag continued to give them perfect coverage of the ongoing situation. Was he about to become one hundred and ninety million pounds richer?

"I thought this would be easy," Clifton confessed, a first crack in his cocky exterior. Svetlana resisted the impulse to feel any sympathy for him, however. "I should burn it, I know that. One task down, four to go, and given what this one is like, the nearer I get, the easier it'll be." He paused, remembering a few game shows he used to watch when he was a kid. "You'll keep offering more until I buckle, won't you?"

"I said you'll only know the next challenge when you clear the previous one. There are no guarantees about anything."

"No, I get this game," he said, shaking his head, getting the thought out of his mind that he was holding nearly ten million in his hands. *Keep your eyes on the prize. You're here for the big bucks, not pocket change.* He reached for the lighter, watching to see any reaction from Svetlana as if she might throw herself at him to get him to stop. He held the object to the corner of the ticket, no flame there yet, his mind asking him if he were crazy. Was he going to burn his chance with that kind of money?

Markovic felt a wave of anxiety, his own chances now precariously hanging in the balance. He'd risked everything by putting forward a simpler task, but by going first, he hoped the temptation would have been enough to force the guy to walk away. Utkin watched with glee, though with a little trepidation himself. His task gave the man no cash alternative, and if Niles could burn what he thought was a winning lottery ticket––the real thing still sat in Markovic's inside pocket––then he might complete the second challenge, though the time element to Utkin's challenge added a new variable.

The flame licked into life as Clifton triggered the lighter, the ticket soon burning. He dropped it into the ashtray, the ticket destroyed, beyond salvation.

"You have completed the first challenge, congratulations," she said, standing up suddenly at that moment.

"Now what?" he said, in protest.

"I said you'll hear each challenge the following day. I'll be in touch," and she moved to the door, taking her bag with her, the watching oligarchs unable to see Clifton's pained expression. But they heard him call after her.

"I'll be ready to knock whatever they throw at me out the park," and he acted out the swinging of a baseball bat as if hitting a home run, something only Svetlana saw, the camera facing the other way.

"A van will collect you from the front gates at eleven tomorrow morning," she said from the door, the bag turned around. "You will get in the back and come alone. Nobody is to know where you are going. Bring nothing with you. I'll see you tomorrow," and she left the villa, back behind the wheel of her car as Clifton came to the door. Once clear of the gates, she spoke for the benefit of those still watching from the built-in camera.

"Markovic, that concludes your challenge, and you cannot win this time. You are all now free to go. We will meet back at the castle tomorrow at eleven. You can watch what happens from the same room. I will meet Clifton as he arrives. I will again explain the entire challenge. My team will covertly record what he does. I will drive ahead to the marina, expecting him no later than one o'clock in the afternoon, otherwise he would have lost the task. I'm looking forward to this one," she ended with a naughty smile. The camera feed switched off moments later, the men saying a few words to each other as they left the room, the sunshine bright on the eyes as they made it back into daylight. Crowds of people milled around the public areas of the castle in the distance, couples sipping drinks outside one cafe, families and at least one school group making their way to the top and the view. A police car sat parked in a car park one hundred metres below, two officers watching the crowds and vehicles from the comfort of their air-conditioned car.

Tomorrow, a naked man would appear from the top of the castle. Suddenly the entire group of oligarchs was looking forward to the chaos that might bring.

17

New York City, USA
Six Months Ago

The deliveries were speeding up, Jeff McKay staying home that morning as yet another package arrived for him from *Gremlin,* a name he had heard the CIA use once for the Russian whistleblower. Jeff didn't know if the CIA knew about the package, or if they knew yet who his Russian source was, or where exactly he was hiding. Jeff had decided not to try digging himself, the source once telling him he could see the Statue of Liberty from his bed. Jeff had never passed that information to the CIA. They would surely have been able to narrow the hunt down significantly.

Jeff enjoyed being the man on the inside, the one in the know. He feared losing the connection altogether if the CIA got involved.

The information in the package that morning detailed a mission by the then President of Russia, Filipov, carried out in Siberia. It was a Russian-on-Russian hit. It listed two oligarchs as killed, no other reports of fatalities.

There were details of a secret underground organisation called *The Machine* controlled by three billionaires which had had its headquarters in Siberia. This was journalistic gold particularly as it looked as if Svetlana was involved.

The accusation was there––did Svetlana Volkov know a lot more than she was letting on?

Jeff made copies of everything once more, keeping his own versions in his locked safe that he had hidden in his study at home. The other two copies he boxed up and addressed for their intended recipients, one bound for Moscow, the other for London. He would fly to Atlanta to visit a friend and courier them from there, deciding this seemed to be the safest approach.

He waited a few days and went unannounced the following weekend. The packages were on planes heading to Europe that very night.

Vauxhall House, MI6 HQ, London

THE PACKAGE ARRIVED first thing on Monday morning, Anissa called down to the post room, checks carried out, the box deemed safe. By that point she already trusted this mysterious source of information.

She ripped open the tab as soon as she was back in the shared office, Sasha closing the door as she took her seat. He dropped into the chair next to her.

They browsed through the information which once again claimed to be official memos, leaked information: the real deal. It fascinated them both to read about the Machine.

It was already clear: Russia had previously had no-one prepared to leak information of this nature, and all so current.

"We need to protect this source," Anissa said after a few minutes, the pair reading different sheets of paper, taking the information at random.

"The whistleblower, you mean?" Sasha asked. They'd been able to continue to work together at MI6 very well. Neither had dared to venture any further in their conversation about where they were relationally. Sasha assumed their relationship was already over, he just wished it was official. They only saw each other during working hours, anyway. That was probably the confirmation he needed, might be all he would get. She seemed so guarded now, though the emergence of Gremlin had shown signs of life once more. The agent in her was on the way back, he could tell.

"Yes. My gut tells me there is much more to come. This is someone who knows how to expose Svetlana Volkov. That has to make him a prime target of the Kremlin."

"The Americans will have him protected, I'm sure."

"No, Gordon said that the CIA don't know where he is." She'd had that conversation with Gordon the other week.

"You believe them? Would they tell us if they did?"

"Maybe not," she agreed, "but it can't hurt to step up cover anyhow. If the Kremlin silences him before we've heard everything, we'll never know how deep it all goes. We'll never know if Svetlana Volkov has even darker secrets beneath that glamorous exterior she carries around." Both knew there was much below the surface, the public Svetlana merely the tip of a very dangerous iceberg.

"I think we should ask Charlie and Zoe to see what they can find out."

Charlie Boon, with his agent-partner Zoe, had been in MI6 for as long as she had. Charlie had been the specialist in Russia, but an indiscretion following the murder of his former girlfriend had put him out in the cold for a while, from both the service and missions concerning Russia. Alex and Anissa had worked with Charlie and Zoe a few times since, however.

"You think they would go?"

"Not if it wasn't a fully sanctioned mission, I guess," Anissa said, conceding that much. She would have to speak to the Director General before approaching the pair. If MI6 could locate Gremlin, could keep him safe, spotting any threat coming from the Russians and most notably from Svetlana herself before it was too late, then they would do whatever it took. Anissa was sure of it. It also gave them front row seats in what could be the biggest political scandal in decades.

"Look, I'll see the DG before I leave tonight. I'll catch Charlie after that, give him the heads up."

"You think the DG will sign off on it that quickly?" He had only had limited involvement with the Director General himself since his arrival in London, the first meeting done with Alex alongside him, the British agent proud to introduce his Russian friend to the top dog.

"It doesn't hurt to prepare Charlie for the inevitable," Anissa smiled. One way or the other she would get her boss's approval. They had given lines of communication and responsibility within Six a sharp overview. For the time being, there was no DDG.

Team leaders in MI6 now reported directly to the DG, all middle management positions done away with, as the Service desperately looked to tighten up, needing to improve its image to those in political power, needing to gain their trust again.

18

Alicante, Spain
One Year Ago

The van pulled up into the private parking area at eleven forty-five the following morning. Svetlana opened the rear door herself, Clifton sitting on a pull-down seat, but there were no windows in the back of the vehicle. Dazzled by the sudden light pouring in, expecting the door to open as the vehicle had finally stopped, he was at least pleased to see the smiling face of Svetlana.

"Did you sleep well last night?" she asked, as if this were merely a coming together of friends, a catching up on old times.

He'd slept terribly. He should have cut his losses and taken the money, he knew that now. He didn't trust any of them, whoever they were. They had set the first task that way to make him think the rest would be easy.

"I slept fine," he said, ducking out of the rear door of the transit vehicle and stretching as he stood there. He looked around for a moment, fear growing during the trip that they had duped him, that this was nothing more than a kidnap situation. Yet the van had not delivered him to some dark warehouse on the edge of nowhere. Quite the opposite.

"This is the Santa Barbara castle, isn't it?" he asked. He'd visited the fortification two years ago, not seen the part they were now in, but the buildings in the distance appeared on most postcards the region produced.

"Yes, we are, and if you'll follow me, I will tell you what your second challenge is." Wall-mounted cameras would track the pair as they threaded through three narrow alleyways, on the way passing the room where the oligarchs were watching, not that Clifton would know this, nor did Svetlana point anything out. She then led him through two interior rooms, climbing stairs between each, heading higher. She stopped in a darkened room, though she turned the lights on after walking in. Outside Clifton could see the viewing platform at the top of the castle, the door in front of him would no doubt take him out towards that area if it were open.

From a window on the side of the room, the walls thick and ancient, the hole now glassed in undoubtedly a cannon point in years gone by, they could see the beach, the pier and the marina beyond.

Svetlana turned to Clifton, who after appreciating the view from the window, turned to face her.

"Welcome to your second challenge. If you accept this challenge and can complete it in the time given, you will move onto the third of the five challenges tomorrow. Today's challenge requires only one hour, so if you complete it, you have the rest of the day to relax and recover." She looked at her watch. "It is now five minutes to twelve, and if you accept the challenge, and by my watch only, your hour will start on the dot of noon. I will wait at the finish line for you to appear there no later than one o'clock."

"The finish line? Where is that?" He'd never been much of a runner, though he didn't yet know what she would ask of him. She wasn't offering him cash this time, it seemed, to tempt him to walk away. He kicked himself internally again for burning that ticket.

"At the marina," she said, going over to the window, Clifton turning and following with his gaze towards the spot where her hand now pointed. "See that second boat, along the front pier?"

"The one with the red and yellow flag?"

"Yes, that one. That will be your finishing point. I will wait right there. Get to me in time, and you will have succeeded with this challenge."

He'd walked there from the beach once before, not as far away as the marina had been, though he'd got lost en route several times. Plus, that had been all uphill. He'd taken around an hour then, maybe less. It was hot, and he had sweated buckets. While still warm, it was later in the year now. And it was all downhill. *He could do this.* His spirits picked up.

She glanced at her watch again.

"You have three minutes to decide, and you can still walk away from this."

"If I walk, I lose. I get it," he said, adding. "I've got this."

"One more thing you need to know," she said, with a smile, the kind that told him he would not like what followed. "You must be naked when you walk out through that door," she said, pointing to the door in front of them, the one leading to the viewing point, the same spot now crowded with people.

He swore at her. "You're kidding, right?"

"No, and you have two minutes before your time starts. The challenge is that you make it from this point to the marina, starting off naked. No shoes, no phone, no money. Nothing with you. And you make it in one hour to the marina, otherwise you can no longer win that one hundred and ninety million pounds."

The mention of the money did what she hoped it would do. It focused his mind afresh, reminded him why he was there, why he'd gone ahead with it in the first place, why he'd set fire to over nine million quid the day before.

"One minute," she confirmed, the silence finally broken. His eyes darted from her to the window and the crowds beyond, then back to her.

"Sod it, I'm in," he said, pulling his t-shirt off, before slipping off his shoes, then undoing his belt, removing his jeans. Standing in only his boxers, with only seconds left, he looked Svetlana in the face. "This is for real? You mean this?"

"I do," she said, counting down the final few seconds in her head, as she moved to the door, one eye on her watch, one hand on the key in the lock. "Three, two, one," and as she turned the key, Clifton removed his boxers, the door opening and without allowing himself any hesitation, he ran, the sunshine on his skin, shrieks audible within seconds. She quickly locked the door again, collecting up his clothes, placing them in a bag. She would take the bag with her, heading to the van, someone waiting to drive her down to the marina. Her team of cameramen and women would relay the rest of the action to the oligarchs. She might review it later, but her focus now was getting into place, being ready. They pulled away five minutes after twelve, passing the police car, the two officers out of the vehicle by then, speaking into their radios as they raced up towards the top of the castle. She smiled. He might not even make it past the first one hundred metres.

As the sunlight hit his eyes, the heat at first seemed overpowering, but Clifton ignored these sensations, shut out the fact he was naked, and raced through the door and into the open. The screams that started soon after didn't help, people turning, some pointing and laughing in the distance, others scurrying to get their children out of the way, hands over their eyes.

He needed to find clothes and knew there was only one way to do that. He jumped a few walls, his feet cutting and screaming at him to stop. The ground was hard, dry and stony. There would be no easy way to move across it, no time to waste. He needed shoes.

Clifton saw the van that had brought him there that morning now leaving. He spotted two police officers running his way, as he darted from view, sure they hadn't laid eyes on him, but aware of his presence. Still voices called out, a few teens with phones following him, no doubt recording or even perhaps streaming this humiliation. Yet, he'd passed up nine million to do this, and if he didn't, he would lose a lot more. That money was his. He could do this. He just needed to get away, slip out of sight for long enough to make it down the path.

He spotted his chance moments later. Turning a corner, the alleyway empty, came a man, probably a few years older than him, but Clifton would take what he could get. The Brit was in front of the stranger in seconds, the local man concerned to see a naked lunatic running at him. Clifton's elbow caught the man clean in the face, his momentum unchanged. It knocked the other man to the ground, his head hitting the compacted soil hard.

"Stay down or I'll hit you again!" Clifton raged, his blood boiling, not knowing if his victim even understood him. Clifton struggled to remove the man's shoes, the local fearing the worst, putting up a fight now, a cry going up. Clifton reached for his mouth, suppressing the cry and then his own scream of pain when the man bit him. Clifton lost it, pounding the victim time and time again until he beat the man unconscious.

At the far end of the alleyway, the way Clifton had come, the cries had apparently drawn the attention of others, or perhaps they'd followed him from the viewing area, but two people appeared, stopping and shouting something from a distance as they saw the fight happening. Clifton heard the word police mentioned, he was certain.

He pulled the man's trousers off, pulled the t-shirt also, and with no time to dress, cuddled everything up into a ball he held tight to him as he raced away from the onlookers. He could soon hear whistles from the two policemen, the ominous sound of sirens in the distance which were all heading his way. If he didn't dress and escape soon, there would be no way down. He had no idea how long he had been so far.

A minute later he was on the outside of the walls, away from the crowds as far as he could tell. He pulled on the clothing, which was too big for him, though the belt stopped the trousers from falling down, which was something. The trainers were a snug fit, and Clifton stood, glad that he was at least dressed now.

The whistles and shouts from behind were only getting closer. Clifton looked down the steep hill which was not an exit anyone took, the ground littered with rocks and loose shingle, hundreds of cacti of various heights dominating the terrain.

There was nothing for it but to run. He couldn't go back the way he'd come, the area no doubt soon swarming with police. He went for it, slipping several times, falling once, which was painful, but he got up. He would have to deal with the cuts and bruises later, the bleeding left unchecked for the time being. He had to make it out of there.

Looking back, two officers had appeared at the spot he had dressed in, and their radios crackled as they reported Clifton's position. He pressed on, his arms now full of cactus needles, his lungs demanding oxygen, his heart pounding in his chest like a marching band at Buckingham Palace.

At the bottom of the hill stood a stone wall which separated the paths leading up to the castle from the area he was now in. The wall was rough and broken, though high. It might have been decades, if not centuries old for all he knew. He grabbed at a few rocks; the stone crumbled away as he tried to pull himself up. Getting frantic, the cops having disappeared from view––heading the sensible way out, not the way he had just attempted––he finally found a hole large enough to get his shoe into, and from there clambered roughly over the wall. He was on the other side.

A few walkers backed away, themselves heading up, unaware of his castle top escapades, but equally wary of a man appearing from an out-of-bounds location. He jogged past them, his clothes dirty and ripped, his arms red and sore.

Down below, two police cars sat on the only road ahead of him. He had to get off the path; he knew that now.

Inside the room from where the five oligarchs stood watching, the coverage remained mostly continuous. A few times Clifton had slipped out of reach from the teams monitoring him, but others, sometimes using long distance lenses until those on the ground got close enough, soon picked up the shots and the show continued.

Utkin looked nervously at his watch while a timer counted down remorselessly on the television relay. There were thirty-five minutes left. The fact Clifton was no longer naked had taken that element of risk, of humiliation, out of the challenge. Now it was a chase. Clifton against the police, him against the clock.

Popov, whose challenge would be up next if the Brit were to succeed, stood a little less comfortable than he had half an hour ago. They'd all watched how brutally Clifton had beaten the man from whom he'd stolen the clothes. Perhaps he would just as easily be able to kill a stranger? He might have even killed this one, had the calls from behind not alerted him that there were people watching.

Avoiding the main paths as much as possible, more often taking the direct line down through the wild terrain than the winding tourist tracks, Clifton made it to the base of the hill, taking his chances along the final small stretch of the paved path, which brought him to some steps, buildings and the start of the tightly packed streets just beyond. He knew if he made it that far he could lose himself.

He sped through a small park; the pathways zigzagging from side to side, Clifton vaulting the gaps when able to and coming to a main road. He paused a moment, to gain his bearings and his breath, spotting that beyond the rails facing him was a road. He jogged over to it, trying to get some energy back, keeping a little in reserve in case he needed a fast escape.

Clifton jogged down the middle of the street, sweat now pouring down his back. He couldn't hear any sirens, that was all he cared about. He'd lost all sense of time.

He cut right, taking him between two buildings, stairs descending ever closer to sea level, and therefore ever nearer to his goal. He turned down another road, desperately hoping he was heading in something like the right direction.

Along that narrow lane he stopped as he got to an opening. He crossed the Plaza De Santa Maria, mostly ignored by the locals and tourists, and continued to the next junction. Beyond the no-entry sign he saw a palm tree, his gut clenching. He was close. He jogged up that street, crossing the next small road, the palm tree still in front of him as he emerged onto the main road, the grass of the junction familiar to him. He'd been here. It wasn't far.

Clifton ignored the strange looks he was drawing from others, his appearance rather startling. He didn't care about that at the moment, a man who usually prided himself in his appearance, bragging about being the sharpest dressed VC in the City. He crossed the road dodging between cars and provoking a taxi driver to hoot in annoyance.

The beach lay before him, golden and crowded, despite the height of summer having past a few months ago. He knew where he was, and turning right, the marina appeared not long after the beach. He still had no idea how long he had been.

Police sirens came back into earshot. Did they know where he was, or were they unrelated?

Clifton spotted the boat he was aiming for, the van parked alongside it, Svetlana hidden behind shades and a large hat, blending in as a typical tourist. If only those passing by knew who really sat there waiting.

She seemed both surprised to see him and pleased at the same time. She glanced at her watch as he closed the final few metres towards her. He'd been only forty minutes.

"Get in," she said, no winner's medal, no handshake in greeting, as she opened the rear door to the van parked up next to the boat. "Those are for you," she said, nodding her head towards the sound of the sirens approaching, showing she knew they were heading their way. "My driver will take you to your villa. Get yourself cleaned up and rested," she said, taking in his state of disrepair, one cut on his elbow looking particularly messy. "I will meet you at your villa tomorrow morning. Congratulations, you've completed the second challenge." She shut the rear door, tapping the side of the van with her open hand, two loud thumps and the driver pulled away. She would not go with him. Wouldn't take the risk.

She got behind the wheel of her own car.

"Utkin, he defied you and sailed through your challenge. You too are now out of the running this time. Tomorrow it's over to you, Popov. You will all gather in the same room at eleven, and can watch proceedings as usual. Have a good day, and we'll continue the spectacle tomorrow." She switched off the camera, driving from the marina, as three police cars reached the junction, two of them stopping, the cops spreading out, the other car continuing further along the beach. She smiled to herself. Clifton had pulled it off again, and the next task would be much less public. But it would raise the bar. How far would he actually go, especially the nearer he got to the prize?

19

Forest Dacha, Russia
Present Day

Rad had taken three calls in the week so far, Kostya surprised the younger man had any reception at all. Kostya had never had a telephone, nothing working that far out of the city, that far into the forest. Rad had let on about his army-issued antenna hidden in the inside of a tree. The older man smiled at that thought, learning more about Rad as the week progressed.

By day four, they had the first two exterior walls up, secured in place by wooden support beams until they finished all the walls, which would then allow them to nail roof trusses into place. Kostya had assured Rad they would get to that stage by the weekend. Looking around, Rad could only see the work they had yet to get finished.

The weather had been superb, the time away from Moscow everything Rad had needed. The calls pulled him back into things all too quickly, updates given on the progress of the hearing from a security point of view. The team based in and around the Law Courts had nothing to do. Rad smiled. He would take that any day. Boredom in his line of work meant his client was safe.

He'd not asked about how the trial itself was going, something his team leader would not have known anyway, security personnel kept out of the courtroom. The world would soon hear the allegations, anyway. Then everyone would know.

Rad had talked a lot more openly with Nastya that week, the time away from Moscow allowing the still newly married couple the chance to talk, and talk about things that mattered. Nastya had been careful not to overstep the mark, but Rad's openness had encouraged her.

He'd still never answered her about what he did for Filipov. He said he couldn't say. Said she wouldn't want to know. He'd told her it was for the best, but knowing there was something, only made her more worried. He promised he didn't do that role anymore. He now looked to stop the bad guys from getting to the Acting President. That was all she needed to worry about, and Svetlana was one of the most popular figures in a generation. There seemed little threat from anyone towards her.

That night, as the third wall came together, built on the ground and ready to go up the following morning, the four relatives once more sat around the fire, the men having showered and taken a banya; the women preparing the food before Rad got on with cooking it.

"We must go hunting again soon," Nastya said. The focus on the house and the nightly feasts that ensued at the end of each long day meant they were getting through the meat supply quicker than they usually would have. She was the hunter on her side of the family, Kostya having initially trained her, but she was far better than him now and had been for a long time. They all knew Rad could hunt.

"We'll go out together, later," Rad said.

"You don't need to," Nastya protested. She knew the labour tired Rad, the work very physical, his passion to complete as much as possible of the building work that week meaning he rose early, was outside not long after seven and worked the whole day, the food finally drawing the men away from the build around dusk.

"It'll be fun," he smiled. They hadn't hunted together for months.

"We must go far, I fear," she said, Rad knowing exactly what she meant. The work there, the fire also, would only cause the game animals to move further away. Nastya had seen no sign of deer in the area for days.

"We'll pick up their trail, don't worry. We'll go once we've eaten," he promised, enough said on the subject, Nastya knowing not to carry it on. Besides, it would be nice to go hunting together, just the two of them. They'd had their very first conversation while out hunting one morning. He'd downed the deer she'd just missed. She had fallen in love with him at that very moment.

When the meat had cooked, Olya passed it around, the conversation jovial, the mood happy. Rad sat there enjoying the food, listening to the steady flow of chatter, the laughter, the love. This was his life now, this was safe. This was good. He was building a home for his wife, a home they might one day raise their own family in, not that the couple had talked about children yet. She was still young; they had time. But the thought excited him.

Svetlana Volkov had offered him all that, a route out of the army and away from all those war zones. He would be forever grateful.

NASTYA WAVED goodbye to her uncle and aunt, their quad bike taking them home, a track they now knew well, despite the growing darkness.

It was nearly nine; the sun had set about thirty minutes before, Rad putting the two weapons on the back of his own quad bike and then several traps. He added three boxes of ammunition into a bag, dropping in another gun, this one a pistol which he'd taken from a collection in the safe. She'd not seen the other weapons before, nor the heavy supply of bullets. She would hold off having that conversation for another day.

Ten minutes later, they too were heading off, Rad locking everything up, always the last to move away from the door. She knew he was checking everything, putting things in place to notice if anyone came searching. She'd once walked in first, getting a sharp reaction from Rad. He'd shouted at her, stressed from something at work, but the first and only time he'd raised his voice. He had told her she'd destroyed any evidence that there might have been, ruining the carefully scattered stones. He warned her never to do it again. She never had. He was merely being careful, she told herself. This was his way of protecting them both. She learned to live with it, learned to accept it and not question anything. She wondered what he would do when the house got finished, the property bigger, the entry points multiple. Surely he couldn't cover the entire perimeter?

"How's the project going?" she asked, the pair now tightly pressed against each other, the bike cutting through the undergrowth.

"It's fun," Rad said. She'd seen him smiling that week for the first time in months. "Kostya seems to think we'll have the roof on by Sunday, some of it anyway."

"That'll be fantastic," Nastya said.

"We'll see. Seems like an awful long way to go before we get that far."

"He knows what he's doing," she countered.

"That's true."

"It'll be a beautiful home, Rad, thank you," she said.

He smiled. He knew it would be, he just hoped they could deliver what they had planned, what they had in mind.

Two kilometres away from the dacha they were at the edge of the water, a stream running down to what would become a sizeable lake soon enough. Kostya and Olya lived further round that lake on the shore near a thick cluster of trees.

"We'll leave the bike here," Rad said, switching off the engine and stepping from the machine once she had moved from her seat behind him. In winter the lake froze over, making crossing it directly a much easier route. He'd once got chased across the snow by a pack of wolves, Nastya coming to his rescue. She wasn't a bad shot with a rifle, either.

They started to navigate their way around the edge of the lake, going in the opposite direction from where her relatives lived, knowing there were not any homes in the near distance this side of the lake. It was twenty minutes before Rad noticed the first sign of animal tracks. He crouched down to examine the markings, sighting some droppings soon after.

"Deer, though a day or two old already," he said, the dryness at the centre of the prints telling him this animal had long cleared the area by now.

"We'll keep moving," Nastya encouraged, both walking in the direction the deer had taken, their ears listening for any signs of movement, their eyes scanning for further evidence.

It was ten before they heard something move in the undergrowth perhaps thirty metres from them. Both hunters stood still, each hearing it, their instincts kicking in seconds later. Rad pulled his weapon into position, the light dim, his night vision lens giving him some visibility. It couldn't have been a deer, the markings old, though after a silence, more rustling.

Rad raised his left hand, showing Nastya to move back along the path they had just taken, her own weapon now raised. She silently tiptoed backwards, gun trained on the greenery from where the noise was continuing to come. Once in position, Rad signalled his intentions to her. She was to move forward, chasing out whatever there was in there.

She gripped her weapon all the more, darkness closing in on her, though she didn't feel in any real danger. A boar might charge her, a deer would run the other way. It could have been a bear, but only a small one, the undergrowth not bushy enough yet to hide anything of significance. She knew it couldn't be a wolf. They never ventured alone, and they would have heard the pack long before getting so close.

Still the noise continued, a rustling through leaves and sticks. Then a snort. It was a boar, Nastya breaking a twig on the ground at that moment as the animal came into view, a fully grown adult. It charged at her through the greenery, Nastya struggling to get her gun in position as the animal darted from her left-hand side. Rad got the shot off a split second later. He emerged from the shadows, alerting the boar moments before, seeing it break cover and begin its charge.

The shot had downed the animal, but not killed it. The boar called out into the night, its dying anger doing nothing to help its survival. Rad put it out of its misery quickly.

They both stood over it, admiring their catch. There was a lot of meat on it. It made moving it back from there even more challenging. There was no way they could get the quad bike to the spot. They would somehow have to move it part of the way.

"I'll grab a sack from the bike," Rad said. "We'll then roll the animal onto the sack and drag it into the next clearing. I think I can get the bike in that far. Will you be okay?"

It was better someone stayed behind, meat an easy meal for any scavenger if they left it unguarded.

"I'll be fine," she said, a little hesitantly, darkness now almost absolute around them, and this the domain of the night hunters. She was used to that by now.

"I'll be as quick as I can," Rad said, already jogging back the way they had come, using his scope to make sure he was going in the right direction and that there were no surprises ahead.

He'd been on the bike for only a few minutes, navigating a route back to the clearing, when the shots first broke the silence. Three shots fired close together from the direction of where Nastya had been waiting.

Rad shouted out, too far away for her to hear, the bike too noisy for that to have been possible. He sped up.

Another couple of shots rang out, the sound of barking heard seconds later sending a cold shudder through Rad's spine. *Wolves.*

Pulling into the clearing, he spotted Nastya, back towards him, gun raised into the darkness from the direction she had just come. He stopped the engine, the only sound now of a pack of hungry wolves attacking the fresh meat.

"There were too many of them," she said, turning to Rad, emotion on her face but no tears. She'd done the right thing getting out of there. The boar was enough of a distraction, enough of a prize, to stop the pack coming after her.

"It's okay," he said, pulling her into him, one eye on the path behind her, but the wolves were keeping their distance. "Let's get out of here. If there are wolves in the area, the deer can't be far away." Having the main predators so close meant there was game nearby. "That boar will keep them fed, they won't bother us now."

Three hours later they were back at the dacha, quad bike empty, the tracks they found not leading to anything else in the area. They would have to pick up where they left off the following night. Now, sleep was the top priority and there were only a few hours left to do that before Rad would once again be up, preparing for another day of building.

20

London
Five Months Ago

Sasha left the pub that Saturday afternoon, the lunchtime's Premier League match finished, the league leaders still in pole position. Ice hockey had always been his preferred sport and he had wondered about getting into that in London but didn't have the time. Anissa no longer liked watching sport so he needed to go to the pub which only showed football. The barman laughed when Sasha suggested switching off the live games for ice hockey; he said there would be a riot.

Two years later, Sasha understood the appeal. He'd adopted one local team himself and was into his second full season of watching them win most weeks. They hadn't played in the match he'd just watched as Sasha ventured out onto the streets in search of some food. The game of the day was the featured top four clash and a derby at that. The pub had held supporters of both clubs, watching in separate rooms, the banter often amusing.

Sasha entered the restaurant that had become a personal

favourite and did a double take as he spotted someone on the first table. He knew her face. She didn't seem to notice him. She sat with another female, the two friends in deep conversation it seemed. Sasha was still looking her way when, as if sensing eyes on her, she looked up, smiling at Sasha moments later, recognition sinking in. The woman said something to her friend, both sets of eyes then looking his way, as the first woman stood and moved towards Sasha. It was in the movement that he remembered where he knew her from. She was the doctor who came to his flat to assess and treat Anissa.

"How are you?" she asked, all smiles, professional to the core.

"I'm fine. Look, I'm sorry to stare, I couldn't initially remember where I knew you from," he said, taking his coat off, putting it behind the chair at a spare table he'd found.

"How is she?" the doctor asked, apparently referring to Anissa, their only shared interest.

"Much better," he lied. It was partly true, though he wondered how much he should talk about his colleague in this context.

"That's good." The doctor glanced over to her friend, who was paying the bill at the counter, her coat on and bag in hand. "Are you meeting anyone for lunch?" she asked.

"No," he said, seeing the other doctor now leave who waved to her friend as she went out of the door.

"Can I join you for a drink then?" she asked, not flirting with him, not that Sasha could tell, anyway.

"Sure," he said, pointing her to the seat opposite him. They both sat down at the same time.

"I don't want to intrude, it's just I never got to work with…" and she paused, not initially knowing how to word the rest of the sentence. "With your lot before," she finally opted.

Sasha smiled. She liked the adventure of working with MI6 and seeing the Russian that afternoon had triggered something inside her.

"Look, it's not all James Bond, you know."

"Oh, I know," she said, serious suddenly, as if she didn't want it to seem she thought it was precisely that. "And Anissa is recovering well, is she?"

She seemed genuinely concerned.

"It took everything from her, we both know that."

The doctor nodded slowly. "A terrible thing to have gone through."

Sasha took the moment to glance at the menu, not sure what more he could say, not sure if he should say anything. Besides, he was hungry.

"Have you eaten?" he asked, the doctor nodding. "Mind if I order something first, then we can talk. I'm starving," he smiled.

"Sure," and she waited for the waitress to come over and take his order. When the doctor confirmed she wasn't eating anything, the waitress left them to it.

An hour later, the pair were working their way through a bottle of Shiraz, a decent one too. Both had ordered dessert, the conversation fun and flirty, but nothing inappropriate. Sasha had forgotten how it felt to be around another woman, without the stresses and pressures. He realised how complicated that side of things had become since Anissa. His mind nudged towards his colleague, the doctor sitting opposite him with a connection to the same agent.

"Did Anissa ever speak to another doctor besides you?"

"I'm not aware that she did, no. I believe they wanted someone outside of the Service, but I think I'm the only one they called."

Sasha seemed to consider that answer for a while, the doctor remaining silent, savouring her wine for the time being, knowing the charming Russian would soon follow up with another question if he were after something.

Those questions landed over the next five minutes, Sasha conscious the topic was creeping more and more towards the inevitable which he asked shortly after finishing the last dregs of his second glass of wine.

"Did she ever ask you to arrange a meeting with someone from MI6?"

She put her glass down for a moment, thinking back to the time MI6 first came calling on her surgery door.

"I don't think she spoke to anyone else at Six, but she wanted me to find a female she trusted."

"Who?" Sasha asked.

"Even if I could remember the name, I'm not sure I could tell you, Sasha," she said, somewhat apologetically. "Not that the meeting ever took place."

"The other woman refused to meet?"

"Oh, no, it was the other way round. I was there with the woman, but Anissa never showed. I guess she got cold feet. I tried calling, but after twenty minutes, the other woman got up and left. I never saw her nor Anissa again after that."

Sasha sat back in his chair, not sure what to do with these connotations, not yet certain they meant anything.

"Was it Bethany May who Anissa wanted to meet?"

The name registered in the doctor's eyes, though her professional front remained.

"I shouldn't say," she said, all she said on the matter. She'd said enough.

"She asked you specifically to contact this person, but you never told MI6 about it?"

"She asked me not to; said they would not allow her back if they realised how troubled she still was."

"How did you find out the address?"

"I didn't. I only had a name and a number. I called the woman, explaining who I was and what I was proposing, and it was the other woman who suggested the venue. The meeting was to be on a Saturday, Anissa's request."

"Why Saturday?"

"I've no idea."

"Where did you meet?"

"Some café if I remember right. A similar size to this place, most of the tables crowded."

That made sense, a public venue, plenty of people around Bethany May.

"But the meeting never happened? You are sure Anissa wasn't there, couldn't have spoken to May in the Ladies or anything?"

She smiled at that.

"No, I arrived first, spotted this other woman arrive not long after me. She came to the table, knew it was me and we sat, chatted a little to begin with, but she kept watching the door. I knew she was nervous, didn't know why that would be. She kept looking at her watch, more frequently the later it got, before bolting from there when Anissa was already twenty minutes late. I'd been calling but couldn't get an answer."

"Did you go with her when she left?"

"No, I waited, perhaps for another fifteen minutes, in case Anissa were merely running late, on the Tube or something and unable to call me. The following week, I was informed that I had completed my task with Anissa and that was that."

"So you never spoke to her again, never asked her about what happened that day?"

"No, Sasha," she said, concern showing for the first time on her face. "Why?"

He already had a sinking feeling about this, certain now that Anissa would have been waiting outside, though from all accounts, the timing of the meeting was a few weeks before they murdered May.

"Where was the café?" he asked, ignoring her last question. The doctor thought for a moment, giving him the nearest tube stop as best she could remember. She didn't know the area or the name of the venue, though said it would be in her records if it was important.

Sasha waved that offer away. The tube station she had given him was the nearest one to where Bethany May lived. Anissa would have picked a Saturday hoping that the former DDG would choose somewhere local to take the meeting on a weekend. Anissa must have followed her home.

He left minutes later, collecting the bill and seeing to it himself, thanking the doctor for her time, warning her not to mention anything they had talked about to anyone.

He still didn't know what to do with what he had learned.

21

Alicante, Spain
One Year Ago

Svetlana sat quietly on the sofa, Clifton pacing around the room, mulling over what she had just told him, his steps agitated, his face angry. Her bag once more sat on the kitchen surface, the camera on, the oligarchs watching from the same room they had met in all week.

Clifton swore again, not for the first time that morning.

"You want me to kill someone?" he said, shaking his head once more in disbelief, Svetlana again confirming that was the third task, the latest challenge.

"Who?"

"A stranger."

"Anyone?"

"No, a certain stranger." She'd already gone over this, the photo of the target on the table.

"Why?"

"Does that concern you?"

"Too bloody right it does if you're asking me to kill him!"

"You aren't to know. He might be a saint, he might be a sinner. For this challenge, to you, he's merely one step closer to one hundred and ninety million."

She placed a pistol on the table now, next to the photo. He took a step back following Svetlana producing the actual weapon.

"I can't," he said, not wanting to look at the weapon, but drawn to it anyway. He didn't know why he had assumed he would need to carry out a kill any other way. Explosives, perhaps, or a sniper weapon, not that he had any clue how to use either in real life. The computer games made it look easy, he knew. But a pistol meant being there, in person, in proximity. The guy would see him, would know it was Clifton who'd killed him.

"You refuse the challenge?" Svetlana asked, surprised with what he'd just said. If he was dropping out now, she had gravely underestimated him.

Popov edged a little closer to the screen, studying his prey, willing him to walk away, call it time, state enough was enough.

"I didn't say that," Clifton responded, however. "Where?" he asked.

"Where to kill him?" He nodded, Svetlana continuing almost uninterrupted. "That's totally up to you. We have given you two locations where this man will be today. One of them he always visits alone. You might like to look at that option. It lists the details in the envelope. You have until midnight tonight. If you talk to the target, if you try to find out anything about him, you lose the task and this will be the last you see of me. There will be no prize. If the man is not dead by midnight, you lose. There will be no reward for killing him after that. Do you understand the conditions to this challenge?"

"I kill this guy, this stranger, who must remain a stranger to me, and must be dead before midnight otherwise I kiss goodbye to my money. Right?"

"Yes. So, do you accept the challenge?"

He paused, his pacing picking up in speed a little, though not as actively as before, the man now needing more focus to think it through. Was he a killer? He was no saint, that much he knew. Even yesterday he might have killed a man, his mind lost at that moment through the shame of his nakedness. Trained assassins killed for much less than one hundred and ninety million. And if the man would be alone later, Clifton provided with a weapon, it would be easy. Pull the trigger and get away from there.

"I'm in," he confirmed, Popov turning from the television screen in annoyance, Ivanov merely smiling at an action needed for his own finale to come good.

"Very well. If you are successful, I will be back here tomorrow morning, same time, to present you with your penultimate task."

She stood, going over to collect her bag. This time she kept the camera turned in his direction as she walked towards the door. The five oligarchs watched Clifton reach forward for the gun, though he hesitated to touch it. He pulled away as Svetlana reached the door, turning to say a final goodbye––she would not wish him good luck–– before exiting as swiftly as she had arrived. Clifton watched her from the window this time, before closing the door once she was out through the gate. He needed something to drink, needed a pill or two. If he would carry this out, he had to be pumped, had to be ready.

Ten minutes later he was back on the sofa. The gun had moved from the table, now tucked into the back of his jeans, his t-shirt covering it all. The envelope detailed that the man in the photo was a golfer and ended each day at the driving range. He always went alone, preferred it that way, and usually had the final spot at the range reserved for him, no other punters anywhere near him. That was at seven, many hours from then, and only five hours from the deadline, but Clifton knew it had to be then or never. He didn't want witnesses.

He reached for the bottle again, topping up his glass to the brim. He had plenty of time to get his courage up.

THE TEAM WATCHING Clifton saw him leaving the villa at six, the three cars tailing his rental as it navigated its way to the driving range. The five oligarchs had joined Svetlana at the marina. That evening's video relay was being beamed directly to the yacht she had hired for the rest of the week. The castle was getting too claustrophobic for the men.

Champagne flowed, the food was exquisite and plentiful, their setting nothing compared to the frantic mind of Clifton at that moment, the two as extreme as was possible. Popov kept a keen interest on proceedings, though most of them watched the screen from time to time, three separate relays showing his progress, a final camera already set up at the driving range. They would all be watching when the two men––hunter and prey––came into view.

Thirty minutes later Clifton ground to a halt on the pristine gravel parking area, a lush and very green looking golf course surrounding him on nearly all sides. The driving range sat next to the clubhouse, a machine visible from where he was sitting, metal buckets stored neatly beside it. A closely shaven man walked over to the machine on the dot of seven, Clifton reaching for the photo, but even from that distance, it was undoubtedly his target. He watched him put some coins into the machine. Seconds later many dozen balls filled a bucket which the man then carried towards the range. He went out of view as he turned left, presumably heading the way he always went as detailed in the notes.

Clifton looked around, though aside from a few golfers several holes away, and the girl in the clubhouse behind the desk, there seemed few others around. It was dinnertime, dusk not long away. There was not enough time to start a round now and get back before sunset. Clifton reasoned that, apart from whoever might be on the course at that moment, there wouldn't be anyone else around. He hoped his target was alone.

He could feel the weapon still pressed against his spine as he sat in the driver's seat. It was now or never, he knew that. He'd played by their rules. The guy had to be a criminal, had to be someone they wanted dead. The man looked the type and the way Clifton had seen him swinging the golf club suggested he'd used it not only to drive golf balls. Clifton repeated the persona he had created in his head as he opened the car door, as he kept taking each step. He had to convince himself the man deserved it, had to know he was doing everyone a favour, couldn't accept that the guy was a good man. Wouldn't allow himself to think of some widow grieving over him, two kids asking when papa might come home.

Clifton edged over the gravel, each footstep making a crunch, each pace taking him one step further to becoming a killer.

Beforehand in the villa he had not had another drink for fear he might be too drunk to hit the target. He had stood in front of the mirror, drawing the weapon, pulling the trigger, the pistol empty of bullets. He'd been able to do it, time and time again. Now he carried a loaded weapon, now a bullet would race from the gun and enter human flesh, and probably not stop when it hit bone. Now it wouldn't be his own reflection looking back at him, but another human face. Was the guy armed? Panic raced through him for a moment, almost overpowering him as if to make him stop, to make him question the stupidity of it all. What if the man drew a weapon of his own and fired off a round before he could react? Clifton might this very second be walking to his death.

He reached for the weapon, the contact with the metal bringing some reassurance. He had once fired such a gun, taken to a shooting range by a high-value client, an hour spent firing an array of weaponry at circular targets. He did at least know what to expect, trusted he remembered the grip and position to control the kick.

But this was for real, and suddenly he wondered if he could do it.

The sound of golf balls being hit one at a time from the other side of the wall told him his target was most likely in his usual end booth. Clifton had not gone through the entrance in the middle that led from the parking area, where he'd seen the man walk before turning left. If there were other players, they would see him, not to mention the chance his target would spot him approaching, without a bucket of golf balls, without even a club.

Clifton turned the corner, the wooden walls continuing a little around the side so he could move parallel to the booth, but remain out of sight. He pulled out the weapon, checking the chamber, checking the safety catch was off. He looked around, the golfers from earlier no longer in sight, the road leading up to the clubhouse up which he had driven minutes before still empty.

He slowed his breathing, the sound of a golf stroke coming from the booth every five to ten-seconds now almost rhythmic. Clifton checked one final time, realising that until he poked his head around the corner, he wouldn't know who stood waiting. What if there were others? Yet the information said the man did this alone, whoever he was. Clifton had seen him enter alone. Clifton realised now that the moment he turned that corner, his target would see him, face-to-face.

Whack, whack, whack.

It was time to act. Clifton didn't know how many balls the guy had left in that bucket. He didn't want the opportunity to pass. It was now or never. He counted the time from one hit to the next. About twelve seconds, the guy apparently tiring. He would go on the count of six, hoping at that point to catch the guy having completed his shot, having watched it sail away, before reaching down, collecting the next ball and placing it on the tee. At six-seconds the target might have bent over, back of his head exposed, vulnerable and unaware.

Four, five, six, Clifton counted.

The movement from the edge of the man's eye of someone coming around the corner had startled him, Clifton with the gun raised, his arms straight, the head shot the one he was hoping to make. As the gun fired, the sound cascading around was not dissimilar to a few of the man's shots as the ball skewed into the wooden dividers between the booths. He had tried to stand, throwing the club in Clifton's direction, but the bullet's impact had made that impossible. Clifton looked down the other booths, terrified that there would be witnesses, but thankfully, they were empty.

The dead man lay on the ground, a golf ball on the tee, the bucket knocked over as he'd fallen, the thirty remaining balls scattered in all directions.

Panic raced through Clifton's veins. He was certain someone would have heard the shot, someone seen the killing. He had to move, had to get away from there fast, though not draw any attention to himself.

He went back the way he'd come, skirting around the end wall, back to the corner that looked towards the carpark and his vehicle sitting there. He slipped the weapon into the back of his trousers, not knowing what to do with it, but preferring to keep it with him until he was safe. He could only see one camera, which looked towards the clubhouse entrance. He looked the other way as he crossed the carpark just to be safe and made it to his car. Seconds later he was putting up dust from the driveway back to the main road.

His hands were still shaking.

ON THE BOAT, the camera feed still showed the fallen mafia man, the blood pooling underneath, confirmation that Clifton had managed a kill shot.

"Popov," Svetlana said, her tone sombre––murder was never something they usually went for, though it was far from the first time. "That ends your chances of winning the money. Clifton Niles is proving to be rather a resilient son-of-a-bitch, I think you'll all agree. It appears there isn't anything the man is not prepared to do to get that money."

The oligarch pursed his lips. He didn't think he would have won the challenge. It had not cost him much, the entertainment value far surpassing any financial outlay in finding the mark. One less thug in the world. It was nobody's loss. Ivanov couldn't help but disagree, sure that the man's father would take it as a personal insult, a way of getting at him indirectly.

"But today he had a weapon, and the element of surprise," she said like a commentator, analysing post-match what they had watched. "Tomorrow it is over to Budny. Will Clifton's survival instinct be enough this time, when there is no weapon, when there is someone fighting back? It remains an interesting prospect. As for tonight, we will dock in twenty minutes. You are welcome to stay as long as you like. Please be back here tomorrow lunchtime, and I bid you a pleasant evening," she said, leaving through a side door, heading for her suite. She would sleep there that night; she had been around the men enough that day. There were emails she needed to check, replies that needed her attention.

22

New York City, USA
Two Months Ago

Agents from what Jeff assumed were the CIA, or perhaps the local FBI, now seemed to follow the journalist wherever he went. He'd picked up their presence the previous month, not sure if they had been there before that.

His increasingly random trips out of state must have put them on alert, as had his continued connection to the Russian whistleblower, Gremlin. Two agents had confronted Jeff the week before, cornering him one block from his office as he grabbed a bagel for lunch, demanding to know where the source was hiding. Jeff had refused point blank to give them anything. He had been pondering that very thing himself, but to demand the information, for them to step in and make him feel like the criminal, they'd gone too far.

Besides, Jeff knew very little. He still held a copy of everything Gremlin had sent him, the originals sent on to their intended recipient as directed, but no-one had more than Jeff did.

He used his journalistic rights and privileges to shield himself from further interrogation by the two agents that lunchtime, but within days of the confrontation, his usual news outlets were going silent on him. Soon they wanted nothing to do with the freelance reporter deemed a loose cannon.

Jeff knew it could only have been the work of the CIA. They were attempting to force him into a corner, convince him to share with them what he knew or see his career and reputation go down the drain.

He would not be moved, not by these practices, not by their cheap shots. Jeff also knew that when the time came, no newspapers worth its salt, despite the threats delivered by the CIA, could resist printing the revelations he would expose. Then it wouldn't matter what the CIA was doing to him. Everyone would know. It would be his scoop, his story––his career-defining moment. And he was getting closer to that, he knew it.

The flowers arrived the morning of July 4. Jeff signed for them, a little bewildered. Nobody had ever sent him a bunch of flowers. He asked the delivery guy where they'd come from, the man confirming Jeff would have to call the shop, he was just delivering the bouquets. Jeff thanked the man, looking down the street as he closed the door behind him, certain the CIA would have been watching, even though it was a national holiday. He couldn't see anyone suspicious.

Once the door was shut, he inspected the flowers. He knew at once where they were from. Far from a bunch of roses or carnations, tulips or lilies, these were all white petalled flowers with a yellow centre. To the untrained eye, daisies, and though these were in the same family of flowers, what Jeff held was camomile, the national flower of Russia.

Jeff went into the kitchen, placing the flowers on the worktop and searching for a pair of scissors. He clipped off the bow that held it all together and removed the wrapping from the outside. As suspected, deep into the bunch, he found a note, presumably placed there at the flower store by the florist. He doubted his source would have ventured there in person.

The note was unsigned, merely listing a metro station in New York with an instruction of when and where to be and including the

The Acting President | 153

phone number of the payphone Jeff was to find. He had three hours to get there, easily long enough to make the thirty-minute walk to that station. Perhaps not long enough to escape the watching eyes of those following him.

He pocketed the card. Once he was in place, he would find the correct payphone. As far as he could remember, they were all along one wall at the station in question, not that he had ever used them.

Jeff left the house five minutes later, a coat on, an old jacket he'd been meaning to throw away, now perfect for what he had in mind. He decided he would walk to the office, located just a block from the metro station for which he was ultimately aiming. The walk would buy him time, help him survey his surroundings, and hopefully allow the agents on his tail to catch his intended destination.

Jeff pulled out his phone, calling the one person he could on that national holiday, the one other person he worked with not having a family and therefore probably not already tucking into a lavish meal.

"Hey, it's me," Jeff said, speaking louder than the busy traffic around him might otherwise have warranted, the pavement crowded with people. Jeff assumed a few of them were federal agents. "I'm heading in now. It's something big. Meet me on the top floor in thirty minutes," and he hung up, leaving the other man in no position to protest. Jeff hated himself for doing that, but there seemed no other choice.

The lobby of the building where Jeff worked was noticeably quiet, though nothing in New York ever sat empty. The office crowd might not be there but there were plenty of tourists and visitors, two social functions in the same building the target for many that day. Jeff stepped into the crowded lift only after the third one arrived. He'd spotted his colleague's car seconds before heading down into the garage. It was now or never.

Several people got in the lift, at least two with dark suits on, shades in place. They practically smelt of the CIA. Jeff pressed the button for the top floor, a few others pressing their own destination on the forty-five storey skyscraper, but neither of the suits bothered to press anything. They didn't even glance at the numbers. The doors closed on the twelve occupants and Jeff wished with everything in him that, like most days, the first stop would merely be the cafe on the mezzanine floor not even ten metres above the lobby, but only accessible via the lift, something the shortsighted architects seemed to have overlooked in the design phase.

No sooner had the lift started moving than it came to a stop, Jeff thanking his luck as a crowd of five stood waiting to get on, no-one getting off, as they pressed into what still was ample space in the twenty-five person capacity lift. Jeff glanced at the reflection on the polished metal, catching one agent eyeing him from the back row, Jeff at least out of reach. As the doors slowly started to close again, Jeff had edged forward enough to make a run for it, doing so with no delay, the doors closing behind him; the lift ascending to the upper floors. He checked there were no other people watching him, and aside from those in the cafe startled to see someone fly from the closing elevator, there were no threats at that moment. Jeff assumed these threats were still ascending, though word would get out, his behaviour suggesting he was up to something.

Jeff ran to the staircase for the garage, the main reason the lift called at the mezzanine most mornings. His colleague was just coming up the stairs towards him.

"I thought you said to meet you on the top floor?" the man said, puzzled to see Jeff, a little sweat and panic visible on his face.

"I don't have time to explain," Jeff said. "Follow me," he added, already on the way to the man's car.

"Is everything okay?" he asked.

"Not now. I'll tell you everything, but I need you to drive me out of here. Please open the trunk."

A second's pause and the man complied, Jeff climbing in and giving an address several blocks from there to which he was to drive.

He took the turns carefully, watching his speed the whole time, now sweating himself. If the cops pulled him over, explaining why he had his boss locked in the trunk of his car would not be easy.

Twenty minutes later he was in a part of the city fewer people went to, run down and crime-ridden as it was. He pulled into a multi-storey carpark, going up five ramps to the penultimate floor, which, given the day, was empty of vehicles. He finally stopped the car against the far wall, quickly getting out and opening the boot. Jeff looked up at him, thankful the ordeal was over, grateful they were away from the office.

"Are you going to tell me what the hell this has all been about?"

"I will, I promise. Just not now."

The man knew that was coming, knew his place.

"Can you at least tell me why I needed to smuggle you out of the office like that?"

"I'm being followed by the CIA," Jeff said, the line delivered emotionlessly, the impact still dramatic. The other man swore.

"Why?" he asked, once he had determined Jeff was on the level with him, that this was no windup.

"I'm onto something big," Jeff said, his face lighting up for the first time. *Big and career defining*, he could have added. He let that thought drop.

"And it involves the CIA?"

"No, not at all. They just want the information, I think. Want my source. But if that happens, I'll lose everything."

"I see," the man said, somewhat sceptically, but he'd heard it happen many times before in their line of work. Nothing surprised him now. "Where are you going to go from here?"

"I'll take the metro," Jeff said, nothing more added. The nearest station was underneath that garage, which was the reason Jeff had decided upon the location. "I'll call you in the morning. You never made it in today, okay. Car trouble or something. Go home, call the mechanic."

"You think they'll come knocking on my door?"

Jeff smiled. "I would practically bet my life they will, yes. Best be quick. Good luck." Jeff held out his hand, a firm handshake needed. His colleague then got back in behind the wheel and raced off, much faster now than when he arrived. Jeff took the stairs down, two steps at a time, the walls covered in graffiti but thankfully empty of the drug pushers who might have lurked there. He entered the metro station without walking onto the street, his jacket already discarded, a hat pulled from his pocket, seemingly a different man entirely to the one who had jumped from the lift not thirty-five minutes earlier.

He had two hours to kill before he needed to be in place, and he would not risk loitering at the phone booth in question for anywhere near that amount of time. He figured he needed to be there only a few minutes before, five at a push. Enough time to locate the telephone in question, assuming he could find it and assuming it wasn't in use, but not enough time to draw attention to himself. Ever since 9/11, people were ever more vigilant to strangers acting suspiciously, especially in public areas.

The metro station Jeff now stood in was on a different line to the one near his home. That would require a change two stops away, and then it was three stops to the metro in question. Jeff was passing through that stop twenty-five minutes later, remaining in his seat. He checked his watch. There were ninety minutes left, and the line he was on went right out to the outskirts of the city, probably an hour's journey time, easily forty-five minutes. He would travel that far out, trains frequent and plentiful as always. When he got to three quarters of an hour, he would get off at that stop, switch lines and head back in, knowing it would take him the same time to arrive back at his home stop.

He was there with three minutes to spare, a little pushing it for time but he climbed the escalator as it rose from the depths of the city and was standing alongside the bank of telephones with sixty-seconds to spare. Only two of the twelve phones were in use at that moment, Jeff pulling the card from his trouser pocket and checking each available phone off against the number noted. Thankfully, it matched with the furthest phone on the right, in the corner. It was free and Jeff stood there, hand near the receiver as if trying to recall a number. On the dot of the hour, the phone rang, Jeff picking it up immediately and placing the receiver to his ear, a quick glance around him confirming he was alone.

"Hello Jeffrey McKay," came the accented voice.

"Please, it's Jeff, but don't use my name again," he said, as an afterthought.

"Thank you for making it on what I know should be a holiday for you all."

It was a holiday for everyone in America, regardless of nationality. "Do you have a notepad with you?" the Russian asked.

No journalist worth their salt would fail to have a pad and writing instrument on them at all times.

"Go on," Jeff confirmed, his pad open, pen at the ready.

"We're getting close now, close to the time when you can reveal everything. One month from now it'll be freely shareable, do you understand?"

"One month?"

"Yes, exactly from today. You have my permission on that."

Jeff noted the date.

"You'll release everything in the order I am about to give you," he started, Jeff remaining silent, letting himself adjust to the accent, his pen jotting the entire conversation down in shorthand.

"Vladimir Putin could not have killed the President," the voice stated, the line silent for a moment, Jeff reeling from the supposed revelation. "And I have the information to prove it."

23

Black Dolphin Prison, Orenburg Oblast, Russia
Present Day

Russia's Sixth Federal Penitentiary was in the city of Sol-Iletsk, near the border with Kazakhstan. It housed mostly lifers, the seven hundred inmates including the worst criminals in the country, there until death.

What gave the prison its most common name, *Black Dolphin*, was an inmate-made sculpture of the same animal, in black, which stood outside the prison.

There had never been an escape from the Black Dolphin, and only one prisoner, reportedly, had ever left the building alive.

For the last nineteen years it had been only accepting the most extreme prisoners, though among the child molesters, murderers, terrorists, cannibals, serial killers and maniacs, there were two other men, neither of whom fitted any of these categories.

Prison guard abuse of the inmates was not widespread at the Black Dolphin. Control was absolute, the prisoners kept in harsher conditions than at any other institution in the country. Sleep was for eight hours, then an inmate had to be on his feet for the rest of the day, no exception. They could not sit on the floor, or lie on the bed, and getting caught doing so would cause swift punishment. Guards patrolled the corridors every fifteen minutes, a constant assurance to make sure that the rules of the prison were being enforced.

For ninety minutes each day, they transferred each inmate to a cage for exercise, during which their cell was thoroughly searched for contraband substances. Every time they moved prisoners around the building, they were handcuffed with their hands behind their backs and forced to bend down, their cuffed hands raised above their waist, in a stress position as they walked forward. This reduced their ability to assess their surroundings, to familiarise themselves with the building. Blindfolded on arrival and walking the corridors to their blocks, the only walls they knew well were those of their cell.

They also used blindfolds to move inmates between the various buildings. No prisoner had made a successful escape in the last two decades.

The guards at the Black Dolphin were mostly ex-military. Strong, hard men who followed orders and expected the inmates under their watch to do the same. When a guard commanded an inmate to do anything, they expected a voiced response every time: *it is so, Citizen Chief*.

The two prisoners, not on the roster of the seven hundred lifers, but still there for the same indefinite time, were housed on the edge of one building, kept apart from the others, even using their own exercise cage only for themselves, but never at the same time. Each knew of the other, a few words shared over bowls of soup, which came their way four times a day.

The guards hadn't known how to handle the pair initially, especially Putin. Those who had voted for change were happy to see the man behind bars. Some had threatened him to his face, as if he were Aslan the lion, shaven and tied to the stone table in CS Lewis' timeless classic. Devoid of power, weak and vulnerable. Still others saw a danger in the former President, and it left those who had supported him most confused of all. They had a job to do, and Putin had killed the sitting-President, but they allowed him extra freedoms.

The same went for the British prisoner, the only Brit in the building, a former MI6 agent arrested for attempting the same feat; the assassination of Filipov. None of the guards could speak English, and Alex had come into the place badly injured, his legs broken. In the three years since, his legs had healed, medical attention provided on arrival. He had been the one prisoner allowed to break the rule about standing, not that any of the others knew. For the first six months Alex had been allowed to rest as much as necessary, in isolation. His legs recovering came with a flip side. Once he could stand a little, they treated him like all the others. Up was up. It took him another six months to make it through without excruciating pain in his legs and back. Two years on, and he was getting used to it all. He saw Putin pass him on his way to the cage each morning; the man stooped and looking nothing like the President who had ruled the land, often with absolute power, for so many years.

Alex had picked up a little Russian. He had memorised the response he needed to give each time, not that he understood what they had said to him. The guards didn't seem to treat him any differently now, their Russian loud and commanding. Alex soon learnt the routine.

Putin stood by the wall of his cell. He knew it was time for exercise; the guards had made their six rounds since breakfast, Putin with nothing more to do than count them and wait his moment to get out of those four walls, a space which had been closing in on him the longer the time went by. A few books lay on his bed, most long since finished. Besides them, they only allowed an inmate access to newspapers and a radio, neither of which Putin now bothered with, sick of the reports of all that the new Acting President did. All the good she was creating for the nation. He knew precisely who she was, however.

The main guard opened the door on cue, Putin smiling at him. This guard had been a loyal supporter, a man merely doing his job now, but not prejudiced against this inmate as he was with all the others.

Putin turned around silently. He knew the routine. They cuffed his hands, the former President turning back around.

"Thank you, sir," the guard said, the only one who addressed Putin in that way. He took the cuffed hands, regardless, and raised them behind his back, Putin forced lower, though not as low as most prisoners might have been. There were no guards around to observe the favourable way the main guard treated their most famous inmate.

Putin stood in the cage, the sky bright, little else of the compound visible. Guards watched from above, the constant presence in a place that gave no inmate privacy. He went through his routine, stretching and bending, before using the bars for pull-ups and then sit-ups and crunches. He took his time on the floor work, the only moment in the day they couldn't force him to be on his feet. He would take whatever he could get, working up to two hundred of each as he honed his abs, not as easy as it used to be two decades before, but easier than when he first arrived there.

When it came time to return to his cell, the same guard opened the door to him. They ambled back to the cell, Putin not even forced to bend this time, something he'd almost missed until a few paces from his cell. He turned to the guard; the man looked him in the eye.

"Is it true?" the guard asked.

"Is what true?" Putin said calmly.

The guard passed him a copy of the newspaper. The headline on the front page of one of the national papers read: *Whistleblower states Putin didn't kill President Filipov.*

Putin merely smiled. "It's true," he said.

The guard left the paper with him, Putin happy there was finally something about which he wanted to read. The back of his cell door, as it did with every inmate in the prison, stated his name and the crime the inmate had committed. It was a reminder to the guards to show no mercy. The current inmates at the Black Dolphin accounted for over four thousand murders alone. And now, perhaps, that morning the country was waking up to the fact that their former President had not, in fact, carried out the most high-profile murder of the last decade.

Once in his cell, the guard removed the handcuffs. Putin had the paper held open in no time, devouring the article even before they locked the first door. He ignored the next two doors locking into place, ignored the opening doors of the next cell down, the British agent being prepared for his time in the cage.

As he read the paper, hope rose inside for the first time since his arrest. Did that mean they knew where he was? Might there be someone coming to release him? Did they then know who had carried out the assassination? Thoughts raced through his mind as the reality of the situation dawned on him.

Alicante, Spain
One Year Ago

THE CAMERA FEED from the plane the following day was perfect, despite the plane now being airborne. The plane had been kitted out the previous day, one camera watched the pilots, one focused on the prisoner Budny's men had dragged and placed into the rear-facing seat, and another camera rolled watching Clifton.

They had briefed him carefully, warning him of the vile man with whom he would have to share a flight. They mentioned nothing more about what would take place, Clifton accepting the challenge despite his reservations. He'd killed someone the day before, beating a man unconscious on the day before that, too. He could share a flight with a rapist, no problem. He was also two steps away from getting the money. The closer he got to the finish, the less he cared about what they were asking him to do.

The five men stood glued to the screens as, with little warning, the next stage of things played out suddenly.

The door on the side of the plane opened, wind rushing in. Both pilots now had parachutes on, the spare one thrown between the two passengers, who looked dumbfounded at the sight of their pilots getting up from their flying positions and perched on the edge of the doorway. Then they jumped.

On the boat, there was absolute silence, something matched by

Clifton and his passenger, save for the rushing wind. The plane began to lose altitude.

Both men got it immediately, their eyes moving from the open door to their opponent and then to the one parachute that lay between them.

Clifton reacted first, though with insufficient headroom he could only lunge forward, the other man reaching out with his hands, fists clenched.

The fight was brutal, the action unstoppable. Both men fought with everything they had, first Clifton grabbing at the chute, then his opponent. At one point the other man, parachute in hand, collapsed from the seat and onto the floor, his arm precariously dangling out of the still open door, chute flailing in the wind dangerously.

Even Svetlana gasped, leaning closer to the screens. If that parachute fell, they were both dead.

The man drew his arm back inside, protecting himself from Clifton's blows. Both were now weak though Clifton had the strength advantage, be it a slim one.

After three minutes, Clifton had him where he wanted him, pinning the other man down against the floor and edge of the seat, his hands around the man's throat, knee firmly on the parachute.

Clifton positioned all his weight on the man, preventing his opponent from kicking or punching, and soon the eyes went wide, the struggle over, the mouth open. *Dead.*

Clifton pulled away thirty-seconds later, reaching for the parachute without taking his eyes off the body, though he knew the man was dead. He hurried to pull on the parachute, clipped it all in place, and moved over to the door. He did not understand what he was doing, but saw the cord he had to pull. He'd never jumped from a plane before. Mountains were approaching in the distance, the course set to take the small plane over the rocky interior, away from civilisation.

He jumped from the plane.

The sensation of falling was exhilarating, though the ground was racing up fast. With his fists thumping in pain and covered in blood,

Clifton pulled the cord, a sharp jerk happening as the chute opened, his speed reduced. He glided down for the next five minutes, landing in an orange grove, part of his chute snagging on the lower branches, but he hit the ground reasonably comfortably, rolling once before coming to a stop.

He did not recognise where he was, but any ground under his feet was much better than sitting in that plane. He untied the straps, freeing himself from the parachute. He would leave it where it was, moving over to an irrigation channel next and washing the blood from his hands, wiping down his face.

In the distance he heard the little plane flying on, miles now from him and sure to crash somewhere in the mountains.

Clifton jogged down to the main road, eventually offered a lift into town by a Spanish farmer. It would be seven that evening when Clifton finally arrived home at his villa, the only one there now that second week. The parties had been constant the first week; at least now the neighbours would be happy.

He felt exhausted, but knew he had only one hurdle left. One more challenge and then Svetlana would hand him her computer, and he would press enter. Then it would all be worth it.

He fell asleep on the sofa at nine, woken only when Svetlana pulled up at the gates the following morning. Half an hour later, showered and dressed, he emerged ready for his final challenge.

"THE MAN you shot two days ago was Luken Zabala," Svetlana announced. She sat on the sofa, Clifton perched on the edge of his chair opposite her. She'd asked him to sit down, his pacing getting on her nerves. It also made a better shot for the oligarchs watching if he was sitting.

"He was part of a large crime family from the Basque region. His father, Don Jose Zabala moved down to this region twenty years ago, owing to the better sea connections with north Africa."

"They are mafia?" Clifton asked, sudden terror in his eyes.

"Yes," she confirmed, cooly. "However, Luken had been threatening to tear apart the dynasty. Drugs, prostitution, trafficking. He brought nothing but stress and shame to his father."

Clifton smiled at that. "Pleased I could be of service," he joked, a little less anxious given what Svetlana had just said.

"However," and, if ever a word could change the whole tone of a conversation, instantly replacing hope with fear, then she had just delivered it. And she knew it too, the pause deliberate, the line rehearsed. She was performing for her audience. Putting on a show they would never forget. "Despite the strained relationship, Luken was still the Don's son. Don Zabala only discovered the news this morning that somebody had gunned his son down. He's taken it as a personal insult."

"But he hated the kid!" Clifton exclaimed as if this were a debate or a trial.

"He was family, end of story. Family drives the mafia, Clifton."

"But nobody saw me," he said, coming back to the facts. They didn't know it was him.

"Correct," she confirmed, Clifton closing his eyes in silent celebration. "However, if you are to complete this final challenge, that situation will need to change."

"What situation?"

"Don Zabala knowing who killed his son."

Clifton jumped up from his seat, pacing like a caged polar bear. "You will tell him I killed his son?" he spat, wanting to damn her to hell if this were her trick, her way of trapping him all along.

"No," she said, her response in no way reflecting or mirroring the anger in his words. She remained calm, absolutely in control. "You will tell him," she added, after a suitable pause. The silence that followed for a moment was deafening.

"Like hell I will!" he snapped, shaking his head.

"Clifton Niles, your final task is this. Do you have the courage to walk right up to Don Zabala and tell the man to his face you killed Luken? That you shot his son. This is your one last hurdle, the very final stage before I send out the money. If you walk away now, no-one will ever know who killed Luken, I can assure you of that. But you will leave with nothing but the blood of two men on your hands."

"I won't get the money?" he confirmed.

"Correct," she said, merely for effect.

He swore more than once.

"His men would kill me on the spot. I wouldn't even get close."

"We'll make an opening. It'll be just you and Don Zabala. He won't have his minders, won't have a weapon. It'll be public, people all around you. You'll be safe," she said, no actual guarantee if that was really the case, not knowing how someone like Zabala would react when confronted with the news.

Clifton considered it for a moment.

"Do I have to tell him my name?"

"No, only that you killed his son." She'd expected that question at some point, Ivanov actually the one to say he didn't need to give any details. Both Russians knew the mafia had ways of putting a name to a face sooner than the police might be able to. The Don would have a name before the end of the week.

Clifton sat down again.

"And I have to do it today?" he asked, aware that each task so far had needed completing the same day.

"Yes," she said, passing him an envelope. "If you accept, Don Zabala will be at this location at three this afternoon."

Clifton's flight back to London wasn't until the following day, and at five in the evening at that. He didn't like the prospect of being around town for twenty-six hours with the mafia hunting him down. He would see what flights he could get that evening, once the money was transferred. Once he had claimed his prize. Then, money wouldn't matter, he could afford anything.

"What choice do I have?" he said, reaching for the envelope.

"You have the freedom to leave now, Clifton, to refuse this challenge and with it have nothing more demanded of you."

"But then this week would have been for nothing. No, I'll do it," he said, tearing open the envelope, pulling the sheet of paper from inside with the details of the restaurant. Svetlana worked hard to suppress a smile, Ivanov cheering back on the boat, despite it being in his best interest if Clifton had turned down the challenge. Ivanov didn't care about the money, didn't need it himself. But the show was enthralling. She had surpassed all his expectations.

"Very good. I'm docked in the marina, flying the red and yellow flag. I believe you know the spot," she smiled. It had been the finishing location of the second task. "Come to me after you have completed the task. I'll be there for two more days. And," she added, happy to do away with any pretence now, "we have cameras in the restaurant watching, so if you don't go through with it, if you try to be smart with us, I'll know. And I'll go." She tapped her bag, Clifton for the first time spotting the lens on the side of the black bag stationed on his kitchen unit. "We've been watching you closely all week, you see. Don't disappoint us now," and she stood, Clifton suddenly very aware of the camera watching him, unaware to whom the relay feed went.

"Don't you want the gun back?" he called, Svetlana turning at the door, Clifton holding the weapon by the barrel, arm reached towards her.

"It's nothing to do with me. Why don't you keep it?" she smiled. "You might need it again before the week is out," and she stepped out through the door, driving away for the last time seconds later.

Clifton looked around the room, unsure if the Russians had bugged the place. He started searching for more hidden cameras that might still be watching him.

24

Moscow City Court, Russia
Present Day

Day four of the hearing couldn't have started in a more extreme way. Svetlana had not even entered the courtroom when her lawyer handed her a newspaper, the same one now in the hands of Putin, the same damning accusation glaring at her from the front page.

She had thought her big moment that morning would be naming some soldier killed in action with the same initials as Rad. It would have put distance between her current personnel and those who had worked for Filipov in the past. Now all that was pointless, the revelations splashed across the newspaper timed to coincide with the hearing itself. It might have even been the Prosecutor who leaked them the story, for all she knew. She wouldn't have put it past him, that much was clear. He was out for her blood, and suddenly it looked like he might get his way.

The article went into detail about the other revelations also, all topics which had come up in the trial that week––the source had to be the same man––but nothing previously known publicly. As the trial was a closed hearing, Svetlana's team had been clear that anything discussed, especially until the panel of judges reached a verdict, would remain within those walls. There were to be no leaks, absolutely.

Except it had now all come out.

If it was the Prosecutor, she would have him stripped of all power and responsibility after this if it was the last thing she did. She faced the same prospect herself, however. Three years in an acting capacity, but now the fight was on.

To her team Svetlana said, "We announce immediately that these are nothing but lies. We bring forward the date for the election, announce that it's time the country put their votes behind me as their elected President, and we move on."

"Are you sure?" her lawyer said, still reeling from the fact one newspaper had released the story. The timing couldn't have been worse with an election imminent.

"This is nothing but a shallow attempt to knock me off course, and I won't allow it to do that." She sounded defiant. Opinion polls were high, but such an accusation, especially if there was any truth in the matter, and these supporters could just as easily go the other way.

Svetlana went to the corner of the room, leaving the others standing there. She didn't want to be disturbed. She read the article through completely, the second and third pages of the paper given over to the report. They even included photos of the same source documents handed to the judges in the courtroom that week. All suggested official Kremlin origin. All pretending to be true. Alongside the slur about the guilt of Putin and whether he had ever entered the Kremlin on the day of the assassination where it stated the murder had taken place, there was the mysterious revelation about the Machine which included news of the death of Sergei Volkov. The article also mentioned Yuri Lagounov, a criminal on the run, believed to have been responsible for at least one death in Moscow. A few oligarchs got a mention, indirectly, as did the Acting President. They didn't have any direct links, not now anyway, but the slur was there, Svetlana's name bandied about for all to connect to the crimes.

The article ended with the hint there was one final sensation to reveal, something which would happen in the following edition. She knew it was merely a sales gimmick. There had been nothing more mentioned in the courtroom. The Prosecutor had thrown everything he had at her, yet she was still standing. They scheduled witnesses to appear on days four and five, though she didn't know who, if anyone, these would be. The Prosecutor had informed her team that the whistleblower would not be present. That much she knew. How she wished she could stand eyeball to eyeball in front of the traitor, her piercing eyes boring into his, searching for why he would lie like this. Why make such stories up about somebody doing so much good in the nation as she was?

To work out if he *really* knew what he was talking about.

THE PROSECUTOR WASTED no time that morning, a copy of the newspaper in his hands, as if anyone needed reminding of what the nation was reading that morning.

"I assure you this did not come from me," he said, addressing the judges, though answering in his usual dismissive fashion the accusation from Svetlana's lawyer. "As you know, I agreed to the terms set by this courtroom before the trial started. I can only imagine that the same source, the person who has sent me this information, has decided the time is right for the nation to know the truth."

"The truth?" Svetlana spat back, getting to her feet. "What do you know about truth?"

It pleased the Prosecutor to have evoked a reaction from her, ready for whatever now followed.

"I'll get right to the point," he said, turning to address her, though his eyes often darted to the four judges, making sure they were hanging on every word he spoke. "As already stated, these documents from one of Filipov's own men, state Putin never left the base he was on."

"Then he is wrong," Svetlana said.

"So you claim."

"Then it is one person's word against another. There is no substance to these lies, no witnesses standing in this courtroom prepared to vouch for these stories. Let me face the person accusing me of god knows what. What is it, exactly? That I knew of some other conspiracy? That I found out Putin had been nowhere near the building? That Filipov got murdered somewhere else? What is it you think I've done, exactly, to warrant all this?"

She went silent, her questions loud, aggressive and forceful.

"I'll get to that, I promise," he said, reaching for another piece of paper, the lawyer fond of physical documents, tangible reminders. "I'd like to call my first five witnesses," he said, reading off the names of five oligarchs from his sheet of paper. All five were men, all known to the judges, known to have been pro-Putin, somewhat resistant to Filipov during the election. All known for being not overly supportive of the current Acting President according to some reports.

"Very well," the Judge said, the door opening to the courtroom moments later, the five men walking in, four of whom took a seat on the front row, the other carrying on and then standing behind the lectern at the front. None of them looked at Svetlana, none of them showed any sign of respect to a woman who had been their President for the last three years.

"Roman Ivanov, thank you for coming to this hearing," the Prosecutor started, addressing a man worth a reported fourteen billion dollars, easily the wealthiest oligarch present.

Alicante, Spain
One Year Ago

CLIFTON STOOD outside the busy restaurant at just after three that afternoon. A thunder storm had passed through over lunch, the blue sky back again even if the streets and pavements in places still showed signs of the downpour.

He'd studied the photograph of Jose Zabala long enough to remember the face, and looking in through the windows, despite the many families still crowded around the two dozen tables, Clifton recognised the Don instantly. Sitting alone, a glass of red wine in his hand, the bottle half empty on the table beside him, the man sat, waiting.

Clifton had come this far; he couldn't back out now. Taking one final deep breath, the warm air doing little to calm his racing heart, he stepped in through the doors, passing a family of four who were waiting for a table, and made his way to Zabala.

As he approached the table, the Don lowered his glass of wine from his lips, his eyes spotting the stranger now walking right towards him.

"Don Zabala?" Clifton asked, his voice shaky.

"Who are you?" the old man barked, his English broken. He looked around the place, looked at the crowds, looked at all the children.

"I'm not here to harm you," Clifton said, taking a seat, though he didn't know why. He wanted nothing to keep him there longer than was necessary, though he didn't want to draw more attention to himself than he already had.

"I wasn't expecting you," he said. "You aren't even Russian."

Clifton didn't know what Svetlana had promised, whether she had said she would go herself, but that seemed unlikely. Everyone would have noticed her. She had one of the most recognisable faces on the planet, not to mention one of the most beautiful.

"I'm the reason you are here," Clifton said, aware of that much.

"Which is?"

Clifton wondered where the cameras were, if they were in fact recording this as Svetlana had said. But they'd been correct about everything until this point.

"I killed your son two days ago at the golf course," he said, the Don's eyes going wide.

"You killed Luken?"

"I did."

The Acting President | 173

The rage was clear in the older man's face.

"And you mock me, is that it? Do you know who I am!" and he thumped the table roughly, sending a fork clattering onto the floor. A few heads turned, Clifton remaining focused, letting the moment pass.

"I'm sorry, and now you know." He stood to leave.

"You're just going to walk away from me?" Don Zabala asked, looking up at the man but remaining firmly seated.

"I've said all I came to say," and Clifton turned, determined not to stop, not to turn back, not to imagine a gun coming up from underneath the table, a pistol in the Don's right hand. A father enraged, a Don disrespected, and despite the venue, despite the witnesses, still prepared to gun down his son's killer.

No shot came.

Clifton reached the doors, pressing out into the warm sunshine and running along the side of the building, one final glance in through the window before passing clear of the restaurant and seeing Don Zabala fixed on him, his eyes having tracked him for the entire exit. Now Clifton was clear and out of sight, though he was not out of the mind of Jose Zabala.

He stopped running at the end of the road, his breath gone, his legs spent. He stood there for a moment, deep breathing, wondering if he might just throw-up. His insides settled, the butterflies beginning to rise now in his stomach. He'd done it. He'd finished all the tasks.

He looked around, the beachfront visible in the distance, which meant the marina was not far beyond. He planned to head straight to the boat, straight to Svetlana and therefore his prize, and then head to the airport, but not fly from Alicante. He would drive to Murcia, an hour further south. He was certain the mafia would have men watching the more local airport.

Ten minutes later Clifton Niles was aboard Svetlana's rental, shown into her private suite. Behind two locked doors in a room at the other end of the boat, the five oligarchs sat watching the video feed, a finale not to miss.

"You've completed all five challenges, congratulations," she said, the smile fixed, her eyes dangerous.

He took the seat across from her.

"The money," he said, cutting to the chase. He didn't want to be there longer than he had to.

"Naturally," she replied. "Shall I call it the Clifton Niles takeover fund?" He smiled at that. She tapped a few keys on her computer, swinging it around to him when she'd scrolled down to the enter button. It displayed the full amount of one hundred and ninety million pounds just above the button he needed to confirm the transaction.

"Isn't that a thing of beauty," he said, a broad smile coming across his face, his finger caressing the enter button on her laptop. "Bloody hell," he added, letting out a long sigh. "I feared you were bluffing me, you know," he admitted.

"Yet you carried on anyway?" she mused.

"True," he laughed. It made no sense, none of it did.

"Are you going to confirm the transaction or aren't you?" She seemed edgy now. *The show's over, get on with it already.*

He pressed enter.

"It's instant, right?" he asked, passing her back the computer once the confirmation said it had sent.

"Yes," she confirmed. She started to stand.

"Wait," he said, one finger up, his arm raised. "You don't move until I see it in my account," he said, pulling his phone from his pocket, opening up an app. He refreshed it multiple times. "It's not here," he said, showing her the display. She turned the device around, the confirmation clear. She raised her hand as if in protest. She moved two steps towards him, a threat he'd never seen in the beautiful Russian and yet enough to cause him to take half a pace back.

"I didn't say I would send it to your account, did I?" she snarled. "Only that you would get to confirm the transaction."

"You bitch!" he said, stepping forward now, but the gun in her hand that she raised stopped him in his tracks from closing the gap any further.

"Oh, it gets better, Clifton, believe me," she started. "That transaction hasn't gone to just anyone, it has gone to someone specifically. *Her*." Svetlana's eyes glowed with a power he'd not seen in her until that point.

"Adele?" he gasped.

"Yes, Adele Spence, her very self!"

"But it's mine! I've worked for that!" Her smirk was as cold as ice.

"And she'll see your name on it, know I meant it for you. She'll also know exactly what you intended for it, too, won't she? Smart girl she is."

He stepped forward another pace.

"Easy, tiger, don't you think for one moment I won't pull this trigger. It wouldn't be the first time, I assure you." Her eyes told him that much.

"Why? Why me?"

Svetlana snorted at that.

"Let's just say it's Melody Southern's payback, shall we?"

"Who?" He seemed genuinely confused.

"I thought as much," she said, no desire to elaborate. "I would get moving if I were you. I think you've got enough to worry about now rather than waste your time talking to me." She waved the gun towards the door, two men outside waiting to escort him off the boat. She would travel immediately across to Ibiza that night, flights taking them all back to Moscow scheduled for the following day. He left, the minders seen guiding Clifton down the corridor not long after, soon to be off the yacht completely.

Svetlana joined the other five men, announcing to them the itinerary for the next few hours.

"Tell me who Melody Southern is," Ivanov asked, eventually alone with Svetlana, the one piece of the puzzle he didn't yet understand.

"She's the first life Clifton Niles ruined. And she was my friend."

25

Los Angeles, USA
September 2005

"And that's a wrap, folks," the Director called, the day's shooting finally over, the crew already stepping forward to pack away the equipment ready for the trip out the following day.

The actors started to go their separate ways, a few having words with various members of the team, some going over lines again, others making small talk.

Svetlana Volkov headed directly for her trailer, not an uncommon practice for the movie's biggest star. Sergei was waiting for her at the door, two security guards standing to one side, allowing the couple a little space. He greeted her with a kiss on the cheek, as usual.

"How did it go?" he enquired, the door open, Svetlana walking up the steps first, followed by her husband, who pulled shut the door behind him. She went left while he went right, though she stopped, turned and called after him.

"Did you get hold of her?"

"No, she's not on set."

"Does anyone know where she went?"

"Didn't show up, apparently," he said, turning at that and entering his room, shutting the door behind him so that he would not be delayed any further. She shook her head in frustration and went to pick up her phone. She dialled the girl's number. No answer after letting it ring for a minute, no answerphone available either. "Where the hell are you, Melody?" she said aloud, to no-one but herself.

Melody Southern was American, at least ten years younger than Svetlana, and just starting out in her career, but the two women had hit it off immediately. Melody felt honoured to have Svetlana mentoring her—for the Russian, she had a friend, someone she could be herself with, enjoy life with, talk. She had no-one else to talk to, ironic when her husband of many years always shared the same trailer as she did.

She'd not told Melody the marriage was a sham, but she wondered if the younger woman had worked that out herself. Svetlana knew Melody would say nothing. In fact, Svetlana felt she could share anything with her and not have it passed on.

Yet, Melody had not showed up for her two scenes that day, production not impressed, though these things happened, and she had only a minor part, anyway. They rescheduled the day to allow for the absence, but Svetlana heard the Director say at least twice that if Melody wasn't back soon, he would cast another woman in the role, someone who wanted to be an actress.

Svetlana knew Melody struggled with self worth, but the Russian superstar also knew her young friend could act. It was what had drawn her to the girl in the first place, why she'd reached out and offered to take her under her wing. Svetlana saw a lot of herself in the American—attractive, bright-eyed, ready to learn yet already broken by the system that often took advantage of budding starlets. She didn't know for sure if that had happened with Melody—there were things they had yet to share— but Svetlana had her concerns. She determined to encourage her, making sure she was safe. Because of Svetlana's connection, Melody had a much bigger chance than almost any of the girls trying to make it big in Hollywood right now. The latest film was a prime example. Melody would not have been on the studio's radar without Svetlana's casting in the leading role.

The Russian went back to the door of the trailer, opening it a fraction and catching the attention of one of her minders.

"Marco, can you let me know as soon as Melody arrives, please?" she asked, closing the door again soon after, the nod of the head from the man confirmation enough.

THE DAY'S shoot that morning began on a downtown block, the studio set not able to produce the filming they needed. As the crews set everything up, Svetlana stood with the Director of the movie, an umbrella held over their heads to protect them from the sun.

"What do you mean she quit?" Svetlana asked.

"What can I say? Melody called up casting this morning, told them she was through with it all and wouldn't be coming back. I'm sorry, Svetlana, there's no more I can do."

She walked away from there puzzled, taking the chance to call Melody again, the scene at least half an hour away from being ready to shoot. There was still no answer, the call being cut short after five rings.

Svetlana didn't like any of it, though she would focus on the day, then see her friend later.

It was past seven that evening when Svetlana's driver pulled up outside the modest building where Melody lived with dozens of other tenants. She went to the front door, calling up to apartment twenty, Melody's voice crackling through the intercom seconds later.

"It's me," Svetlana said, the door buzzing, the Russian pulling it open, taking the stairs to the third floor. Melody's apartment door was ajar when Svetlana got there. She entered, closing the door behind her. Melody was sitting on the sofa. She seemed vacant yet pained and her friend knew there was something wrong.

"What happened?" Svetlana probed, slipping her shoes off at the door—something Melody had always said she didn't need to do, though for Svetlana, it was an old habit—and moving across the space between them quickly to get to her friend. Melody stood, now in tears while Svetlana hugged her, nothing but sobbing coming from the younger woman for a while, as the Russian held her tight. She let go after a minute. "Talk to me," Svetlana pleaded. Melody sat back down on the sofa and Svetlana did the same.

"I'm done," Melody said, holding back the emotion for the time being, but Svetlana knew that might not last long.

"What the hell does that mean?"

"I'm done! Okay?" Melody confirmed, far more forcefully this time, taking Svetlana by surprise.

"Just like that?"

"Just like bloody that, yes," she snapped, not able to look Svetlana in the face, her eyes mostly low, focused on the carpet only.

Svetlana went to put an arm on the shoulders of her friend. "Something happened to you, Melody," she started, Melody jumping at the touch on her neck, pulling away a little. "Relax, it's only me," Svetlana said, her internal radar now on overdrive. She'd felt like that before: dirty, unclean, worthless.

"I met someone," Melody said, still no eye contact, a slight tremble in her shoulders evident. Svetlana stayed quiet, allowing space for the story to come out. Allowing her friend time to speak. "We laughed a lot. He seemed nice, cute accent, you know. He was in town for business, said he had the best view from his penthouse suite."

"You went up to his room?" Svetlana probed, fearful already of where this was going.

"He offered me a drink," Melody continued, not confirming one way or the other though Svetlana soon assumed she had gone with him. "I didn't see him again, woke up when it was dark, the cleaner there to make up the room. She found me on the bed. Someone had drugged me," she said, tears streaming down her face now, her arms wrapped around her stomach, knees coming up, almost in a foetal position.

"You poor darling," Svetlana said, though Melody resisted any more physical contact for the moment, curled up now on the sofa, head resting on the side cushion. "He raped you?" Svetlana asked, though she knew the answer before the wall of tears broke, Melody unable to respond, unable to speak for the sheer release of emotions. The tears gave Svetlana her answer. "I'll find out who did this," she said, eventually.

"He's gone," Melody confirmed, after a long pause. "Back to England, to London, I think. It's okay, I'm safe now," but she looked far from okay, the situation far from safe.

"Look, you're the victim here, and we can do something," Svetlana started.

"NO!" Melody screamed on her feet now, a side to the American that Svetlana had never seen. "I don't want anyone to know about it! It'll destroy my parents, destroy everything!"

"You can't let this man get away with this!" Svetlana stormed back, also on her feet.

"He already has!" Melody spat back.

"No," Svetlana said, shaking her head, her history as a young actress in Moscow coming to mind, the things men had made her do. She'd done them, semi-willingly, fully conscious. But this was different.

"Listen to me, Svetlana," Melody said, her tears stopping for the moment, though her voice was loud, her words crisp and biting. "I'm thankful for all you've done for me, for the opportunity you've given to me, but I'm done. I can't do this anymore, I don't want to be here anymore, to live this lie, to..."

"What lie? You're an actress, Melody."

"No, I'm not! I wanted to be, I thought I did. But I can't. Not anymore. Not after this."

"Look at me!" Svetlana demanded, Melody refusing to glance her way, shrugging off her hand when Svetlana tried to turn her face to hers. "You can't let one scumbag take everything away from you."

"He's already taken everything from me, don't you see?" Now she looked at Svetlana, the eyes enraged, the joy gone. "And don't you see it's what happens here, in cities like this, to people like me?"

"You're being over the top, Mel," but her friend laughed back at her.

"Really? You can't stand there and tell me this kind of stuff hasn't happened to you, too!" and Svetlana went silent, her mouth open, words failing to come forth. "See, I knew it," Melody said, her finger pointed at Svetlana accusingly.

"Nothing like what happened to you has happened to me, Mel," she clarified.

There was silence for a moment.

"What will you do?" Svetlana asked.

"Go home, live with my parents. Go back to college, get a degree. My father runs an accounting firm, said I always had a career with him there."

"You'll become an accountant?" Svetlana laughed. Some come down in her books from being an actress.

"It's something I know I can do," Melody countered.

"You can do this! I've seen you."

"No, I can't, not like you."

"I've told you, stop comparing yourself to others. You don't have to be me; be you!"

"Yet I don't know who that is now."

Svetlana took a step back at that, shaking her head in disbelief.

"What, because some loser cowardly raped you while you were bloody unconscious?"

Melody swore at her, a frosty silence following.

"Look, I'm sorry, that was harsh," Svetlana said, stepping two paces towards Melody now, the women at arms length from each other. "I just don't want to see you throw away your career over this."

"My career?" Melody snapped sarcastically. "Look around you," she said, waving her arms at the mess, the cracked walls, the rundown building, the boxes piled high in the corner because there was no room for any storage in her apartment. "I don't have a bloody career."

Svetlana hadn't meant that. She could have a career if she kept going.

"So you'll just quit, walk away. Is that it?" Svetlana had not thought of Melody as a quitter.

"I can't carry on," she merely said.

"We can catch this guy," Svetlana said.

"No!"

"We can go to the police, together, okay?"

"NO! Look, I don't want you to get involved. This stays between us."

"But why? You've done nothing wrong, Mel."

Melody didn't offer an answer. "It's over, okay."

"What will I do without you?" Svetlana asked, her mind at a loss why the girl would give everything up when it wasn't her fault. What those men did to Svetlana in Moscow had always been the driving force behind her career. She had to show them, she would show them, and one day, however long it took, she would make them pay. She would make them all pay.

Melody smiled at that question. "I think you'll be just fine," she laughed. "You need nothing!"

Svetlana realised how little Melody knew about her, the things they had yet to discuss. She needed the friendship possibly even more than Melody needed it. Svetlana bit back the emotion inside, knew this was a losing battle not worth fighting over, having seen defeat in her friend from the moment she walked in through the front door.

"I'll miss you," Svetlana said, holding open her arms, Melody this time stepping forward, the embrace lasting only seconds. "When will you leave?"

"Rent is due the end of this week, and I don't have it, so I'll go tomorrow."

"Tomorrow?" It seemed so soon. "Look, if it's money you need," Svetlana started, but Melody raised her hand in protest.

"I don't need a handout, Svetlana. I pay my own debts. It's time I went home, okay?"

Svetlana nodded. She got it. Home. She too missed Russia—this beast that beat you up and spat you out, yet, despite your better sense, you kept going back, kept giving it another chance. She had big dreams ahead of her too, a gathering of oligarchs coming together, a proposal and idea she had to put before them. She too would be home soon.

"Look, stay in touch Mel, I care about you deeply. You're worth more than this. I'll miss you but you know I'm here for you, even if I'm far away."

From the look on her face, Svetlana knew she wouldn't hear from Melody again. The woman wanted to close the Los Angeles chapter, with all that it meant, and move on.

SVETLANA WOULD WRITE *a few times over the coming months, had tried calling when able, but she never heard from Melody Southern again.*

After leaving her friend's apartment that day, Svetlana went back to the trailer, walking in on Sergei as he was on a conference call with two other men.

"I'll be out in a moment," he confirmed, Svetlana waiting in the lounge, pouring herself a drink.

Five minutes later Sergei sat in front of her.

"I need you to find me someone," she said, well aware of the connections her husband had.

"Who?"

"I need a name, that's all. He flew back to London two days ago, stayed in a penthouse suite at one of the better hotels. You'll know you have the right suite when the cleaning lady admits to finding a girl asleep in the bed when she came to change the room."

"I see," he added.

"Once you have the name, let me know."

"That's all?"

"Yes, don't concern yourself beyond that," she confirmed.

"I'll see what I can do," he smiled, getting up and returning to his room.

It took only two days for Sergei to hand a piece of paper to Svetlana as she left for that day's shoot. Melody had already moved by then, and opening the information her husband had passed her, she read the name as she walked onto the set. Clifton Niles. The address of the firm he ran was underneath his name.

26

Moscow City Court, Russia
Present Day

The final two days, as they turned out, had not gone the way the prosecuting lawyer had assumed they would. One after another, the oligarchs he had called in––whom he knew had dirt on the Acting President if only they would divulge it–– instead went the other way. First Roman Ivanov spoke in candid fashion, admitting he had been unsure about her suitability as Presidential material initially, but a thorough look at her had changed his mind. He said he would back her in an election.

The prosecution had then cross-examined him, their own witness, asking him what had changed his mind. Ivanov gave nothing of an actual answer, the line of questioning and revelation the Prosecutor had been hoping to draw out of Ivanov heading in completely the opposite direction. He removed the man from the stand, and Svetlana's lawyer refused to ask anything more from their own side–– the oligarch had already done a brilliant job by himself, there seemed no need. A man of Ivanov's standing––and the judges knew of him well, as they did all five star character witnesses––coming out and actively saying he would back Svetlana, went a long way in their minds as they continued to hear the case.

Then Vladimir Popov stood before them, the oligarch with perhaps the best reputation for honesty of all present. Popov unanimously now also gave his backing to Svetlana Volkov, the shock evident on the stunned face of the Prosecutor across the aisle from her, the man looking over to her, fearing some treachery in play but lost for how she might have got to them. He removed Popov from the stand, again no follow-up questions needed by the lawyer who smiled delightedly at the unexpected turn of events, though Svetlana had not been so shocked. Alicante still lived fresh in their memory and was having its effect.

The Prosecutor turned to the remaining three, rapid whispers of conversation rattled off as he tried to see who still held the same view of the woman as when he had initially contacted them. None of them did.

"Your Honour, I would like to dismiss the remaining three witnesses," he began, though on cue her lawyer jumped to his feet.

"On what grounds?" he demanded.

The Judge looked at the Prosecutor. These were his witnesses, the finale of his defence given that the source of these leaks was not to appear in person.

"On the grounds they have all changed their stories, and I don't know why," he attempted.

The lawyer scoffed at that.

"Then I call them myself!" he shouted, the Judge waving the next man forward. Timur Budny took the stand and the lawyer stepped out from behind the table to address him.

"Tell me, what is it you now think about the woman who wishes to become President?"

"Let her stand," Budny said, not quite the dynamite the lawyer had been hoping for, though he would take anything positive he could get. He felt that the last three days had been brutal and that the balance was still tipped against his client. "So what if this country has only ever had a man in leadership? Does that mean the right woman cannot one day be President?" The lawyer smiled. This was more like it.

"And might Svetlana Volkov be such a woman?"

Budny looked across at her––the image of Clifton in the plane strangling to death the rapist he had captured still burnt into his retinas––and nodded his head.

"Yes, I've met no-one like her," he said, adding for good measure. "And I too will give her my full backing in the election."

The Prosecutor threw down his pen, taking his seat in disgust, appalled at what he was hearing.

The Judge turned towards the Prosecutor moments after, and with a smile on his face, asked him; "I take it you have no further questions for your witness?" The Prosecutor waved the offer away, Budny returning to his seat, not even looking at the lawyer who had summoned him to court that day.

By the time both Arseni Markovic and Motya Utkin had taken the stand, the Prosecutor's case was hanging on a knife edge, the Judge about to call time on the whole process. The backing of these men, their wealth, influence and connections, not only in the legal sphere, but right across the country, made them men not to mess with lightly. Given everything up to that point was hearsay––one faceless voice against that of Svetlana––and that the prosecution had failed to produce the witness, the Judge was inclined to give her the benefit of the doubt. Especially given the presence of the five men now moving towards the exit door.

However, in one final desperate lunge for survival, the Prosecutor threw out his final play, his one last trump card that brought a deathly silence over the entire assembly for nearly a minute.

"Your Honour, this woman also has access to unlimited financial assets stolen by Filipov from a bank in Zurich, illegal riches placed there by criminals and royalty alike from right around the world."

"I'm sorry?" the Judge said, caught mid-flow in his thinking of how best to dismiss the case. He took in the raised arm of the Prosecutor, holding yet another piece of paper aloft, and then the crestfallen face of Svetlana, confirming there was truth in the matter.

The five oligarchs had stopped at the door, Ivanov turning around at the mention of the facility looted three years before, the contents assumed destroyed, the motive unclear.

"It's in this report, the final piece of information my source has given me. Trillions of dollars, at least."

The Judge knew about the Bank. He knew of several people who had lost everything. He took the information when it was passed to him. A glance up to Svetlana at that moment told him she knew it all to be true. She had the money. She subtly shook her head from side to side. *Leave it, you don't have to make a big thing of this.* Watching from the back of the room, Ivanov spotted the movement, spotted her eye contact with the Judge, took in his reaction.

"Well, I think we've heard enough from you, now, haven't we," he said, picking up the paper but pushing it to one side as he addressed the Prosecutor. "Trillions, you say. There is no person on the planet who has that kind of money, let alone this woman standing not ten feet from you, I can assure you," he said, the Prosecutor dumbfounded, his mouth open. "I see this whole hearing as nothing but your attempt to fling dirt at her and see what sticks. You've provided no concrete evidence, nothing that we can verify as trustworthy. The five witnesses you produced seem only too ready to help her become the next elected President. Then you cap it all off by possibly the most ridiculous suggestion of them all, proving finally that either your source has a twisted and warped imagination which you've been a fool to believe, or, more disturbingly, there never was a source and you've concocted this whole charade yourself." He turned to his fellow judges. "I motion to dismiss this entire hearing forthwith and propose we discuss if we think there is anything criminal in the prosecution bringing this matter forward in the first place," he said, pointing to the Prosecutor who looked as if he'd just been hit by a train.

"Case dismissed!" the Judge ordered, having got a consenting nod from his three colleagues, banging the gavel hard on the desk.

The four judges stood, leaving no lingering doubt in anyone's mind that the hearing had come to a halt, and they vanished through the door behind them saying no more. Svetlana turned to her lawyer, who seemed delighted it was over, though he couldn't really understand how. The Prosecutor gathered his things up, stuffing everything into his bag, Svetlana coming over to him before he could scurry away.

"Nice try," she said, her grip firm on his arm, but she let go before he pulled away.

"We both know it's all true," he glared at her, their conversation kept between them.

"Who is your source?"

He smiled at her final attempt.

"I don't know. He just sent me this stuff."

She took that in, aware Roman Ivanov was waiting in the wings ready to approach her once she was free, but far enough away to not yet catch what she was saying.

"Do the packages come from Russia?" If they did, it would have surprised her.

"No, the US." She closed her eyes at the thought, the United States probably the last country on Earth prepared to do Russia a favour.

He moved as if to go, Svetlana holding his arm, pulling him back towards her for one final word.

"What you said about *the Bank*," she started. "That stays here, you hear me." He smiled at her, one final little victory in what had been a catastrophic loss.

"Too late," he said, pulling a printout from his bag, passing it to her. "The source went viral with it an hour ago," he added, a dirty smile on his face. "Good luck fending them off," and he pulled his arm from her, Svetlana glancing down at the Bloomberg article, the revelation damning. She would have every tyrant on the planet knocking at her door before the week was out.

Ivanov stepped towards her the moment the Prosecutor walked away, closing the gap in seconds, her hands still holding the article, her mind racing with the connotations.

"I take it the rumour is true?" he said, taking her to one side, wondering whether he should, though they'd had an understanding for some time. "You control the money?"

"How do you think I pulled Alicante together?" She was wealthy herself, though he saw now, not ready to give away one hundred and ninety million for nothing.

"I see," he said, his connection to her now even more important. She would need help, men to stand alongside her. "You have our support," he said, his hand waving to the other four oligarchs, Ivanov apparently the official spokesman for the group. Either that, or he would get them in line immediately.

"Thank you," she said. She waved her lawyer away as he passed—he knew his place, his role completed. He knew there had to have been truth in that final leak, the way everything had changed, the reactions between the men in the know. That was not his fight anymore, he was happy to walk from the building.

"Do you have your team nearby?"

"Some of them," she confirmed. "I must bring in my main guy, get him up to speed."

"You can travel with me, if you like." It was unlikely there was anyone waiting for her outside at that moment, the news still to filter through. But they both knew before the weekend was out, many would raise their heads. She had their money, and they would demand it back.

"Thanks, but I'll be okay," she said, gathering her things together, leaving Ivanov on the spot as she passed him, sweeping elegantly back through the doors, a smile to the other four oligarchs as she passed, but no words needed. Her mobile was at her ear.

"Get back to Moscow immediately," she said, ending the call with Rad as her security detail moved across the room with her. Once they were outside they opened the door to the armour-plated vehicle and the convoy pulled away from the building at speed soon after. Twenty minutes later, she was safely inside the Kremlin.

Forest Dacha, Russia
Present Day

"I've got to go," he said, putting his phone away, Nastya looking over, the brevity of the call telling her that much before her husband voiced the confirmation.

"When?" They were due out again later to hunt, the building work making good progress, but the food running short.

"Now," he said, Kostya looking up from the piece of wood he was hammering into place.

"I thought you had the whole week off?" Nastya questioned.

"I did," he said, already starting to collect some things together. "Something must have come up. She wouldn't have called otherwise."

Nastya started to protest, but it was actually Kostya who intervened.

"Honey, he works for the President of this country. She wouldn't have called him out of the blue like that if it wasn't urgent." He looked across to Rad, whose help he would not now have over the coming weekend, the hope of getting the roof on taking a big hit. "You go, sort out whatever needs sorting, and I'll do what I can here."

"Thanks," Rad said, grateful Nastya's uncle saw it that way, needing their support and backing to help him leave things in a good way with his wife. They'd made inroads with the build, but his departure would definitely scupper their plans and progress. If he knew anybody he could trust with the build, he would have paid for some extra hands to come and help. He didn't want anyone else knowing where he lived, however.

"How long will you be?" Nastya asked as Rad dropped the last of his things onto the back seat. He didn't enjoy leaving her like this, but it had to be something urgent, like Kostya had said. Svetlana had known how important building a family home was to Rad.

"I don't know," he said, Nastya looking like she felt she was being fobbed off. "Look, she didn't say, okay. Didn't tell me what had come up so urgently, only that I needed to come in immediately."

Nastya didn't like that revelation, didn't like the reality that if Svetlana needed Rad so urgently, there must be a threat of something very serious. His only job was to protect her. Why did she now suddenly need protecting, unless that wasn't all he did for her? Nastya had been suspicious from a month after the wedding, when Rad had vanished to Spain for nearly two weeks, no explanation given why he'd taken a week longer to come back since events in Madrid had wrapped up.

He kissed her on the lips.

"Stay with them both," he said, nodding to Kostya and Olya, though she knew precisely who he meant. She didn't enjoy staying in his dacha alone when Rad was in Moscow. He intended the construction of their new home to change that, giving the couple an actual house, not just a large shed.

"We'll look after her, as always," Olya said, coming alongside Nastya, pulling her away so that Rad could get into the car. She looked like she wouldn't let him go.

He waved one final time, before pulling away, the dust of the track soon making the car vanish in a cloud.

"What if he doesn't come back this time?" she said through tears, everything about the sudden emergency putting her on a knife edge since he'd ended the call.

"He'll be fine," her aunt said, holding Nastya tightly, a look of sadness across to her husband, who then picked up the hammer, and carried on the best he could.

She dried her eyes.

"You will need another pair of hands now, won't you?" Nastya said, coming over to him.

"I'll be fine," he said, struggling to move the panel he'd just completed by himself.

"You can't do this alone, you're not as young as you used to be," she warned. "Here, let me help," and together after a struggle they got the piece up, Kostya holding it in place. He passed the hammer to Nastya.

"Secure this one in place, like the others."

"I know," she said, already reaching for the plank of wood before he'd started speaking. "I've been watching you both all week, remember."

She decided she would do what she could. Whenever Rad made it home again, they would have made progress. It would help her keep her mind off Moscow, anyway.

27

London & Alicante
One Year Ago

The flight from Spain had been uneventful, though for Clifton, every passenger moving up the central aisle posed a threat, every knock into the back of his chair a potential killer moving in for revenge.

Clifton got off the flight amongst the first half dozen folk; good, honest passengers he believed. He made his way at pace towards customs. Surely, he reasoned, once back home, once he had passed the border, had his passport returned to him by the official, then he would be safe? They couldn't touch him in London, could they?

As the taxi pulled away, Clifton couldn't help look over his shoulder, watching the other cabs, the other passengers. Straining for any telltale sign that someone was onto him. It took a full ten minutes before the Venture Capitalist sat back in his seat, eyes forward, his breathing slower. He'd not seen anyone. They weren't onto him.

His thoughts, the closer he got to London, focused in on Adele Spence; former partner, former lover. She was many things, in fact. He'd not spoken directly to her in years––slagged her off repeatedly behind her back in the meantime, though he knew she'd done exactly the same. Now she had the money. *His money.* Money that changed everything.

He swore at Svetlana once again, not for the first time since taking off from Alicante that evening, and it would not be the last, either. He remained at a loss why the Russian President had targeted him.

He'd searched the name the Russian had mentioned in the last few miles of the cab ride, though nothing conclusive came up. As Melody never succeeded as an actress, there was nothing showing online that produced a result that might have triggered his memory.

It convinced him he was the innocent victim, plain and simple. Made a fool of by someone the world was heralding a saviour. She'd picked him out for no other reason than to have him carry out her dark deeds. There had been no other oligarchs involved, he was now sure. Not any Melody for which Svetlana was making him pay.

It was her doing.

He swore again; the driver glancing his way, the ride complete. Clifton paid him and grabbed his case, the taxi pulling away moments later, the Brit standing outside his home address. Was he safe there anymore?

He went inside, turning on all the lights, moving through every room, checking each window. All safe and secure. He was alone.

He hated how he felt caged, watched. *Vulnerable.* It should all have been so different.

It took Don Zabala's men thirty hours to produce the name of the man who had killed his son. They handed him the information at the end of the funeral service, his son now buried, an estranged relationship suddenly ended, yet the man's only son.

The fact Clifton had seemed so confident to confront Zabala in person, telling the man face-to-face what he had done, was a mockery. The Don would not allow him to get away with it.

Zabala studied the name carefully. Had it been a rival group––the murder a threat, the motive clear—he might have thought longer about what had to follow. Yet the killer was a nobody, a rich City trader of sorts, but no-one in their world.

Four men were on the next flight to London, tickets booked individually, seats purposely apart. They would meet up once on the ground, once away from the airport. Then they would find out everything they needed to know. Where he lived, where he worked, who he knew.

They would pass this information to Don Zabala, who was clear that he would make the call on their final move. He might even pull the trigger himself, though travelling to England was not a possibility. Zabala doubted Clifton would be back in Spain.

Three days later, the four-man unit sent by the mafia Don was stationed outside Clifton Niles' London address. The Brit hadn't left home that whole time.

ADELE SPENCE HAD WOKEN to the sound of a notification on her phone, but only stirred enough to come from her dream state. A minute later she was up, bleary eyed, make-up smeared. She'd fallen asleep on the sofa again, another night out, another late one home.

She went into the bathroom, splashing water on her face. She would shower, but not before a strong coffee and probably an equally large batch of painkillers. Her headache reminded her she wasn't as young as she used to be, and that if she kept pushing the drinking as she was doing, she would go the way of her father, and his father before him.

She would not repeat their mistakes.

Adele picked up her phone, only then seeing the notification from her banking app. There had been a significant deposit.

She swore under her breath, sure there had been a glitch, some error either inside the app, or a colossal balls-up at the bank.

She stopped dead when noticing the details included against the transaction. *The Clifton Niles takeover fund.*

"What in the world?" she screamed, the house empty. She lived alone. The one hundred and ninety million pounds she had in her account at that moment could not be a coincidence. A colossal error, but from neither of the two sources she had imagined. It made no sense. She called up the office, sure her assistant would already be in––it was after nine, Adele not usually in most days before eleven now.

"It's me," she stated, formalities ignored. "Look, what's the enemy worth today?"

"Still less than us," the lady replied.

"Give me a figure, nearest million."

Adele could hear keys being tapped, the ten-second silence broken finally with the words she expected.

"Still at one-eighty-nine," she confirmed. "We're a million up," her assistant added, with excitement in her tone.

"Are there any messages for me?" Adele asked, sure that the mystery financier would have reached out to make contact before sending her such funds.

"No, nothing. What are you expecting?"

Adele paused. She hadn't been expecting anything, least of all this.

"Nothing. Look, I have some errands to run," Adele said, her assistant well versed in what that really meant. "I'll be in before lunch," she concluded, ending the call.

She went back to the app, the money still there, the balance enormous. Yet this was her personal account. The office didn't know it. Who would, besides her? It made no sense. All transfers from clients came into the firm's client account, no exceptions. She'd never traded privately, not aware anyone had her details.

She called her accountant.

New York City, USA
Present Day

The Acting President | 197

"And you do not know where he is?" Charlie Boon said to Jeff McKay who was sitting behind his desk in the office.

"No. I've never met him."

"But you said you thought he was in the city?"

That had changed in the half an hour Charlie and Zoe had been with the journalist. Originally, he'd said he thought he was in New York.

"I think he's smarter than I gave him credit for."

"He's not in New York?" Charlie asked, puzzled.

"I'm not sure he's in America at all," he whispered, hardly daring to say anything aloud. They had swept his office for bugs several times, the latest that morning before he met with the two British security agents. Since Anissa had arranged the trip, Jeff had felt somewhat calmer about meeting them as MI6 was one of the two main recipients of the information. They knew nearly as much as he did.

"Why?" Zoe asked, the two agents edging a little closer to his oak desk.

Jeff looked a little uncomfortable as if he felt he'd done something wrong, something an agent in the Security Service of any country might deem a criminal offence.

"We last spoke two months ago. He gave me everything, and the order I should leak it all. Told me when to release the information to the newspaper."

The final piece, initially appearing on Bloomberg before going viral, had gone out that morning. It was the somewhat cryptic announcement––to the uninformed, at least––that Svetlana Volkov now sat on a huge fortune possibly amounting to trillions of dollars. It claimed Filipov had stolen it from the secret savings of many of the planet's worst dictators, but she now kept it for her own use.

"I always questioned whether he was actually in New York."

"You said he could see the Statue of Liberty from his bed?"

"Yes, he told me that early on. The CIA found no-one in the area matching his details."

"It doesn't mean the source isn't there though."

"His final call to me," Jeff carried on, ignoring the previous comment, knowing what he had to say next would make it much clearer, "came to me at the subway. He'd arranged an elaborate scheme to speak to me. I think he knows they are hunting us. Anyway, he told me everything, as I mentioned. When we ended the call, I used an old trick I think only journalists, and perhaps cops and crooks, know. I dialled a number to confirm from where the inbound call had come. It won't give a specific number, usually the State, and often the city, too."

"And?"

He passed them a sheet of paper. The number started with the code +52.

"Mexico," Jeff confirmed, their blank faces showing the British agents didn't know the relevance of the discovery.

"Gremlin's in Mexico?"

"I think so, yes," Jeff confirmed. It was his best theory. It made a lot more sense now, the way the packages came to him, always via a different route, a different state even. That reference about July 4 being *his* holiday.

Charlie looked at Zoe. It made things a lot more interesting.

"Do you have contacts down there?" Charlie asked Jeff.

"In Mexico? I've had a few connections down the years, but nobody I could trust. Why?"

"Because the CIA might not know, but the FSB soon could."

"You think they would go after him?"

"He's a hell of an easier target in Mexico than he would have been here. It makes sense now," Charlie said, everything falling into place. "I'd always wondered why he hadn't sought their protection, the CIA I mean. If he had information, if he was here by himself, why not tell them what he knows?"

"He's told them next to nothing."

"You mean, we know more than they do?"

"Hell, yeah," Jeff confirmed.

"And besides the Moscow lawyer you mentioned, does anyone else know?"

"Not everything, no. The guys here know I'm onto something, naturally." It was clear to both agents that Jeff meant the office he worked in, where they were sitting at that moment. "But I've not confided in anybody."

"Why?" Zoe asked.

"It's my story," he said, matter-of-factly. "If you've been around the block as long as I have, you learn how it goes. Even involving our own CIA. Something leaks, someone's happy to turn a quick buck, and us poor sods, the ones who got the information in the first place, get screwed. Time and time again. I knew this one had the potential to be huge."

"And you want to guarantee your payday, is that it?" Zoe asked, torn between understanding him and her anger at him for putting career advance over serious intelligence information.

"We've all got to eat," he said, with a pained smile. His final piece to Bloomberg that morning––he had a standing agreement with the three main broadsheets, which published the stories in their morning run––had already earned him half a million dollars, the final payoff in his month long release of information. Firms had started a bidding war for the exclusive, something he'd eventually signed with those four outlets only forty-eight hours earlier.

Charlie saw things from another angle. Besides Jeff, and assuming the Russians weren't onto Gremlin, MI6 were now the only other people who knew the potential whereabouts of the biggest whistleblower in modern Russian history. His mind started racing along a different chain of thought.

"Do you have access to the list of people banned from travelling to the United States?" he asked Jeff.

"No, but I can get them. Why?"

"I'm trying to work out why Gremlin didn't come here, and I've landed at that."

"He's banned from travelling here," Jeff said, catching up fast, an even bigger smile filling his face. "Brilliant, bloody brilliant," and he picked up his phone, dialling a number from memory without saying another word. Evidently, seconds later, the call got answered.

"Cass, it's me," he started. "I need you to fax me the current *No Fly List* and *Sanctions List* for all Russian nationals. Include everyone making that list in the last five years." There was silence at their end for a moment, the other person speaking, before Jeff thanked her, ending the call.

"She'll send it over before close of play," he confirmed, fax still his preferred choice of device for such matters, faxed documents much harder for the government to intercept. "I'll call you when I have it," he added, Charlie standing at that moment, ushering Zoe to follow.

THE TWO AGENTS sat at a table in a diner one block from Jeff's office, a coffee each, Zoe scanning through the menu. They ordered something to eat, a few hours expected to pass before they would hear again from Jeff.

"Look, I've been thinking it through. I think we need to split up," Charlie said. "Ordinarily because we know the CIA have been watching the journalist, I would suggest sneaking you out, but I'm not sending you to Mexico on your own."

"You want to go to Mexico?" Zoe asked, not impressed with being left behind, nor the thought he didn't think her capable enough of going herself, but knew his intentions were honest enough.

"I think we have to do both, yes. One of us here, visible. Get the CIA tracking us, searching for this Russian locally. If they know where he is, they'll have teams onto him in no time. I can leave, as if heading to Europe. I'll change somewhere and head to Mexico and see what I can find. You get a name from Jeff, someone he knows, someone he thinks could help."

"Will you inform the Mexican CNI?" Zoe asked. The look on Charlie's face at that moment told her all she needed to know.

"No, for even more of the same reasons we won't let the CIA know."

It wouldn't be his first time to Mexico, either, not that Zoe knew that, not that anyone at MI6 did, as far as he was aware.

"Do you think you will find him?"

"It depends what happens between you and Jeff. Once you get the list, get Gordon and Sasha to look into it. See if there is any name they spot that matches what Gremlin knows. It has to be someone who, until a year or two ago, still worked in Moscow. If you get a name, I think I'll be able to find him in Mexico."

"You'll be safe there?" she asked, concern in her eyes.

"I can handle myself," he said, not the answer she was looking for.

The food arrived not long after that, the bustle from the tables around them constant though for the moment the two agents ate in silence, Zoe looking up from her meal regularly at Charlie, but he didn't seem to notice.

28

The Kremlin, Moscow
Present Day

Her team had written the press releases the following morning, Svetlana reading through them one final time. She'd been dealing with press releases for decades, exclusive reports, often the latest film role they had cast her in or something on similar lines.

She'd never released such a report to the press as this one, the announcement that there would be an election in six months. Russia was to go to the polls again, only four years since they last elected someone to a six-year term, but Filipov's assassination had changed all that.

It was time the country decided.

While the timing could have been better––even a week ago, opinion polls suggested she would have walked into the position, officially this time, with a bigger margin than even Putin managed––yet now, that all had changed. The stories circulating that week, these leaks from someone who should have known better, had done damage. She needed a change of focus, needed the newspapers and media outlets across the country to talk about something else.

An election would be just the thing. She also needed to flush out any rival to her crown, the date of an election setting into stone the cut-off points when candidates could announce themselves. First the independent candidates not connected to any of the established parties had to say they would stand then later the party candidates themselves. Six months only gave the independents two months to prepare––hardly enough time, in her opinion. She didn't know of a single person able to challenge her. The political parties weren't in much better shape, either. A date pulled everyone into play. She signed off on the releases, buzzing her assistant into the office moments later, the announcements hitting the airwaves later that evening, in time for the rush-hour commute and nighttime news shows.

THE COMMUNIST PARTIES––THERE were two in Russia, weakening their already small numbers by dividing the vote––were the first to make waves the following morning. They called Svetlana out for her capitalist attitudes and that, once again, a billionaire had put themselves forward for a position. They stated the opinion that her wealth should exclude her from challenging.

She refused to comment when questioned about these comments by journalists. She'd long looked down her nose at the communist supporters, whose views she saw as three decades past their best, at least. Yes, she had wealth, but that was what every Russian wanted, what everyone of her countrymen and women deserved. She'd even known communists who themselves were billionaires––she'd had one such oligarch in her Games events for years. He'd never seen the hypocrisy in his actions––he too had been outspoken against Matvey Filipov when he first put his name forward. He too had no effect on the ultimate outcome.

Not having the support of a few communist-voters did not bother her in the slightest. She could have reached out to them, bringing back Soviet rule, teaching Marx in every classroom and they still wouldn't vote for her because of her background in America and her vast personal wealth.

Plus, they'd all been reading the papers. They all believed Svetlana had much more besides her own fortune now under her personal control.

Moscow Subway Network, Various Stations

They timed the blasts between nine and ten on Monday morning, four stations hit, platforms and trains packed with the heavy throng of commuter traffic making their way into work at the start of a new week.

Svetlana Volkov had stayed at the Kremlin all weekend, Rad and his unit at maximum alert, the FSB drawing up a list of all known threats, blacklisting anyone they could from travelling to Russia, and all known associates. It had been four days since the news about the Bank broke, ninety-six quiet hours where Svetlana sat in the shadows, waiting.

The news of multiple bombs detonating across stations that morning was the confirmation that they had broken the silence. She could even see smoke from one station rising into the air as she looked out of the windows of her new office, the complex in lockdown. They had suspended tourist visits that weekend.

"How bad is it?" she asked her aide who was bringing in fresh reports every ten minutes.

"It's bad," she confirmed. "Dozens killed, probably many more. Four locations hit so far, the network has shut down, all remaining stations emptied. Teams are now scouring the stations, though there are too many to check."

Moscow had an established and vast underground network. The four attacks were probably the only ones planned, but she knew the units had to follow procedure.

"I want to visit the one nearest here," she said, waving at the window, the smoke darkening an already ominous skyline.

"I don't think that's safe," the aide protested.

"Nonsense," Svetlana barked. "Make sure there are journalists there. I'll show these terrorists I'm not afraid of them. I'll use this to remind my people who I am, remind them I'm no pushover, remind them I'm their President."

The aide remained silent. Using a backdrop of an attack as political leverage was nothing new in the world of politics––Presidents and Prime Ministers around the world had done it––but it wasn't anything Svetlana had stooped to yet.

The aide left the room, Svetlana following her out, calling to another member of her team.

"I'll see Rad in my office," she ordered, turning and closing the door behind her.

Three minutes later the sniper-turned-head-of-security for the President was sitting opposite Svetlana.

"Rad, as you know, terrorists have struck at the heart of Moscow this morning," she started. Rad was aware of the news and his team was on the highest alert as a result, though he was not afraid of the Kremlin being targeted. The metro was the soft option, attention grabbing, weak, the attack below the belt, but it got the headlines. It spread fear.

"I want to visit the station, right away. To stand in front of the cameras and tell these people, we will not let these terrorists wage war against our nation," she said. Both knew, though there had yet to be any communication, that this was personal, knew they would make contact privately, not publicly. It was a first move of an infinite number, from an unknown mass of individual threats. All because she now had their money. All because of a leak of information and its public sharing, her public shaming.

"I think that is dangerous," Rad informed her, there for that very reason. He knew nearly everything about danger. In the wild, in the war zone, you don't put yourself in the line of fire. You move the other way.

"I'm doing it," she informed him. This wasn't a discussion, testing the risks before they might have settled on a decision. This was her instructing him to do his job, get the team ready, be in place for when she turned up at the scene of one of the bombings.

Rad nodded. "Which station do you have in mind?"

"Aleksandrovsky Sad," she informed him, the one with smoke rising from it which she could see in the distance from the window.

"You know they might have picked that station for this very reason," he informed her.

She stood, shaking her head, refusing to take in the idea Rad had suggested.

"You'll plan a random route to the scene, something less direct. But I have nothing to fear, not really."

"Why?" he dared ask. If she had a death wish, he was in the wrong job.

"We both know this is *them*," she said, the collective name for all the threats now out there, these cross-border, international, ethnically diverse group of tyrants, criminals, dictators from whom Filipov had stolen their hidden loot. Loot she now controlled, riches only she had access to. "And therefore we both know that if they kill me, they still have nothing."

He saw her point, though that seemed to assume an awful lot of these people, only some of whom might be that rational. For too many, it often seemed, death was the price you paid for overstepping the mark. There could be no compromise, no negotiation.

"Have you heard anything yet?" he asked, unsure if she might hide something from him.

"Rad, when I hear, you hear, you know what I said to you," she reminded him, a promise she'd made to him the day he took the job.

"Okay," he said, thinking through the next few minutes. The longer they left it, the more time any threat had to make a move.

That was assuming the danger wasn't already in place, waiting for the prey to walk right into the trap. "We'll head out in twenty minutes. I'll have a team look at a route. I'll have an advanced group on the ground, scanning for secondary explosives," he continued, though the local units would already do that most likely, standard practice now in these types of situations. It wasn't the first time they had hit the metro systems in Russia, Moscow and St Petersburg suffering previous attacks. "I'll travel with you and once I get the all clear, you'll make your speech. You get five minutes at this. No longer."

She smiled. Five minutes would be plenty. She enjoyed the dedication he showed to his job, enjoyed having him close to her. She'd been the secret guest at his wedding, in disguise on the day--only Rad knew she had been there, Nastya still unaware--watching from the edge of things, happy for him. He'd found love, the real thing. Something which had always evaded her, and now she was too busy for such nonsense, too old for such distractions, too broken to allow anyone in close enough.

And it seemed like certain corners of the world now wanted her dead to top all that--dead or forced to hand back the money she controlled. Yet, she was having too much fun with it to contemplate repatriating the wealth to its former owners. Most, if not all these people, had no legitimate claim to the capital. Nobody used the Bank for legal deposits. This was ill-gotten gain, blood diamonds and Nazi gold. The bounty of wars and revolutions. The proceeds of criminal activities and robberies--and she had assisted Filipov in pulling off the biggest robbery of them all.

Half an hour later they were outside the metro station, fire crews seen behind her racing back and forth, police units erecting barricades, keeping the crowded pavements controlled. Ambulances stood waiting, bodies and bloodied survivors already on the way up from the platform.

In front of that backdrop, Svetlana Volkov stood before a group of waiting journalists. Cameras flashed, microphones were crammed together as newsrooms across the country lined up to report the story.

Her white fur coat fluttered in the gentle breeze––the purity of her covering a stark twist on the scene evolving behind her.

"My dear nation, it devastates me that there are people out there who not only think up such atrocities, but then carry them out. They hit our capital city and this not for the first time. The heart of this nation has been struck. My heart, too, bleeds for the losses suffered by so many this morning. Husbands who will not arrive home tonight, mothers and fathers who will not be there to tuck their children into bed. Students who will not be at class tomorrow. Hardworking folk, men and women of my great nation, of our great nation, going about their everyday lives, heading into work, heading to university, heading to the airports of this city. All gone. In a moment of madness, and a premeditated madness at that.

"This morning as the news came in, I could see the columns of smoke from my office window inside the Kremlin, an office I have sat in for three years as Acting President, and an office I officially expect to hold for at least another six years, now that the mechanisms are in place for an election in just under six months.

"In these last three years I've seen so much good happening, been around the work of many wonderful people. Men and women who are striving to make an impact, starting businesses, or getting an education. Good people. The same people caught up in all this today, right across this city. This station, as we know, is only one of the four struck this morning. These cowards, these terrorists, from wherever they might have come, whatever hole they climbed out of this morning as they set about their destructive purposes, will not stop our progress. In my three years in office, this is the first time we have all been involved in such a tragedy. I've not had to stand before you, journalists here and viewers watching at home, and relay my sadness at an event that has taken place. That changed this morning with these four attacks.

"And I take them personally. In a country gearing towards an election, this scum has now appeared, planting their devices of death and scurrying away. At no point in my time in office have I needed to deal with such insolence, such disrespect for human life. So let the perpetrators hear this: I will hunt you down, and I will bring you to justice. My government, my term in office, will be hard on crime, hard on this tiny minority who think subway stations on a busy Monday morning are the right places to make their voices heard. There is a special place reserved in hell for such people, and believe me, plenty of prison spaces across this land to accommodate them in the meantime. And I'll build more prisons if we need them, I'll put more police on the streets, use more security personnel to protect our borders and send more soldiers across those borders to hunt down and eradicate these threats. Because, hear me today, my voters, people of Moscow and citizens of this vast yet beautiful land we call home. I will not let these lives lost today count for nothing! I will not be that President, that woman who looks the other way, turns the other cheek. They come at one of us––they come at all of us! And we will not back down! No, we will fight. I will fight! I will lead the charge with you. These terrorists can never have the final word, because victory belongs to the people! Victory belongs to all of us!" She swept away from the microphones, the finest speech of her political career to date behind her, no time allowed for questions. She'd seen the pride on the faces of many of those standing there, journalists who might have criticised her a week before now about to gush for days in countless columns with what they deemed one of the greatest speeches in a generation given by any Russian leader.

Rad met her at the vehicle, a smile on his face, though he said nothing as he opened the door, allowing her to get into the back of the car before shutting it behind her, taking the front passenger seat himself. They would go a different way back to the Kremlin, the route decided on before they had left that morning. Rad watched Svetlana in the rear mirror, seeing the passion in her eyes, a fire that had ignited into something stronger, something forceful the closer they got to the Kremlin.

Ushered in through the gates within minutes, the President now safely returned home, Rad breathed a sigh of relief.

THE MESSAGE CAME through within an hour, Svetlana handed it by Rad, who had been passed it by a member of the cyber-security team. They had sent it through a secure server, to Svetlana's private account. It originated in Dagestan, a troubled region in the far south of the country. It held the name of a known Yemeni organisation, on the US list of terrorist groups.

"Give us back our funds otherwise what happened today gets repeated and repeated until you comply," Svetlana read aloud, a message Rad had already noted.

She passed the printout back to Rad. "Do we know how they did it?"

"They've never attacked Russia. The organisation has its headquarters in Aden, Yemen. We have known them to train fighters, most heading to Syria. They've carried out local attacks in the region, often on American installations."

"But now they have turned their focus to me?"

That much was clear. She had their money.

"It would appear they are in contact with groups in Dagestan," he confirmed, a region and a threat the Kremlin knew about; the fighting had been going on behind the scenes for decades already. "I believe it would have been these men who carried out the attacks here."

"Any idea if they had money in Zurich?" she asked, though Rad was less versed in all that than she was, the reference to the Swiss city enough to tell him she was talking about the Bank. Zurich had been the secret location, its whereabouts until Filipov's inauguration meant to be something few knew.

"It is clear they have enough private means," he said, the four bombings testament to that.

She stood there pacing, thinking through the right way to respond. She wouldn't work with the Yemeni now, not after this. That much she knew.

"Gather me a list of all known Russian criminal networks. Not the street thugs, but the real deal. The ones who might also now have a grudge against me. Ones who might have lost money in Zurich. I know the oligarchs involved, so ignore them."

"And then what?" he asked.

"Then I want to make a deal," she smiled. *Get her in power, keep her safe, and they could have their money back.*

29

London
One Year Ago

Adele had spent an hour with her accountant, someone she usually had her assistant deal with, someone she required a telephone conversation with at most.

She'd not once stated the actual amount, though it was clear she was talking about a significant deposit. She let him believe it might be seven digits, even.

That had been enough to make him concerned. He mentioned money laundering more than once.

She left his office more confused than ever, but something had become clearer. The money had nothing to do with the business; no-one knew about it. She needed to know the source, needed to know the reason. For now, she would take the advice of her accountant and let it sit there. It wasn't a high interest account––something like point two percent, given the state of the economy at the moment––yet even then, she'd done the maths. The sum would earn nearly four hundred thousand a year in interest, just by doing nothing.

She had broached the subject of a takeover with her accountant--the man laughing the question off, something she'd been asking for months. He reminded her both firms were an equal match, with neither having anywhere near enough liquid assets to mount a serious attempt. She backed off, leaving things at that.

She knew she couldn't use the money in that way, therefore. It would pose too many questions--namely, where did she get it? It left her a little deflated.

Adele sat in a cafe near to the office pondering her situation. Her buzzing phone pulled her back into the moment.

"Hello, Jonathan," she said, answering the call from one of her longest standing clients.

"I've just had a call from Clifton," he said, the name making her skin prickle. The fact the enemy was trying to poach another client was nothing new, though Clifton making it personal like that rarely happened.

"Look, you know that lot will try anything," she started, but the caller cut in quickly.

"Adele, it's not from his firm. It was from him, personally."

"He wants to sign you personally?" That made no sense.

"Yes, and I'm not the first he's tried."

He explained what he knew from friends at the golf course. Clifton had been making calls for the last couple of days, some successfully, asking all of them to sign with him personally under a new name.

"Did he say why?" she asked, her mind still racing.

"No, and let me tell you, it has not gone down well at the firm, either." Adele smiled at that comment. Anything that caused havoc in the Niles Ventures' ranks was good in her books.

"They didn't know?"

"Apparently not."

"I take it you told him where to shove his offer?" she asked, only half concerned.

"Naturally," the man replied coolly. He'd worked with Adele for a long time, liked how she ran things, liked the returns she generated. He'd never trusted Clifton either, regardless of all the dirt he'd heard from Adele that last decade. If even half of it was true, it delighted him to no longer be working with Clifton, glad the split had happened. Adele had also always been flirtatious in his direction, though he had long since given up expecting it to go anywhere, despite her public split and very obvious singleness once more.

They ended the call, Adele lost in thought as she looked out of the window. Clifton had overstepped the mark in going for that client; she knew it. But it made little sense to sign him to another venture, something other than the enemy itself. Unless the firm was in trouble? She'd not heard anything, had quizzed her accountant that morning about rumours of any other firm stepping up their game, if there was anyone looking to force a takeover. There was nothing, though rumours could only suggest so much. She well understood the best moves got carried out before anyone knew. It was how she preferred to do business herself.

Yet someone had sent her the money to take them out. Still, she was cautious.

Adele picked up her telephone, calling a man she thought she would never speak to directly again, but annoyed he'd tried to poach the client she'd been chatting with just now.

"What?" he demanded, picking up the call after four rings, knowing it was her. She'd not changed her number since the split.

"Jonathan just called me," she said, sure it would all sink in; the reason for her call, the smugness on Clifton's face certain to vanish quickly.

"And?"

"And? That's all you've got to say for trying to take one of my closest clients."

He laughed at that. "Look, I don't care anymore, okay."

That stopped her in her tracks. Didn't care about what? Money, business, life, the rules of the game? She'd never had him as a quitter.

"What are you up to?" she demanded.

"As if I would tell you, you thieving bitch!" The anger in his tone was clear. He had also called her all these names many times, something she assumed was past them since the legal case concluded and that they had a settled solution.

"Still on about all that, are you?" Nothing but utter contempt oozed across the airways.

"I'm not talking about then," he hissed.

She lent forward in her chair, cradling the empty coffee cup in her spare hand.

"You know about my money?" she said, almost at a whisper, wondering why she was even mentioning it to him.

"Your money?" He laughed at that. "However do you work that one out?"

"It's in my account, isn't it!"

"And who put it there!" he screamed back.

Confusion reigned. Were they actually still talking about the split, when she'd stolen money from the firm's account before telling him it was over, or did he know about the millions now there?

"What figure are you talking about, exactly?"

He paused, a snort suggesting he could work out what she might be thinking.

"The one-ninety," he said eventually.

"You know about that? How?" It could only have been the accountant, though she'd never once mentioned the amount, of that she was certain.

"How? Because I earned it. Me, not you. Me. And that bloody bitch screwed me at the close, sending it to you instead of me." He went silent.

"What?" she demanded.

"You heard me!" he snapped. She had, though she still had no idea what he was going on about.

Then the penny dropped.

"You attempted to take over my firm?" she said, the full force of that statement hitting her like a sledgehammer to a glass table.

He didn't answer––couldn't answer––but the silence told her everything.

"Who?" she demanded thirty-seconds later.

He said something which she couldn't make out. Fire burned inside, as the full understanding dawned on her. It hadn't been some outsider who had sent her this money--some unknown stranger keen for her to close the other firm. Clifton had intended to get the money to buy out her firm, to give him the weaponry to close her down.

"Wow," she said, words almost failing her, an utter disgust at the man as she began to see him in a new light. "You really are something else, aren't you," she said, swearing at him so forcefully that most heads turned towards her in the café, not that she took any of it in. "You were coming for me?"

He didn't have an answer for that. They'd both been going at each other since the day of the settlement. Gloves off, every client up for grabs. Neither had managed the killer shot, however. Until now, that was.

"Well, you really cocked it up big time, didn't you," she laughed, seeing the complete comedy of the moment. She had the money. In some bizarre twist of fate, somebody, someone stupid, had sent the transfer to her personal account instead of his. Or had that been intentional?

"You can't use that money!" he demanded, though she was through with him making demands to her. That had ended years ago, ended with all those whores he had in tow.

"I'll do whatever I bloody well like!" she screamed, heads once again turning her way, at least one mother walking her child out at that moment, presumably to save him from further expletives.

She knew this changed everything. It was like finding a gun, something you didn't know how to use, didn't know why it was there, so kept it hidden. Then you found out another had ordered the gun, intending to kill you with it. You now had that weapon. You now had the target.

It wasn't her money, and it wasn't something she had planned to use, not yet anyway. She hadn't known who had been behind it. Now she did. Now she knew her personal account contained the ammunition intended to wipe her out. Now she had the firepower to do precisely that to him in return.

Further insults were traded between the pair—nothing new there—and they ended the call both more enraged than when they had started it.

This was war. Everything had changed and Adele could march in at leisure, picking off whatever she wanted. And she would take it all. The money could remain her little secret for the foreseeable future, hidden away, accruing interest all the while. A very rich nest egg for her someday, not that she would ever really need it; the game was about to shift dramatically and her business and salary were about to get a sharp boost before the year was out.

Forest Dacha, Russia

NASTYA PUT THE PHONE DOWN, a tear in her eye, Olya coming over to hug her. Nastya always cried after speaking to Rad. He'd been in Moscow for the last fortnight. The day the bombs went off at the metro stations had scared her and Nastya was desperate for her husband. Kostya told her she was being stupid, Olya scolding her husband for such a remark. He left the women to it after that, able to finish the roof on the dacha which he managed after another week.

"He doesn't know when he'll be back," Nastya said, composed enough to voice part of what Rad had told her.

"He knows what he's doing," Olya comforted, holding her niece tightly for the time being.

"I'm scared," she said.

"I know you are," Olya confirmed. She'd seen that look in Nastya's eyes once before, the setting a little different. Nastya had fled an abusive boyfriend in Moscow, arriving at their dacha with nowhere else to go. They'd taken her in. Now that fear was back. Not fear of escaping somebody, now just fear of losing someone she loved.

"You need to take your mind off things, dear," Olya said, letting go of Nastya, returning to the pots of paint she'd been sorting through on their worktop. She handed one to Nastya. "Try this one," she encouraged.

They'd been testing colours on the bare walls of the new home, with one room nearly ready to paint. Nastya wanted to have it ready before Rad returned.

Nastya took the tray, the colour warm, inviting, homely. She smiled, her face lighting up, her natural charm shining through.

"Thanks," Nastya said, taking the brush offered to her by her aunt, and walking across to the new dacha, over the bricks that would eventually be a front porch area, and in through an open doorway into what would be their entrance hall. She went into the room on the right. A windowpane lay on the floor underneath the hole it would fit into. This would be their bedroom, the view out back towards Rad's old dacha, the shed he'd been using for years. She painted a few small patches on all four walls, the light slightly different in each spot. She loved it. It would be perfect. Rad had always insisted she design the inside of their home, and with the roof nearly finished, the windows ready to go in, that phase of the build was so nearly upon them.

She couldn't wait to live there together, just the two of them, her uncle and aunt further into the forest, close but not too close. She missed Rad desperately. She hated not knowing what he was doing, if he was safe; if the next call she took from Moscow might be the news she dreaded hearing most of all.

Central Moscow

ROMAN IVANOV always cut a handsome figure, his tailored suits costing more than most families spent on their car, though he'd pulled out all the stops today. A new high-rise building was being opened that day, another of Roman's projects, yet another of his businesses. He was in the top one hundred richest Russians alive, the upper half of the list at that.

After his short speech, the questions started. The initial three were regarding the building—the process from planning to construction, how he felt now they'd finished it, questions about planning permission—but soon it moved onto other things.

"Mr Ivanov, will you be standing in the Presidential election?" someone asked, the question left of centre, though soon everyone wanted to hear his answer.

Roman smiled. In the week since the bombings in Moscow, they had bandied one name about as a suitable candidate for the Presidency, a gifted man who had held the deputy position in the State Duma, and one with twenty years' experience in the political sphere. Before that he'd worked with Roman Ivanov who might now be ready to back him.

"No, I'll leave that to the more experienced people," Roman smiled, doing his best to push away the question and move onto other things, though that only threw petrol on the flames. A barrage of questions followed.

Did he therefore think his former employee, a man with decades of experience in the political sphere, was that man? Would he back him? Did he see him as his future President?

Roman let the noise die down, until they were silent, the reporters all watching him, the oligarch's mouth slightly open, clearly about to speak, about to answer them.

"I'll be supporting our current President, Ms Volkov," he said, a few of the people present now gasping at his words, "because she has shown me she has the makings of a President."

"But you talked about experience?" one reporter called.

"And that she possesses, far more than you know."

"That might be, but your friend has been in the Duma for twenty years," which wasn't true, though he had been deputy there for the last twelve.

"This friend you speak about; I've not seen him in, well, a long time. Probably over ten years."

"And Svetlana Volkov?" A question loaded with accusations.

"President Volkov has done an incredible job," he repeated, his words different but tone the same as moments before. "I've nothing but respect for her, and I will put my time, money and voice behind her, all the way."

"And your friend?"

Roman smiled at the simplicity of it all, this assumption that someone who worked for him twenty years ago in his fast-track management programme, who he hadn't spoken to in a decade, could still get called a friend. Oligarchs had very few friends.

"I suggest he saves himself the disgrace of putting his own name into the hat," Roman said, looking directly into the camera, his message aimed at that one man.

30

London
Two Months Ago

Sasha had made all the arrangements, a table booked at their favourite restaurant, Anissa informed a few days before of when and where. He'd not suggested they do something together outside of the office for months.

She'd assumed they were already through with all that.

Anissa arrived second, appearing at the crowded entrance way, a few families waiting for a table. She wore a simple but beautiful dress, her hair done, a clip holding it up, just the way he liked it. She spotted him through the crowd, a smile on her face, as she made her apologies and moved from that spot, making it to the table set for two as Sasha stood. He kissed her on each cheek.

"You look fabulous," he said, taking her in. He seemed nervous, an unease there that Anissa rarely saw in him. She brushed his comment and the thought away, taking her seat, Sasha returning to his. She looked around the place. She and Sasha had shared many happy memories there over the last few years. It was the only other local, high-quality family venue she had not previously been to with her husband and boys.

"Well, this is a surprise," she said, taking the menu offered to her by Sasha, aware it hadn't changed since their last date there. She already knew she wanted the salmon. He smiled at her, though not the warm smile she enjoyed so much. His eyes darted away for a moment, his mind taking him elsewhere.

"Are you okay?" she asked, Sasha looking back towards her.

"This isn't easy," he said, Anissa reaching for his hand instinctively across the table.

"We can still eat here as friends," she started, wanting to help him, wanting to take the worry from his strained face. He pulled his hand away.

"It's not that. This isn't what this is," he said, his eyes on her. She felt a bolt of something unpleasant shoot into her gut.

"Then what is this then, exactly?"

He paused for a moment, allowing her to calm a little. He'd picked the venue to not create a scene, to force them to chat quietly, to confirm he would not turn her in without speaking it through with her. He still didn't know what to do.

Sasha lent forward, arms on the edge of the table, head less than two feet from hers. "I know you killed Bethany May," he whispered, almost too quietly, almost inaudibly, yet she heard enough.

"How?" she reacted, somewhat shocked, somewhat taken aback by the sudden change in her reading of the situation.

Sasha sat back, his final hope that he was wrong about Anissa now gone, her response the confirmation he'd been dreading. Not *what are you talking about*? Not *are you crazy*? But *how? How did you know it was me? How did you find out?*

"It was the cemetery the last time I met you."

She didn't seem to connect the dots, nor could she remember anything recent.

He continued. "The anniversary of their deaths. I called by to pick you up." Recognition filled her face.

"That was months ago."

"Yes," he said, something that hardly seemed relevant at the moment. He'd just told her he knew she'd lied to him. Knew she'd overstepped the mark. Knew she'd murdered someone, albeit the woman responsible for the death of her three loved ones. But murdered her.

"I still don't understand," she said, calmer now, yet her world was imploding. The clever mind inside her head raced with a thousand thoughts, none of them good, none of them ending well for her right now.

He opened up with her over the next five minutes. Told her what he remembered of the day in question, him waking, her gone. Her need for closure, for permission even, from her dead husband. Her need to have run straight there to the cemetery in the early hours of the morning after the night they had first slept together. Her telling him where she'd been, why he needed to say she was at home. How she couldn't have proved where she was that morning. How he lied for her when the body of their former DDG was found at home. How he'd seen the camera at the entrance, known she had lied to him. Bumped into the doctor, heard the story of Anissa's no-show at the meeting she had requested. Everything.

She swore, tears on the edge of her eyes but now wasn't the place for that, she knew it. The fact they were in a restaurant full of families and not in a detention cell at Vauxhall House told her something. She still had time.

"Who knows?" she asked, once she'd composed herself a little from the shock, once Sasha had gone silent again.

"I've not taken it to the top," he said, dodging a direct answer but confirming ultimately what she was needing to find out. She breathed a slow, long breath out, her pulse settling a little.

"Thank you," she said, as if he'd done her a huge favour, though he knew he had. She would lose everything if the truth came out. She would definitely go to prison.

"I don't understand why you lied to me," he said, hurt showing more evidently for the first time now.

"You don't?" she said, somewhat flippantly. "I thought that was obvious now, no?"

He shook his head. "Is everything we had together a lie?" he asked, pain in his eyes, his accent coming back stronger than usual, his voice wavering as he spoke.

She didn't know how to answer. She loved him, liked him for certain. But she'd needed him, needed someone to cover for her. Needed an alibi.

"Our happiness was real," she said, something she knew to be true.

He swore now. "I don't believe it!" he snapped, reaching for his glass of water but unable to take a mouthful, just holding it there, midair. "Everything we did together. It was all an act for you?"

"No, Sasha, it wasn't," she said, her eyes pleading. She didn't need him hurt like that, didn't need that reaction. She hated herself for thinking it, hated the fact even now she was managing the situation, managing their relationship so he would say nothing. So it would all be okay, the issue pushed to one side, life moving on. "What we have together is real," she said, attempting to reach forward, though he pulled his hands away from her this time before she could make contact.

"What we have together is nothing but a lie," he said.

"No, it's not," Anissa whispered, yet Sasha could not look at her. The waiter came over at that moment, Anissa flustered, ordering the first glass of wine her eyes landed on from the menu. Sasha waved the man away, said he wasn't ordering anything, wasn't able to stay much longer. She was losing him, she feared now.

"Sasha, you mean everything to me," she said, now it was the two of them again.

"I'm nothing but your freedom pass," he said.

"No, that's not true!" she protested, knowing that was exactly what he had been since he covered for her that day.

There was a long silence, the wine arriving midway through, Sasha confirming he wanted nothing from the menu. He needed a drink all right, but not there. Not now.

"I will not report you to the boss," he said, reluctantly, something he'd decided upon before this meeting, something which his strained emotions hadn't yet talked him from doing.

"Why?" she asked, hope rising in her heart as suddenly as she raised the glass of wine to her trembling lips and downed half of it in one go. He watched her silently for a while, his dark Russian eyes boring into her as if searching for her soul, seeing if there was anything redeemable about her before he answered.

"Because of what she did to you," he finally said, Anissa nodding at that understanding. "I get why you did it," he added, having had time enough to think about that since his lunchtime chat with the doctor. "I just don't get why you involved me in it."

"You're not involved in it!" she said.

"The moment you asked me to lie, I became part of it. Is that why you tricked me into it?"

"No," she said through tears now, the glass long since finished, the waiter desperately slow at spotting the fact.

"You aren't the person I thought you were," he added. She considered that comment for a while, took it in, mulled over the truth of it all. She'd not been her real self in a long time, ever since her last trip to St Petersburg. She knew that now. She should have got help, proper medical help. She'd pushed it all away just as she had pulled the wall of evidence from their office wall, the cork boards free of the secrets that had previously lived underneath. Then Alex, then Phelan, then the bombing. She'd lost herself somewhere in that mix, she realised. Sasha had fallen in love with a broken version of her, but a fragment of her real self, a real self she wasn't sure existed anymore.

"I'm sorry," is all she said after an awkward pause following his previous comment. "I really am. Sorry for everything I've put you through. Sorry for this situation you are in now."

"Sorry we slept together?" he probed. She shook her head through tears, words unable to form, her hand to her mouth, silent.

He believed her, aware there were feelings showing. There was a woman––part of a woman anyway––behind those eyes, behind those tears. The hurt hadn't swallowed her, the death of her family had not totally snatched her soul from within.

The waiter appeared and Anissa asked for another glass of wine.

"I was a mess," she said once it was just them again. "When I woke up in that bed, I knew immediately what I'd lost." She was talking about the hospital, Sasha having been keeping watch over her for days, weeks even, as she slowly recovered. "I knew it would change my life," she continued, a focus returning to her the more she spoke. "I knew I had to make them pay. Make her pay, when I found out what MI6 had done with May."

She took the wine when it arrived, the break allowing her a little more time to compose herself, to draw her thoughts together.

"Yet none of it made any difference, did it?" she said, Sasha unclear what she referred to specifically. "Life goes on. Volkov takes office, Alex is still missing and every bloody day I live on, my family is still dead!"

He allowed the emotion to die down somewhat. Everything surrounding Russia had threatened to get the better of Anissa, that much he knew. A fresh thought hit him, something that could move them on, move them from this impasse, offering them a workable solution. Someway they could get through this, carry on, rebuilding their relationship.

"We can't bring back the dead, Anissa, but we can do something about the other situation."

"Volkov?" she said, unimpressed. They'd tried that once before with a Russian President.

"Alex," he corrected.

She repeated the name.

"We go after Alex," Sasha said, a smile on his face for the first time since they had started talking.

31

Kazan, Russia

It had taken a few days to arrange but Svetlana was in the city of Kazan, an eighty-minute flight east from Moscow. She couldn't have people watching her this time.

The FSB had foiled an attempt by the same Yemeni group from carrying out an attack in St Petersburg, her silence to their initial demand meaning they'd followed through with their threat. She had kept that attempt from the media. It would only play to the fear these terrorists were trying to cause if word got out.

Svetlana hoped that by the end of the day, she could control most if not all the threats there might be to come.

She'd taken a big risk by going personally, she knew that, but there was no-one else she trusted more.

The venue on the edge of the city was mostly derelict and had been picked for that very reason. She had used such areas herself in the past for the Games. Nearly every major Russian criminal organisation had someone representing them––quite the risk themselves, given her speech from two weeks before about being hard on crime. Here stood a room full of people devoted to the art.

"Thank you all for coming," she said, a trip she'd made with Rad and just a handful of his most trusted men, though only the former sniper was in the room with her. The others patrolled the perimeter, deliberately kept at arm's length.

"As you now know, Filipov looted the vault of the Bank. He'd discovered its location and let me in on his secret only late in his plan. What you will not know was that it was I who got the combination which enabled Filipov to gain access to the actual treasure. I did that from within a prison cell," she said, not elaborating, though a few knew the connection, knew of her arrest and sudden release in the weeks before the theft.

"And what you all now know is that I alone have access and use of these funds, something that I had kept secret for three years,"--most assumed Filipov had destroyed it all--"until a traitor within my own ranks turned on me." She'd still not found out who that was. All those who might have been the leak were already dead, or so she thought.

The room shifted uncomfortably as she spoke. They knew the rumours and had read the reports, but hearing her tell them in person somehow made it even more raw.

"And I'm here to make a deal. I can give you back everything you lost in Zurich," she said, with a smile. The room didn't move, these men all too familiar with how the world worked.

"For what?" one man asked after a few seconds. There always had to be a flip side.

She nodded in appreciation. "Yes, that is a good question. Why would I give you back millions of dollars for nothing? You all get back what you claim is yours, provided you can prove it, naturally. But I'll let you have it. As long as you protect me," she said, the room left a little dumbstruck.

"You want us to be your muscle?" another said, looking at Rad, who seemed perfectly capable of handling that side of things himself. Most in the room knew of him by reputation already.

"No, I have that covered," she said, a slight turn of the head towards Rad, a smile confirming what they all knew. "What I need from you goes broader than that. A Yemeni group carried out the Moscow bombing. On their own they had no access to our country. They needed units on the inside. Now, my government can work on watching the borders, but if men are already in the country, it does get a lot harder."

"You want us to snitch?" another said, jumping ahead to where he saw her going.

"No," she said, aware from her husband Sergei that there was nothing a criminal hated more than being made to turn on their brethren. "But these outsiders, these terrorists, monsters happy to blow up babies and children, have to get their supplies from somewhere. I want you to be that somewhere. You get me into office, you help me rid the country of any threat, and I'll settle your accounts with you. We will return the money. You can do what you like with it."

"We need that money now," another man growled from the side. "You closed down my entire enterprise when you stole it from Zurich."

Svetlana snapped. "I didn't steal it!" she said. "Filipov did, and he would have destroyed it all," she added, which was a lie, though no-one there could prove it. "Be thankful you even have the chance to get some of it back."

"But without it, what good are we to you?"

"You'll find a way," she said, aware they'd been in this position for three years already. Another six months wouldn't break them, she was sure. But she wouldn't risk giving it back before the vote. She needed the legitimate handing over of power first.

"So we become the invisible shield heading off trouble before it gets anywhere near you?" another asked.

"Invisible, visible. However you want to play it works for me," she smiled, ever able to hold an audience, forever the performer.

"And after?" another said, aware she'd made promises to crack down on crime once she was President.

"After, we shall see," she said, aware of their concern, aware of her promises, though they would soon learn there was two sides to her.

The one in front of a camera, speech inclusive, words warm and open. And then there was her real self, in contexts like this one.

"Do we get a choice?"

She laughed at that. They had no choice. They had nothing, she everything.

"If you want your little empires back, want your many ill-gotten gains returned, I suggest you agree with my proposal. But you have a choice," she winked. "I'll give you a little time to discuss amongst yourselves," she added, stepping to the door, Rad following her through before pulling it shut.

"We'll give them one minute," she said, both knowing it was not nearly enough time for a group that size to reach any consensus, though that was the point. She wasn't presenting them with any real option.

Sixty-seconds later she was back in through the door, heads turning towards her, a few faces red with rage, a few more smiling at the obvious one-upmanship she was showing them.

"I take it you all agree?" she said, the room deadly silent for a moment, before a few of the men at the front started nodding their heads, the room soon erupting into a confirmatory roar of acceptance. "Very good. I would like a word with you, Pavel, before I leave," she said, pointing to a man at the front, the head of a large Moscow-based crime syndicate. Rad stepped to one side, allowing Pavel to follow Svetlana back through the door she'd just come through.

Once outside the room, Pavel waited for Svetlana to speak.

"I need two things from you," she said. "I would like you to be my contact for this entire group," she started, waving back at the room they'd just left, though he knew what she meant.

"Not everyone will like that," he pointed out. They were all rivals with a long history with each other just as they were rivals with the law.

"Well, find a way of working out your differences. Build your own team, if you will. I can't openly meet with any of you."

"Bad for business?" he smirked.

"We all have appearances to keep up," she snapped back.

"I'll act as spokesman," he said, not sure how to make that happen, but he would do what she required.

"And my second request is a little more personal," she said, taking a list from the inside pocket of her jacket, something she would have passed to Sergei in the past.

Pavel looked at the names on the list, none of which meant anything to him.

"Find them all," she said. "They aren't to know, and some of them might be old, some might be dead already. But I want every address you have for those still living."

He nodded. "Consider it done," he said, Svetlana smiling at that, glad that her assessment of the man whose background she had looked into thoroughly had turned out to be right for the job.

He walked back into the main room, Rad coming back through the open door to join Svetlana, the two then heading towards the car. Rad's unit would follow in convoy to the airport, and the Acting President would be in the air within half an hour, on her way back to Moscow, her mission for election taking a giant leap forward with the events in Kazan.

32

London
Past Eleven Months

Clifton had been back from Alicante one month, and since that time when he had arrived home in a hurry, the taxi bringing him to his front door, he had left home precisely once. That had been enough to show him the many shadows who now seemed to follow his every turn. They were onto him; he was certain. He'd dashed home with his shopping, slamming the door shut behind him for fear they would grab him on his own doorstep, and he closed every curtain he had.

He ordered home delivery from the local supermarket from then on, insisting on using the same delivery driver every time––he would not take any chances––and going through a careful routine of allowing the driver into the underground garage before accepting the order. The store had got used to his peculiarities after the fifth visit.

Conducting business from home was a little more straightforward, though in his industry, the lack of face-to-face contact with his clients and potential clients had quickly become an issue. Rumours soon spread about an illness––some said Aids––though Clifton rubbished such statements. Nobody at his office knew the reason he was suddenly housebound. He had asked no-one to visit him there. Clifton had never acted like that.

The confirmation that it was the mafia standing close on the street outside came five weeks after he arrived back in the UK from Spain. Don Jose Zabala called him, Clifton's private number taking longer to discover than they had wanted.

"We speak again," the man said, his accent thick, but unmistakably the same voice Clifton had heard in the restaurant as he told him he had killed his son. Clifton had been expecting something like this to happen for weeks, had even started wondering if he was merely being paranoid, seeing things that weren't actually there. Seeing men on the street who were no more interested in him than the pigeons flying overhead. Yet the call confirmed his sanity––which was little consolation.

"How did you get this number?" he asked.

"You might ask how I had men locate your home address within days of you running from me. How I've had men visit your office, take one of your secretaries for coffee, play a round of golf with some of your employees. You might ask many things but there is only one thing I want to ask, and one thing I will tell you in response. Why did you kill my son?"

Clifton didn't know what to say, didn't imagine in any of the nightmares that last month that he would ever talk to the man again. In all these terror-dreams he couldn't speak, couldn't make a sound. His voice silent, his attacker vicious. In every nightmare he died a gruesome death.

"They framed me," he said, finally.

"Framed?" It'd not been the answer the Don had assumed, though he'd never been able to work out any motive. Clifton wasn't into crime, there was no turf war, no fight that he appeared to have with their family. Yet it could only have been personal. Clifton had even confirmed that fact by daring to confront the Don in person and admit to the killing. "By whom?"

"The President," he said. "The Russian President," he clarified after the few seconds of silence that followed.

Don Zabala laughed at that. The man was more delusional than he had thought.

"And why would the Russian bloody President want anything to do with someone like you?" The laugh had gone, only biting hatred present now.

"I don't know," Clifton admitted, something he'd been asking himself for the last month, something for which he still had no answer.

"You're lying to me," the Don said, "and listen carefully. I said I would ask you one question and then give you one response. My son had lost his way, and some of my associates warned me he was leading the family down a dangerous path. Anyone who knew the pair of us knew we weren't speaking. I couldn't control my boy anymore, hadn't really known him for some time––too many years. I understand that now. In so many ways he was a real pain to me." He laughed. "I know, it's crazy."

"So I did you a favour," Clifton said, the Don's laughter snapping in a second at that comment.

"Oh, not so fast. You see respect and kindness and responsibility are important in my circles; but honour, family, blood, even revenge are king. You killed my son and for that you will die." His voice was calm, too calm, the Spaniard suddenly in total control of his words, his tone and emotions.

"I thought you said he was dragging your family down into the gutter?"

"Not my choice of words, but yes, you could say he headed that way. Still, he was my son, and you stepped in and killed him. For that you will die."

"Why haven't you topped me already?" Clifton demanded, his eyes darting to the curtained windows––there was nothing to see––as if the Don might be outside his building at that very moment, his team of men ready to break in, force the door and kill him on that very spot.

"That is a good question," the Don mused. "I wanted to know who you were, understand why you did what you did."

"I told you why," he started to protest, the Don having nothing of it.

"Oh, the President, right? You mentioned that," he said, mockingly not believing a word of it. "I know she was in Madrid the week before, but that is from where she left, too."

"No, that's not true. She was in Alicante."

"Don't lie to me!" he screamed at Clifton, the Brit silenced by the outburst; the threat of a man who knew how to command an audience was plain. There was silence, before the Don's voice, now calm, now almost melodic, started down a new line of conversation.

"You can't stay hidden inside forever, can you?"

Clifton thought about that. His men could have tried to come in if they were able. Being inside gave him an advantage it seemed, though he knew it was temporary. There would be no life to live stuck indoors.

"Who says I'm even home?" he asked.

"Come, Clifton, we both know precisely the answer to that one," the Don mocked.

"Then come and get me yourself, old man!" Clifton snapped.

"Oh, manners, boy," the man said. "Didn't your bitch of a mother ever teach you anything?"

"I'll go to the police!" he said, getting desperate.

"And say what, exactly?" the Don posed; he was way ahead in his thinking, having played out this question for days already. And suddenly Clifton got it. What could he say? Such a move would only prove his guilt. Nothing but life in prison for murder would await him. He would take his own voluntary house arrest over decades behind bars.

"So you think you have me, do you?"

"Think? Oh no, Clifton, I don't merely think it. I know I do." The confidence in his voice caused Clifton's stomach to turn, the Brit now sharing that same certainty about his own inevitable downfall.

"However," the Don said, a tone and word Clifton had never

expected to hear, a sound that suddenly turned on light at the end of his endless tunnel. "You appear to have some friends in high places, I'll give you that." Clifton stayed silent––he wasn't immediately aware of anyone remotely fitting the bill. "And one of these men has reached out to me."

Clifton wanted to ask who––who knew about all this, who had reached out, what had they possibly said that might have altered the inevitable in any way? But he couldn't speak for the internal struggle now taking place inside him.

"I've accepted this man's proposal," the Don added, apparently not about to divulge what the proposal might be.

"And?" Clifton begged.

"He will contact you shortly," Don Zabala confirmed.

Clifton didn't like the sound of this any more than the call out of the blue, yet this third person seemed to have caused the Don to pull his figurative gun from Clifton's face. He knew it could have been a literal gun instead of a phone call when the pair did finally speak. And Clifton knew they would have done, eventually.

"And then what?"

"Then I suggest you take what he offers," the Don confirmed, his final words in fact, the call ending immediately after those words.

Clifton sat there in silence, looking at his phone, thinking through the conversation.

It would be two days before a knock on his front door would alert Clifton to the appearance of this mystery stranger.

CLIFTON HAD BEEN asleep when the firm knock of a fist on the front door woke him with a start. Peering through the peephole he didn't see the gun wielding henchmen of Don Zabala as he had been fearing for weeks, but a stylish man with dark hair and an expensive suit. Had he not been waiting for such an appearance, he would have left it, shunned the stranger, grabbed anything to protect himself. But since the call from two days ago, he'd been waiting, and hoping.

Clifton opened the door cautiously, edgy that it wasn't some form of trap, that this wasn't what he'd been told it would be; his way out, his lifeline when faced with otherwise only bleak options.

"Can I come in Mr Niles?" the visitor asked, his accent strong. *Russian, by the sound of it, perhaps Eastern European. Not Spanish.*

The Brit eyed him cautiously, looking beyond the visitor's shoulders, searching for fear there were others nearby, waiting to pounce, waiting to take him. There were no others. He stepped back, allowing the stranger to walk on past him, Clifton closing the door firmly once he was inside, turning to face the man now, though waiting for him to speak.

"I work for a very wealthy man," the visitor said, no name given, no other information offered.

"A Russian?" Clifton quizzed. The stranger merely shrugged his shoulders, either unable or most likely unwilling to divulge more than he had already said. If the Russians were present, it brought things all closer. They'd got him into this mess––surely they had the means to get him out of it too?

"You've been expecting my call, I take it?" Clifton nodded. "Very good. Shall we sit down somewhere more comfortable?" the Russian asked, the two men standing in the hallway, shoes cluttering the floor despite Clifton living by himself. He had a thing for shoes.

"Be my guest," Clifton said, arm raised towards the lounge, hand ushering the visitor forward. Clifton followed him in, the room tidier, but only just. Cooped up alone, he hadn't needed to bother much about visitors. The Russian took a seat, Clifton letting him settle before taking a seat on the opposite chair.

"They have advised me about your predicament, Mr Niles, and I'm here today to offer you a way out."

"A way out?" Clifton pleaded, the lifeline he'd been hoping for, though fear soon filled the void, terrified as he was at what they might ask him to do, whom they might demand he kill next.

"You killed two men five weeks ago, Mr Niles, not to mention the middle-aged man you put in hospital when you attacked him and stole his clothes," the Russian started, well versed in all he needed to say, well aware of the truth behind the accusations. "You caused a small aircraft to crash, resulting in a sizeable amount of localised damage."

"I had no control over the plane," Clifton protested, not sure why he was fighting such a minor point, surely the least of all his crimes.

"That may well be correct, but in the grand scheme of things, I think you've missed the point. And we've not even reached your most pressing need yet, have we?"

"Getting the mafia off my back?" Clifton said, assuming they were talking about the same thing.

"Precisely," the Russian smiled.

"You can do that?" he asked, the Russian initially shaking his head, Clifton somewhat alarmed before the words filtered through into his brain.

"I can't personally, no, but the man I work for can––he has, in fact. If you take the deal. He'll make the four men standing guard on the street outside walk away. He'll make Don Zabala stop pursuing you. You'll be able to walk out of this door, a free man."

"Free?" Clifton asked, barely able to force the word from his mouth.

"For a time, yes."

The smile left Clifton's face. "For a time? What does that mean?"

"You've not heard the deal yet, Mr Niles."

"Enlighten me," Clifton said, resigned to the fact he would not like what he was about to be told, though sitting there, a prisoner in his own home, he knew he didn't have a choice.

"You've committed two murders. It doesn't matter who these men were, what these men had done. In a criminal court, you are the one who will be held responsible. And believe me, there is video evidence."

That comment brought Clifton to the edge of his chair.

"They recorded it?" he said, more alarmed than ever.

"In minute detail," the Russian confirmed. "There is no doubt of your guilt, no mystery in your crimes. Any court, any jury, any judge. You're guilty, plain as day."

Clifton knew that much.

"And added to that, there is this angry father, a violent man with a vast reach, demanding revenge for the murder of his only son."

"Enough already, you can cut the theatrics. Get to the point!"

The Russian pulled a mini tablet device from his jacket pocket, switching it on, setting it on a stand then facing it in towards Clifton. Nothing but a blank screen waited, the white triangle *play* button in the middle of the screen. The Russian pressed it, sitting back and watching Clifton's expression change from confusion, to surprise, to dread then to utter despair.

"Where did you get this?" he demanded, one minute into the recording, the climax to the clip not even yet reached.

They had taken the video from his villa in Spain, during his first week in Alicante. The camera was mounted somewhere above his bed, maybe around the door to the en suite. The replay showed, through his open bedroom door, a party happening in the distance. Clifton himself appeared in shot several times, drink in hand, very much the host with the most.

In the centre of the shot, filling most of the screen, was his bed on which a woman was lying. She'd not moved once in the minute he'd been watching.

Then Clifton appeared at the door, the video without audio, the screen appearing to show him speaking as he poked his head around the door, spotting the guest on his bed. There were a few seconds where his head had disappeared from the doorway, seemingly a man returning to the party, but Clifton knew what followed, knew what he was inevitably about to watch. Sure enough, the video showed him appearing in the doorway again, this time coming in through it, a glance behind him before closing the door gently. It showed him locking the door now that he was inside the room.

He walked over to the bed, his face less than a few feet from the camera, the shot picking him shaking the sleeping girl by the shoulders. First gently, then with a little more vigour. She was out, stoned or drunk, but dead to the world.

Clifton looked away as the video of himself showed him lowering his jeans, climbing on top of her. He knew the rest.

He passed the device back to the Russian.

"You planted this camera in my villa?" he demanded.

"Mr Niles, you can hardly demand such information now, not in your position. And this isn't the first time you've done such a thing, is it?" It wasn't a question, Clifton looking at and then seeing the certainty in the eyes of the Russian, both men aware of the truth in that statement.

"Thirteen years ago you did the same thing to Melody Southern."

"Who?" he said, still unsure of the connection, though the link now came back to him, the mention of the name from Svetlana as they parted in Alicante finally making sense.

"In Los Angeles," the man confirmed.

Clifton sat back, eyes to the ceiling. She'd been the first person he had date-raped, the first woman he'd seduced and used, unleashing a thirst for more. More risk, more power, more control.

"I never knew her name," Clifton confessed.

"But you know exactly who I am speaking about now, I assume?"

Clifton nodded.

"Then it is time you confronted your past," the man said. "You turn yourself in for these two offences," he said, holding up the device, clear he was talking about the two rapes. "We won't even use this video evidence if you confess to it all. Say you reconsidered, felt the weight of your guilt, whatever. Just see that justice gets done."

"Or what?" Clifton asked, though the deal looked a lot better than his predicament of an hour ago.

"You know the answer to that."

"How does this make any difference to the mafia?" Clifton probed, unsure of the connection and unaware of why his confession for a crime of over a decade ago in a faraway place might appease the man wanting revenge for the murder of his son.

"Let's just say, the person I work for can be very persuasive."

Clifton didn't doubt any of that. His whole final week in Spain had shown him just a glimpse of what they could do. He was through with the lot of them.

"Why now?" he asked, the thought pressing for a few seconds. "I mean, it was years ago when I last went to Los Angeles. The authorities could have tracked me down if there had been any reports of trouble, I wouldn't have been too hard to find. So why now?"

"That's an answer I can't give you," the Russian said, unclear to Clifton right away whether that was because he didn't know or was not at liberty to say.

"So I just walk into a police station and confess to two crimes that happened in America and Spain?" he asked incredulously.

"Yes," the man replied, matter-of-factly.

"But they won't try a case here for a crime committed elsewhere," Clifton said.

"Have there been similar incidents here?" he asked, Clifton going silent, not prepared to answer that one, though happy he wasn't being shown a video again to prove his guilt. It appeared the Russians only had one video of his rapes.

"I still don't see what it'll do," Clifton said.

"Mr Niles, do you still think in today's era, that if a man like yourself walks into a police station and confesses to the drugging and rape of women they will merely turn you away and demand proof before arresting you?"

"So I face the music for these two crimes and the rest goes away?" Clifton checked, the sentence sure to be harsh––if they could even trace the victims––but nothing compared to facing a murder charge, with the mafia on his back.

"That's the proposal," the Russian confirmed.

Clifton sat back in his chair, eyeing the man across from him, the two not speaking for the time being. Clifton blew out a long breath, his pent up fears melting somewhat, his nearly impossible predicament changed over the course of their conversation. Sure, he would face some heat, face prison time, but that would compare little to what it could all have been.

"How long do I have?"

"To decide?" the Russian checked, Clifton nodding his response. "I would say time is already up, wouldn't you agree?"

"Okay," Clifton said, aware he had no better option. An hour ago he had nothing. "Tell them I agree. I'll do it. Get the mafia off my back and I'll turn myself in, confess to my crimes and face whatever they throw at me."

"Very well," the Russian said, pocketing his device, tapping the cover as he did so, very much the threat that remained if Clifton didn't follow through. *We've got the video now, don't forget.* "I will let my boss know."

A minute later he was out through the front door, nothing more said, Clifton closing it behind him quickly and walking to his drinks cabinet, his hand trembling, tears welling up. With his hand shaking, he poured himself a large drink, taking a large gulp right after, allowing the liquid to swill around his mouth for a while, burning his throat as he swallowed.

He mulled over the name Melody Southern a little more, finally with some context: a location, a year, and a reason. He wasn't sure if he had ever known her name––they'd been chatting flirtatiously; her drink easy to spike, the rest plain sailing. He'd never been able to find any firm reference to her when he'd come back from Spain, Svetlana's final words still fresh in his mind.

He went back to the computer. Los Angeles was the home of Hollywood, and Clifton knew all about Svetlana Volkov as an actress. He clicked through to her IMDb page, the list of films she'd starred in appearing under her name. He went to 2005, Svetlana listed in one big film that year, details of the film in question showing she would have been in the city at about the same time. Clifton pulled up a new window on his browser, typing in Melody's name and this time adding the word actress after it, a few results now starting to appear. Melody had a few small roles, the films listed, the last three, once he checked the previous page, coinciding with films Svetlana was starring in. There was nothing past 2005, Melody apparently off the grid from then on. The penny finally dropped.

CLIFTON'S ARREST was big news—the circulating stories of his fall from grace resulting in several women speaking up for the first time, all UK based, claiming he had drugged and raped them too, only now finding the voice and confidence to come forward.

They took Clifton into custody immediately, bail denied, his trial scheduled for three months from that first incarceration to give the authorities time to investigate his crimes.

The police traced and contacted Melody Southern. Married with two children, she lived in the same town she'd always lived in—besides her brief stint in Hollywood—and wanted nothing to do with any trial. She'd told no-one about what had happened to her, besides Svetlana, someone she'd not spoken with since the day she'd left, two lives travelling in very different directions ever since. They informed Melody there were many names, many cases—Clifton would go to prison for sure. She contented herself with that information, but hurried the police away, desperate to keep her own life unscarred by the crimes of her past.

During the months leading up to the trial, Niles Ventures went into free fall, Adele Spence and her firm there to move in for the spoils, as were several other firms. It would be six months before they lost the business, but the warning signs appeared immediately. With Clifton out of the picture, with his high-profile arrest and very public fall from grace, his clients couldn't leave the firm quickly enough.

Spence Securities would eventually purchase the building which the now defunct firm had utilised, doubling her working capacity overnight, keeping most of the employees from the troubled firm. She had her millions still stowed away, the money not needed to bring her enemy down. His own confession had been enough.

She bought her first Caribbean holiday home, safe knowing that business was so good and that nobody would question such a spend.

She toasted her former partner on that first trip to the property, mocking him all the more.

Clifton remained in custody, his trial due to start the following week, twelve charges of rape before him, which didn't include the name of Melody Southern or the incident in Spain. If that video were to emerge, he knew all hell would break loose. But he was alive, the mafia couldn't touch him, and with his life falling down around him, remaining where he was for the time being felt about the easiest place to be right then.

London Crown Court
Present Day

JOURNALISTS PACKED the auditorium high above, the doors shut for visitors twenty minutes before the jury returned their verdict, every available seat in the courtroom already taken. A hushed silence fell upon the room as the Judge presiding over the trial took his seat. He asked the spokesman of the jury to stand, a piece of paper in her hand.

Clifton stood in the defendant's box, his suit crisp, his hair slicked back. His defence team had done their best—they presented a man with a new image, who had confessed to his crimes, who was looking to confront his demons. The prosecution claimed this was a travesty. The two rapes he had confessed to which had started it all and happened overseas were not the ones being tried in the UK court. Why had he made no mention of these other cases, rapes carried out in the UK where there was the jurisdiction to raise a criminal charge? Why had he only confessed to two other rapes where no victims had been identified, no witnesses coming forward? It had only been the media coverage that had given the twelve women who did come forward the confidence to speak up for the first time. It was the reason why the trial had even gone ahead, despite the man's confession of those other rapes.

"Have the jury reached a decision upon which you all agree?" the ageing Judge asked, a seasoned professional who had handled far more high-profile cases in his forty-year career, though not one this large for a while.

"We have," the spokesman said, the Judge turning towards Clifton next.

"And I understand you wish to make your own plea?" he asked, Clifton's lawyer having got word to him during the break. It was highly unusual to permit the defendant to change their plea, but given the nature of the case, the victims there in the courtroom, the Judge would permit it this time. Hearing the man confess to his guilt might go someway to helping these women move on.

"I do," Clifton said.

"And how do you plead to all these crimes we have presented you with?"

"I'm guilty," he said, little emotion showing on his face, the spokesman in the jury box a little lost for words, the moment taken from her, the result of the jury now not heard, not even considered, even if they had deemed him innocent.

"Very well," the Judge said, aware that this change in plea bore no difference to his sentencing. "You have confessed your own guilt to these twelve counts of rape and I have no other option than to sentence you to the maximum this court allows, regardless of your plea of guilty. I sentence you to life imprisonment, with a minimum term of nineteen years behind bars."

They led Clifton away a few minutes later, the jury already filing out, the Judge vacating his bench. Clifton glanced briefly at those sitting in the courtroom––four of the women he'd raped and who had come forward following the media coverage were still sitting, a few with tears in their eyes, having given evidence at the trial and been there every day since. They couldn't believe it was finally all over. Clifton didn't react as he met their eyes, didn't smile, acknowledged nothing. They had caught him, he'd confessed his crime. Inside he smiled, however. He would live to fight another day.

33

Russia-1 Television Studio, Moscow

Dmitry sat across from her, the camera initially on him, though the interview would focus on Svetlana. She'd sat in the same studio months before the assassination. It had been at that interview, with the same interviewer, when she had first suggested she had a taste for politics. His exclusive. The ratings had been one of the highest that year, and now she was back. Now she was the Acting President, on the verge of yet another election, one that, regardless of what opinion poll you looked at, she would win.

The red light on the main camera blinked into life, the crew giving the interviewer his final cue, the experienced Russian host kicking things off soon after.

"Tell me," he said, when the initial niceties were over and the interview was getting underway. This was why she was there, this was why she'd arranged a discussion like this. The arena was friendly, the interviewer respectful. She could get across what she needed to say, without it coming directly from an opponent. While she knew those debates would come––where rival candidates went head-to-head live on air––she needed to use this opportunity to rubbish certain stories.

"Many rumours were shared in the media in recent months. The main political party challengers are calling for your head, demanding you respond directly to them. You've failed to take them up on this offer, so far," he said, aware she would soon have a face off with them all in front of a local audience in that very studio. Right now it was just them, and the film crew working behind the scenes. "Surely you can't stay silent forever?"

She smiled, the questions shared with her before the interview.

"Let me be clear, Dmitry," she said, keeping with the informal approach she had started when he'd first interviewed her. "When any new challenger comes onto the scene, others will always try to stake their claim. The election will put everyone in their place," she said, clearly meaning: *They would vote her in as President.*

"But these allegations, these leaks, they will not go away," he prodded.

"No, Dmitry, they won't, but these are all linked to situations before I took office." She raised her hand, counting off on her fingers as if recalling a shopping list. "This money, for example. I learned that Filipov destroyed it only after he seized it."

"So that's nothing to do with you now?" he said. Dmitry thought, like most ordinary citizens in the country, that these wild allegations of countless resources had been ludicrously exaggerated. Her PR team had done a fantastic job getting that message across.

"Of course not," she smiled, charm switched on to maximum, a face of innocence flashed before the cameras. "I was as shocked as you all to hear about it, believe me."

"Second," she said, "the death of my husband. Filipov had not informed me of that matter, something you can imagine it was natural for him to keep from me."

"Why would that be?"

"Come on, Dmitry, we both know why that would be," was all she said, moving the conversation on before he could clarify what that might be exactly. "It hurt to find out in such a way, the story splashed across the papers, lies, even suggesting I knew something about it."

"And the link to your current head of security?"

"The oh-so-conclusive initials, you mean?" she elaborated, as if the whole idea Rad might have had anything to do with it was as fanciful as anything. "Once the allegation came out, naturally I looked into it all thoroughly. The man used by Filipov to kill my ex-husband died in battle six months later. A brave soldier, decorated too, but not the man who looks after my personal safety now, I can assure you," she said with a smile.

"And the reference to the Machine?"

"Yes, this mysterious entity. It's connected, if it existed, to the same situation I just covered. If it existed, it ended in that gunfight. I don't know if my husband was in any way involved. It was Filipov who carried it out, apparently Filipov who ended whatever threat they posed. I've found no files in my office suggesting there was any threat," she said, her beautiful smile covering a well told lie. She had plenty that Filipov had left behind on this group.

"So again, nothing to do with you?" he asked, for the sake of clarity.

"No, not at all," she confirmed.

"And what of these rumours about Putin's involvement in the crime? You were the one who first reported the killing to the press. You stepped in, recorded the facts, told us Putin had killed the President."

"And he had!" she stated.

"But these allegations…" he started.

"Nothing but hot air, I assure you. My legal team is already looking into a law suit against the newspapers who published these lies. Where is this man, this supposed source of all these insights? As I've shown you already, they relate to a time before I came to power, albeit a temporary power, something fresh elections will resolve. Believe me, there are many men in powerful corners of this nation who can't stand the thought of a female President."

"You think this is a smear campaign?"

"Of the highest order. Yes, I do," she stated, something that was news to him, though until that moment, to his knowledge anyway, she had not publicly addressed any of the rumours.

"To whose advantage?" he asked, the interviewer in him happy to move away from the scripted questions when the discussion went that way.

"Perhaps it's just the thought of me running the nation? You know my record, my stance on open government, a transparent Presidency. You all know my success in female focussed projects right across the nation these past three years. We're really making progress; I'm making progress. For some men, they don't like what I am doing. They will stop at nothing to discredit me."

"And your links to Yuri Lagounov?" That had been one of the more recent leaks, the man's crimes happening during her time in the Kremlin. This was not something that could be brushed off as Filipov's responsibilities.

"I agree these allegations are frightening, and if they are true, a worry for everyone in government, not just me. I've said for weeks now that my government will be tough on crime. I vow to clean up our cities, making the streets safer for everyone. I vow to clean up the way our nation does business. To bring in reforms that punish firms who bribe their way past legislation, making them accountable for their actions. I vow to take drugs off our streets too, by going after the people who control that market. And if there is any truth in the rumours about this man you've mentioned, then I will see that he faces justice along with everyone else breaking the law."

"Your office issued the arrest warrant for Lagounov," Dmitry pointed out, catching her in her words for the first time, "so you must at least admit a semblance of truth in this allegation?"

She smiled, regaining composure on the inside, her mind navigating herself out of the dead-end she'd reached unwittingly.

"I informed my office to follow procedure. When the allegation broke––and remember, much of what they leaked to the press I've now proved false, so there are no guarantees about this, either," she said, though in his mind she'd done nothing of the sort in their twenty-minute discussion. "But because it came out, I asked them to draw up the warrant. If people have died at the hands of this man, then we will bring him to justice. The same for every criminal out there."

She paused, a member of the crew showing Dmitry they had five minutes left, and needed to wrap things up. He moved the conversation onto safer ground, a line drawn under these allegations, it would seem. She answered him fully, talking about life in the Kremlin, travelling to meet world leaders, and her strong desire to do that from an elected position of power for at least the next six years. When pressed, she said she wanted to remain for a second term in office. She concluded with all that her government would achieve in such a timeframe, all the possibilities there would be for women to step forward, and men to continue to innovate, continue to play their part in the nation's future.

Ten minutes later the two of them were standing, the cameras off, the crew going about their task of packing everything away. Dmitry thanked her once again for the interview and she left the studio shortly after, Rad ever in tow, aware she'd lied to cover him yet again, this time in an interview that would air to the nation.

The Cage––Outskirts of Moscow
Eighteen Months After Filipov's Assassination

TWO HANDLERS STRUGGLED WITH CORDS, getting the tiger around the neck, pulling the animal away from the body, out of the cage.

The winning oligarch moved away from the building, heart racing, gut churning. Lagounov had surpassed himself this time.

The winning Contestant left the cage, not looking at the mangled body of his challenger. In the year and a half since Lagounov had hosted these events, they'd seen nothing like this. People had died in the cage before, that much was true. But not like this.

As if a fight to the death for millions of pounds wasn't enough of a thrill––and after the first half dozen times, for Lagounov it very much wasn't––he had taken on the advice to move things up a notch.

Today's fight had twenty-million on offer, non-negotiable this time. A straight fight, though not only against the other man; there was a tiger in the cage too. The first person to make it to the computer, the first one to confirm the transaction, would be the one to claim the prize.

Lagounov came to the cage, now that they had led the tiger back into the van. Only the bloodied corpse remained.

It had been electrifying.

He returned to the changing room, the room he emerged from alone each time. There was a window in the room, looking onto the cage, though only with one way glass. You couldn't see back into the room from the cage.

"You did well," a voice from the darkness said, the eternal presence at each of these events since they started. It had been her idea to bring in the tiger for this one.

"It's made a mess," Yuri said, glancing back through the window into the cage. The view from there during the fight must have been quite something.

"And it'll be the last time for you, I'm afraid."

"Why?" he asked, taking the document offered to him, reading through the warrant issued for his arrest.

"Someone knows."

"Who?"

"I don't know," she said, turning to face the window, the fallen contestant on the floor, his face looking her way, through eyes that looked like horror personified.

"You signed this?" he asked, taking in Svetlana's name on the arrest warrant.

"I had no choice," she said. "You have time to leave," she added. "Burn everything. Destroy this building. Get out of Moscow. It doesn't matter where you go. I'll file this next week."

"And the money?" She'd promised him a regular monthly salary if he pulled together these events and ran them for her.

"It'll still come to you as always," she confirmed, Lagounov rubbing his face, two days of stubble on his chin.

"And what about you?" He'd been around enough addicts in his time to recognise an uncontrollable desire when he saw one. Her drug was violence, fear, the contest. She thrived on putting people into situations that forced them to do the unthinkable, always for a prize beyond their dreams. Even he had feared she'd gone too far this time bringing in that tiger.

"I'm working on something new," she said, her thoughts on Clifton, her plans coming together nicely.

"You'd better get out of here," he confirmed. She was always the last to leave, sometimes hanging around for half an hour while the oligarchs cleared the scene. Today they'd both gone quickly. She'd laughed out loud at the look on both faces when the tiger pounced. They wouldn't forget that in a while.

"You'll be okay," she confirmed.

"I know," he said. "Thanks for informing me of the warrant. I won't say anything."

"I wouldn't have assumed anything different," Svetlana said, moving from the room now, her twentieth event there concluded, the curtain down on that arena. Alicante would be next, and she would front the show once more. She couldn't wait.

34

Moscow and Forest Dacha, Russia

The Acting President could move a little more freely around the capital now, one month on from the metro bombings which claimed the lives of fifty-four people and injured over three hundred. A few were still in hospital, their condition serious but not life threatening.

Pavel had come through for her, pulling the underworld on-side, a part of Russia few wanted anything to do with––a criminal element Svetlana stood in front of cameras right across the country saying she would eradicate. Yet, for the woman with more enemies now than ever, these groups and organisations offered her layers of protection, an ever increasing network of listening ears and ready informants.

If they watched her back, she promised them she would do the same.

The Yemeni terrorists had never attempted a third wave of attacks, their Dagestan contacts arrested en route to St Petersburg, the network within the Russian Federation silenced.

Three weeks after the bombing the terrorists had been neutralised by a special elite unit led by Rad. Now, a week later, Rad was reporting back in the Kremlin. Rad had finished debriefing Svetlana, who had also brought him up to speed with what Pavel had shared about the local threat.

"Go home," she urged him, finally. He'd been on duty for a month, not seen Nastya at all in that time, the bombings cutting his holiday short, all hell threatening to break out in the days that followed.

"Are you sure?"

"Things are different now," she encouraged him. "You'll see." The election was less than five months away. No independent candidate had put their name forward yet, and they expected it to stay that way. The few names that were mentioned––with their degree of support, their background, wealth, experience or all three making them initially seem a real threat––were nearly all forgotten the next day. Something would break, a scandal taking that one out, an affair taking another. Then it would be an oligarch, always a different one each time––Roman Ivanov had them well drilled by now. The oligarch would restate their backing for Svetlana Volkov. Their reputation and status meant that people listened and the would-be challenger was scared off. There was only a month for any other independents––apart from the political parties who had to submit candidates––to put their name into the hat. Only four weeks were left for any genuine threat to emerge.

"Take a month, finish your house building project," she added. She was well aware of why Rad had taken the previous week off and that she had cut his holiday short. Things would get busier the closer they got to the election. She would spend the next month in Moscow, not leaving the Kremlin much. After that, she would travel, do the rounds. For now, there was little Rad needed to do.

Rad didn't know what to say. "You call me if you need me," he said, finally.

"You know I will," she smiled, before adding, "but I won't call you all month. I promise."

Rad bowed, backing out of the room, closing the door behind him. He spent the next ten minutes making sure his unit understood the situation, knew their place, knew the procedure. Having Svetlana in the Kremlin was easily the most secure way of protecting her. He was confident they could manage without him.

He walked to his car. Since joining the army at eighteen as a blue-eyed recruit, he'd never had a month's rest. He hardly knew what to make of it. He thought about calling Nastya, telling her the news, telling her he was on his way, but left his phone in his pocket. He would be there in three hours. He didn't want to ruin the surprise.

THE SOUND of a vehicle driving over the loose stones of the forest track was enough to bring Nastya out from the dacha. Olya joined her as they saw a cloud of dust rising, heard a vehicle, but because of the dry summer they were having, couldn't yet see who it was. The track led only to their two dachas, as far as they knew. Strangers were not welcome around these parts, visitors not expected.

Nastya gave out a shout of joy as Rad's car emerged around the final bend, her husband beaming at her from behind the wheel, as he pulled into their plot, braking hard. Nastya already had the door open, Rad struggling to get his seat belt off.

"You didn't tell me!" she squealed in delight.

"I wanted to surprise you," he said, now free. He lifted a bunch of flowers off the passenger seat and handed them to her, as she threw herself at him. The flowers dropped to one side, the couple kissing for a long while. Finally they broke away, Olya coming forward at that moment, embracing him as Nastya took the flowers and pulled them to her nose, the scent overwhelmingly beautiful. Kostya's head appeared over the top of the roof, hammer in hand, sweat dripping from his forehead. He called down his greeting to Rad.

"My goodness!" Rad exclaimed, looking up towards Kostya, the roof all but complete, the interior showing painted walls on at least three rooms. Paint covered Nastya in blue and white spots all over. She'd never looked more beautiful to him. "How have you got so far?" he said, astonished at the transformation.

"You didn't think we would just sit around waiting for you to return, did you?" Kostya joked from above, his head not in view anymore, a few blows of the hammer confirming he was finishing whatever he had just been working on.

"And you," he said, turning to his wife. "It looks like you've been busy too!" He pulled her into a tight embrace, the smile on her face as if going from ear to ear.

"Want to see?" she teased, leading him towards the dacha. There were lots of things he wanted to see right now. The progress in the dacha would have to do for the time being.

"Wow!" he said, the place unrecognisable from the shell he'd left in a hurry one month before. They had not even completed the roof then, Rad fearful that his absence would mean things just sat there, the internal wooden walls exposed to the elements.

"Close your eyes," Nastya said, leading him to a door that stood closed. The fact any of the internal doors were on seemed unbelievable right then. She stopped after a few paces, Rad hearing the wooden door swinging open, a change of light through his still-closed eyes, and she led him in three further paces. "Open your eyes," she said, as excited as a little Russian girl on New Year's Eve awaiting all her presents.

What Rad saw nearly took his breath away.

"It's our bedroom," she said, though he'd known that much from the outside of the door.

They had painted the walls, the colour two-tone. There was a large window in the middle of the main wall, looking back to the car outside, the old dacha beyond. There was a bookcase there too though still empty, the floor as yet unfinished. But aside from the minimal furniture and the beautifully painted walls and ceiling, and the double-glazed window, the thing that took his breath away most was the lavish decadence of the bed in front of him. Covered in a dark blue duvet, packed with more pillows than he could ever imagine, there stood an elegant wooden bed with a thick mattress. It looked showroom quality, hotel standard, and only the like found in the top hotels at that. It looked wholly out of place, otherworldly, given the still-paint-splashed floor, given even the absence of a proper front door.

"Where did you get this?" he asked, touching the frame of the bed. He didn't dare touch the sheets; he didn't feel clean enough.

"We bought it," she beamed. The bed had only arrived three days before, the accessaries, a little over-the-top even by her standards, picked up in IKEA. She wanted one room ready for his return, and though the floor was not done, she didn't regret for one moment his sudden appearance. "You earn a lot now," she added, as if the thought of spending money on a bed was something beyond their reach. "I've not slept in it. It's waiting for you," she said, a twinkle in her eye. He knew that look. Through the window outside he could see Olya. There were no curtains up yet, not sure if they needed them. Didn't need them for privacy, but mostly to keep out the light.

"We'll christen the bed tonight," he confirmed.

"Too right we will!" she added, kissing him forcefully on the lips. They'd never owned a proper bed, not since the wedding. The shed they lived in wasn't big enough. They'd been on a mattress on the floor together. Happy, but simple.

They prepared food earlier than usual that evening, Kostya done with the roof within half an hour of Rad's arrival, Olya already cutting vegetables before five. The older couple looked knowingly at each other over the course of the next hour, Kostya stating he'd finished for the day when Rad asked how he could help. A meaningful glance from the older man to Rad suggested Kostya knew very well that Rad and Nastya needed an early night.

"We'll head back now," Olya said, the time barely half-six that evening, the sun yet to set for at least another three hours. They hurried away soon after, Rad clearing away the meal, Nastya washing the plates before leaving them to dry. The sound of the quad bike leaving had not even died away fully before the couple were embracing, a passion inside forcing contact. They moved inside, still kissing, still embracing. Rad laughed as he pulled the odd patch of dried paint from Nastya's hair, and they dropped back onto the bed, soaking in it, enveloped by it, drinking in love and passion and connection as if their very existence depended on it.

RAD PASSED Kostya the final plank, something measured and now cut, the older man hammering it into place. Rad called Nastya moments later, his wife emerging from the back door, paintbrush in hand, smile on her face.

"We have a deck!" she exclaimed, joining the two men as they admired a job well done. The deck covered the back of the property mostly, but also wrapped around one side. It looked out towards the stream that ran near the dacha, though they could only hear a slow trickle from where they were. Steps led down to ground level, the forest and wilderness beyond. It'd been the last main job to finish outside, the inside coming on hugely over the last three weeks. They planned to have it finished by the end of summer.

The flooring would be the final thing they put down, the decisions about this not yet fully made. They painted three of the rooms, doors on, furniture awaiting construction. The dining room was close to completion too, a large table in the middle, something Kostya had built for them. It would suffice for the time being, especially if covered. Rad had promised one day to pick out something extra special. She'd done that for him with their bed, by far their most enjoyed item of furniture that month. The kitchen was coming on, a little tiling remaining and sockets that needed finishing.

"Now that we've moved in," Rad said, the home suitable to stay in the whole year in fact, not just the warmer summer months, "I want to let you know what we'll do with my old place." The shed had been Rad's lockup and summer hangout for years, perfect for what he needed it for, but not a home. "It'll become your workshop," he said.

"My workshop?"

"You are an incredible designer," he said, not for the first time, Nastya blushing, brushing the comment away. "I'm serious. I've always known it. Look at this place," he said, the interior her design, the colouring her inspiration. "You have a gift. And now that we're in this place, it's time you had a space to grow your gift."

"I can't," she said, though Rad put his finger to her lips.

"Don't speak such nonsense," he said. "I won't allow it. You can buy anything you need. Sewing machines, looms, you name it, we'll get it," he said. The space wasn't huge, which limited getting everything, but it was enough.

"We'll gut the place first, get the heating working properly. It'll be a great place to spend your energies when I'm not here," he said, aware she needed a passion. Her effort on the dacha had shown him that. She couldn't pine when he was away like a pet dog, moping around, waiting for his return. She needed to focus her mind on something else, something creative. He'd often heard her singing to herself those last three weeks as she painted, lost in the moment, lost in the colour. He liked the singing side very much.

"Okay," she said, the dreamer in her allowing the thought to take hold. With an actual studio, an actual space coupled with the permission to create, she could go wild. She could do all she had ever dreamed of doing yet never dared to expect she could.

As the final week came about—Rad hadn't specifically said it was the final week, he'd not given an end date at all, in fact—he seemed to check his phone more frequently, taking in the news more closely. There were four months to the election, when Nastya watched TV there was news of each candidate's marathon tour of the country, visiting all the cities before election day. She knew this would take Rad away from her soon, knew it with no need to be told.

As the last night came around—he'd told her the previous day he needed to head back to work, hadn't said for how long—they were alone in the lounge, sitting in silence, the sunset visible through the window.

"It could be awhile, couldn't it?" she asked.

"I'll get home every chance I can," he confirmed, not able to be any clearer than that. He didn't know himself.

"It's safe what you do, isn't it?" His mind raced to Yemen, another life ago but barely over a month in fact.

He'd not shared with Nastya half the things he'd done around Moscow that last month, knowing she couldn't handle the worry. He would not mention Yemen, his days of active service in conflict zones supposed to be behind him because of the new job. Besides those calls, which often involved many tears from his wife, Rad had not seen Nastya since leaving the forest.

"Yes," he said, his eyes not able to meet hers. She knew there was danger. He wouldn't have that job if there was never a threat.

"You'll be careful?"

"Always," he said. "You need not worry."

She went silent for a while.

"I can't help but worry," she said, turning to him, her eyes wide, on the brink of tears already. "Every time you go, I tell myself you're coming back, I make myself say it. But there is never an absolute guarantee Rad, is there?" He didn't know what he could say to that. Life had no guarantees, besides death, the same fate awaiting everyone, eventually.

"No," he settled upon. "And worrying about it will help no-one." He pulled her head into his shoulder, stroking her hair for a while.

"I want us to try for a baby," she said, out of the blue after two minutes.

"What?" It had not even been two years since the wedding, she was still very young.

"I'm serious," she said. The home was now finished, save for some internal cosmetics. They had the space, had the income.

"You're not even twenty-three," he said, Rad over a decade older than her, but even for him, the age issue and starting a family hadn't felt pressing.

"I love you," she said.

"And I love you too," he replied, not sure how this had anything to do with the timing of children.

She started to cry, Rad initially taken aback by the emotional change, holding her close for a time, the sun now setting, no words needed for several minutes. She gave one final sob, the emotion spent, then sat up.

"I'm scared of something happening to you and being left alone," she said, her eyes dry now, though passion and raw emotion filled her gaze.

"Nothing will happen to me," he said, both knowing he could not make any such prediction.

"I'm ready," she said. "I'm ready to raise children with you."

He studied her for a moment. He'd always wanted children, never assumed he would have a wife, let alone a son to teach to hunt, a daughter to take to a sports game. A family to enjoy fireworks with on New Year. He thought it might be years before she was ready, and he was happy for that. They were still newlyweds, she not long into adult life. But not having to be an older dad sounded good, he knew that now.

He kissed her on the lips. "Then let's do it," he said. The smile enveloping her face now seemed to take all the pain, all the emotion that had sat heavy mere minutes ago. He stood, leading her to the bedroom.

35

Guadalajara, Mexico
Present Day

Charlie studied the information in his hand, checking off the address with the street in which he was standing. The British MI6 agent had no Spanish, and for a man who'd mastered Russian, he kicked himself for not having at least attempted to pick up some words before the trip.

Three days before, in the capital, he had been finally given the name––Arkady Petrov, location Guadalajara. Charlie had travelled there immediately.

He'd been in touch with Vauxhall House all week. Zoe remained in New York, the CIA watching her closely. The technical team at MI6 ran the name against their database. Sasha looked into whatever he could find, but all his previous sources were no longer open to him. He felt in the cold regarding anything Russian for the first time since defecting.

Nothing appeared to come up on Arkady Petrov, and for a man who was supposed to be supplying firsthand information, that raised an issue. Either it was all made up, or the guy was so senior, so secret, that nobody outside of Russia knew anything about him.

Sasha finally spotted something, a newspaper report from a year ago. An explosion on a military truck––the obvious work of terrorists, though there had been no arrests for it––had killed all eleven men of the same unit. A *Colonel A. Petrov* was listed within the group.

The timing of the attack worked with what they knew––if this was the same man, alive and not dead as previously assumed, then he would have been around everything about which he claimed to know. Charlie felt confident it was the same man. He stood on the street, once glimpsing the male occupant leave the building he was watching, the man not local himself. Charlie prided himself on recognising a Russian when he saw one.

The agent had been standing in the same spot all day, among bushes, a clear view across to the target address, though the target was not visible, when a rustle and the unmistakable feel of a weapon pressed into the back of his head told him too late that someone had crept up on him.

"Who are you?" the accented voice said, in English, the man distinctly Russian.

"I'm friendly," Charlie said, hands raised outwards, palms open, as he turned slowly, looking into the face of Arkady himself, standing less than two feet in front of him, weapon raised to his forehead. "I'm British Security Service," Charlie continued, "here to protect you, nothing more."

Arkady considered that for a moment. Finding out Charlie was not FSB was a huge relief. He'd picked up the tail the day before, seen the same man watching his home later, and had crept out through an attic window to do what he'd just done. He lowered the weapon.

"Who told you I was here?" Arkady asked.

"Nobody," Charlie said, meaning it wasn't the Americans or, heaven forbid, the Russians. "We worked it out ourselves."

"How?"

"It doesn't matter. I'm here to protect you, that's all."

"You think I need protection?" the soldier asked, putting his weapon away at that moment. Charlie saw his point.

"If I found you, there's no saying your side won't also work it out, eventually."

"I'll be out of here long before they ever make it this far," he said, hinting that he had an advanced way of finding out if they were coming. Given Charlie's proximity at that moment, perhaps his confidence was misguided.

"We share the same goal," Charlie said.

"Which is?"

"Exposing Svetlana Volkov for who she really is."

Arkady considered that for a moment. How the British might have known that was news to him, though it offered him an unlikely ally at that moment, something he hadn't had till then.

"The British government know who she really is?"

"No," Charlie conceded, "but they will do, if we work together."

"I've shared all I know," Arkady conceded. "I'm out of the loop now."

"You were a Colonel in the army, correct?" Charlie asked, Arkady nodding, his head hanging in shame. According to Sasha's reports, the terrorist incident with the Colonel's truck had happened days after the Filipov assassination. Several newspapers had covered that story, the death of eleven soldiers filling pages. Yet Arkady had survived.

"How did you get out?" Charlie asked.

"Not here," the man replied, shaking his head, looking around him. He didn't move from the spot, Charlie not sure what any of it meant.

"Do you want to talk somewhere else?" the British officer quizzed.

"No, I've said all I have to say. The journalist in New York has everything."

"We've met with Jeff," Charlie confirmed, closing the circle a little more, showing they were on his side, proving they knew what they were doing.

"It appears none of it makes any difference," Arkady added, his tone defeated.

"Sorry?"

"Everything I shared. From all I read online, she's pressing forward with an election, will get the vote with ease if the polls are to be believed."

"That's why I'm here," Charlie said, not purely his mandate, as after locating the Russian whistleblower, he hadn't yet worked through what they would do with that information. "If you go public, become the face behind the rumours, everyone will take it all seriously."

"No!" he said, shaking his head, stepping back. "I'm not revealing my identity."

"Why?" Charlie said, aware of the danger, though they could protect him. Perhaps not in Mexico. He could try the US, or come back to the UK where MI5 would station agents to keep him safe.

"You don't understand," Arkady said, getting more agitated now. "I had to do something. After everything I learned, after all I saw. It was those last six months when I got suspicious. Filipov was running roughshod over anything and anyone who got in his way. He executed twenty Russian guards just because they helped Putin flee the country. I thought Volkov might be different, thought she might bring balance.

"She killed Filipov in his own office. Putin hadn't left the base. I suspect it was Volkov herself who laid the trap.

"I knew then that it was all a plant, suspected immediately she'd staged her own coup, done so subtly, so cleverly on many levels, that nobody suspected a thing. Yet I had the evidence. I'd been making copies, except I couldn't get out. I had no choice."

The man's eyes sank to the ground.

"You firebombed the truck?" Charlie exclaimed, the only logical explanation now. Arkady remained silent, not giving any confirmation, though a slight nod of the head, just a fraction, after thirty seconds confirmed what Charlie had realised.

"They were good men," Arkady said. "A fine unit. I slipped out the country that night, documents in my luggage, arm badly burnt from the fire."

Charlie took a step back, knowing this changed a lot, though not the facts of the information he had shared.

"I had no choice!" the Russian said, seeing the look on the face before him, the disgust, the disbelief.

"It's not my place to pass judgement," Charlie said. That might come later, but it wasn't why he was there. Wasn't for MI6 to get involved in, either.

That comment seemed to settle the Russian for a while, a silence falling between them, two men standing amongst bushes, the sun still warm despite the late hour of the day.

"Will you report what I've told you?"

"No," Charlie said automatically. He didn't want Arkady fleeing, not before they'd come up with a plan, a strategy for what to do next.

"Thank you," the Russian said.

"Only me and my immediate team know your location. You are safe here. If that changes, I will let you know."

Arkady nodded, moving back out of the bushes, crossing the road moments later. He glanced across towards Charlie as he got to his front door, but the British agent had already left the spot. There was no need to hide there anymore. He had a call to make.

Black Dolphin Prison, Orenburg Oblast, Russia
Present Day

A BITTER WIND blew from the north, bringing much colder air that cut to the core. Alex sat huddled in the corner of his cell, unwilling to move from his position, having lost all track of time, all hope of release.

The guard called as usual, the watch on each prisoner almost constant.

"Up!" he barked, prisoners required to remain on their feet the entire day, and allowed ninety minutes in the open air for exercise. Alex didn't move but by the time the various doors had been opened, he was on his feet. He didn't want to take the beating that would come if he didn't comply.

"Out!" the guard demanded. They would search the cell, as always, to make sure the prisoner had nothing with him that shouldn't be there. He'd had no visitors, they had kept him from seeing the other inmates. Besides Putin, who occupied the next door cell, the walls concrete, the interaction kept to a minimum, it seemed like all had forgotten this prisoner.

Alex stood on the edge of the exercise cage, his usual walk of humiliation allowing him no real sense of his surroundings, his back bent, head lowered, hands cuffed behind his back and raised high above his hips. His observational skills had shown him more than most, and that didn't comfort him. There was no way out, no opening he could see. Death would be the final escape, Alex knew that much already, the three years eight months he had spent there might as well have been ten.

A few months ago, the exercise yard gave him a delightful change from his cell. Sunshine on his face, a different angle of being watched by the guards––from above instead of from in front of his cell––and a breath of fresh air.

Today, however, snow lay on the ground, the sky promising much more, the cold penetrating even his thick prison-issue Russian jacket. There were noticeably fewer guards around when the weather turned this cold.

"Move!" the guard shouted behind Alex's back, the man's use of English accommodating Alex's lack of Russian, but limited to one word commands, it seemed. Alex would have traded the next ninety minutes that day for the entire day in the cell, but policy dictated each prisoner had to exercise. If Russian institutions loved anything, it was bureaucratic rules.

The guard released his arms and Alex steeled himself to go outside. The door was locked behind him while a guard watching from above sneered. Even he looked cold, looked like he wished to be anywhere else than there right now.

The icy chill at least did something. So numbing was it after an hour, it forced movement, forced him fully awake. The clouds of darkness and depression which hung over Alex lifted, albeit temporarily--there was no changing his predicament, he knew that much--but it allowed him to think sanely again, if only for a time. He made himself move, his muscles needing activity, his mind needing escape. He punched the air, nimble footwork suggesting he was some boxing champion. Where the snow hadn't covered one corner--the freezing cold concrete little relief--he went to work on his ground routine. Planks, squats, sit-ups and then burpees.

By the end of his allotted time, sweat ran from his forehead, though that started freezing around his cheeks and in his beard. They did not allow razors in the cells. Alex had become accustomed to growing out his beard, particularly during winter months. He would take any extra warmth he could get.

The cage door opened, the signal that time was up. The same guard appeared who had brought him there earlier. Alex turned around, allowing the guard to cuff his wrists once more, his arms soon forced above the hips, his back bent, as they led him back along silent corridors towards his cell.

Standing outside his door--the charge written on the door stating *izmena*, treason--he saw Putin through the open bars of the adjoining cell. The former president sat on the edge of his bed, a copy of the newspaper in his hands, books scattered across his bed. He looked up at Alex, the two aware of each other but nothing much more than that, and he smiled at the British agent. Raised the paper and smiled.

The guard ushered Alex back in through the door to his cell moments after that. The guard showed no sign he'd seen Putin sitting, seen him smiling towards them.

"Stand!" the guard reminded Alex, who was standing in the corner flexing his fingers, the cold in his bones yet to leave. The doors slammed noisily shut once again behind him, one after the other.

Alex paced around the ten metre square cell. Food would come later, sleep allowed in five hours. He pressed his head against the wall, the cold of the bricks and solidness of the stone reminding him once again there was nothing he could do, no hope beyond these walls, just cold, snow and endless wilderness.

36

Eighth Presidential Election In Russia

Svetlana had joined the campaign trail late four years previously, flown in at the last minute to endorse Filipov. Now it was her turn, the schedule less hectic, the vote far less in the balance. She had the numbers, her team knew she had the numbers, the polls continually suggested she had the numbers.

Yet until they counted the results, she would take nothing for granted.

Significantly, no credible threat had emerged to stand and challenge her. In a combination of oligarch interference and gangster intervention, the date came and passed without another name being added to the ballot. The main political parties would put forward their candidates, naturally. She knew who these would be; they were the same also-rans who had appeared in nearly every election modern Russia had held since its first in 1991. In the previous election, Filipov's emergence had taken Putin to a second round but no-one with any knowledge of the subject predicted a second round this time.

Where Svetlana had a huge advantage was during the debates.

She was a natural in front of the camera, a master of the political speech by now––a well-written speech was no different to reciting a well-written screenplay––and she looked her stunning best each time too. The men seemed less aggressive with her than they might have been, even the communists didn't know how to rattle her. Opinion polls showed spikes in support the day after each of her live debates aired.

What stood out a mile in the poll demographics was when they took gender into account––among females who answered the pollsters, Svetlana ran at ninety percent support. No pre-election poll had ever before had one candidate that dominant, something her team reminded her of constantly. Three years of hard work into that very target group was now paying dividends.

The more she fronted debates, the more her pictures were splashed around the newspapers, the more the male vote shifted her way, though it still hovered on or just under fifty percent, remarkably low considering there was no other significant contender. It seemed a female President might still be too much of a stretch for some Russian men. However, they made up not even forty percent of the likely voter turnout. She knew their support didn't ultimately matter.

Rad travelled with Svetlana constantly for three months, able to stop off home overnight and see Nastya when the Acting President covered the cities in and around Moscow. Nastya confirmed she would vote for Svetlana; Olya and Kostya did too.

On the night of the election––voting underway for hours, the count already happening in far-Eastern cities––Svetlana Volkov sat alone in her Moscow residence, her security detail outside, the place under watch, but the woman herself unbothered. She nursed a vodka, the television on in the background.

Four years ago Filipov had been around his team, Svetlana included by that point. Results were either cheered or booed as appropriate; there was a collective spirit. They were all in it together. Yet Filipov had always been his own voice, his own strength. She'd seen that, she'd known it herself for so long.

A wad of papers lay on the table in front of her, something Pavel had passed her the last time they had met. He'd found the people she had listed, their photos included on each sheet, though two of the men she'd asked him to track down were already dead. She had looked through each photo, the faces aged, the hair receding, but there was no doubting it. It was them. All except one of the remaining seven survivors still lived in Moscow. The other lived in Germany.

Pavel told her he had found nothing criminal on any of the men, which surprised her a little––she assumed once crooked, always crooked––but she wasn't after them for what they might have done to others. This was far more personal.

"We have the first results coming through," the presenter on the television said at that moment, Svetlana holding her glass to the screen as a resounding victory came in for her, the Vladivostok vote going her way with sixty-five percent of the count. She knew the closer they got to Moscow, the higher her winning margin was likely to be.

At three in the morning they called the result, Svetlana standing with her team––she'd joined them for the final half hour, somewhat drunk, though there were no cameras. Nobody would begrudge her at that moment.

"The country has decided, and it is my huge honour to announce officially that the fifth individual to hold the office of President of the Russian Federation is also the first woman to do so––President Svetlana Volkov!" Her name and image now flashed across the screen, the result no shock, but officially crossing the line was definite cause for further celebration. Her team gathered around her, handshakes given––she was not a hugger, never had been; and now she was President. That set her apart from the other more than ever.

Rad stood in the doorway, Svetlana walking over to him.

"Congratulations, Madam President," he said, Svetlana smiling at him. He'd taken a call earlier that day, the news yet to sink in, no chance yet to share his own moment given the bigger story. Now they had confirmed the result, now that the night could draw in, he felt he could share.

"I will be a father," he beamed, Svetlana embracing him, the first time she'd ever done that.

"Congratulations are then in order for you too," she spoke into his ear before pulling away and standing in front of him. "It's a double celebration, it would seem."

By four in the morning, they were all leaving for home. Svetlana Volkov would remain in her residence. She'd moved out of the Kremlin, as was tradition, before the vote. She would face the cameras officially tomorrow as she moved back in, now with her mandate to lead, now with the freedom that came with such a resounding victory.

Nobody could touch her, she knew that. Foreign governments would have to listen now, relationships would need fixing. Those who had come for her would pay dearly, those who had published the lies, the leaks, those secrets in countless papers across countless nations—not only her own—now they would have to answer for it. Now she had the mandate, had the authority, had the backing and the resources.

And she would start with her list of seven names, men who had been let off for long enough. Old men long retired, but they'd been younger men once, as only she knew. Svetlana the even younger fish, caught in the pool of sharks. Now she'd grown her own teeth. Now she had the command of all, the fear of all and a threat even greater than a Great White. Now she would bite back.

EPILOGUE

Santa Barbara Castle, Alicante & Wandsworth Prison, London

Roman Ivanov stood in the historic fortress overlooking the city for the second time in a year. He was fond of the region, even considering buying something in the area, though he wasn't there to house hunt this time.

Following the week-long event Svetlana Volkov had run, he'd been back once to discuss with Don Zabala a proposition with the man. The Don had agreed to the offer and Roman's man had gone to London to put the proposal to Clifton. When Clifton accepted, the mafia had backed off and Zabala's men had been on the flight home the following morning. The oligarch was now back at the castle to make good on his promise.

Jose Zabala walked in, the cane he lent on nearly as iconic as the reputation he had in the region in certain circles. Roman liked him, the Don a hard man, but honest. His word was his bond, he wasn't a man to double cross anyone with whom he did business.

"Thank you for meeting me," Roman said, by far the wealthier of the pair––crime paid, but not as handsomely as the breakup of the

Soviet Union had––the Russian offering a chair to the ageing Spaniard.

"I take it you have good news for me," the Don said, Roman reaching for the portfolio he had prepared for their meeting.

"Everything you need to know is in there, delivered as promised."

"You have the name of an insider for me?"

"Three, actually. You get to take your pick," Roman smiled. "It's all there."

"I hear congratulations are in order," the Don said, his eyes hard to read at the best of times, impossible in the darkness inside those rooms of the castle. "You have a new President," he concluded, the result announced that morning, the timing of the meeting in his mind no doubt deliberate.

Roman smiled at the Don. "I didn't vote," he said.

"You didn't need to," Jose smiled. "You'd already done enough for her." He'd seen Roman's speeches, not understanding a word, but aware the oligarch had gone on record more than once to back the former actress.

"This was her doing, wasn't it?" he asked, waving the papers a little, his arm taking in the castle.

"I don't follow," Roman said, unusually lost for a man of his intuition.

"Everything that happened here that week, the week my son died. It was her, wasn't it?" He didn't seem to question it; he knew.

"Clifton Niles murdered your son, Don Zabala, nobody else."

The older man smiled at that. "He pulled the trigger, for sure," the man said, "but someone put him up to it."

There was silence for an awkward moment, the two men assessing the other in a new light for a while, looking for any threat.

"She did not target your son, Jose, I give you my word on that," Roman said, his eyes focused.

"Very well," the Don nodded. "I'll take you at your word, the word of a gentleman," he added the last part after a short pause. "I'll keep my eye on her, anyway," he confirmed.

"And Clifton?"

"You said you didn't want to know," the Don said. Roman didn't move.

"I shall be acting on this information," the Don said, indicating the portfolio he had been given then headed for the door. Roman watched him slowly cross the courtyard outside, getting back into his car, his driver taking him from the area.

The oligarch stood there pondering it all for a moment, not sure if there remained a risk or not, unaware how much Don Zabala knew, certain he knew much more than he had thought, probably more than Svetlana realised. Roman moved away from the window, now heading to his own car. The beach beckoned, one last soak of sunshine before the real work started once again in Russia. His country had a new President, and he now had an inside track.

CLIFTON SHUFFLED down the corridor behind the other inmates, his blue prison garb a huge comedown for a man who had power-dressed for the last two decades.

He'd been inside for a month, the trial a distant memory, the routine of prison life starting to settle down. He'd read in the prison library the various financial papers they had, his company in free fall, his clients jumping ship, his name and reputation in tatters. It had all finished him; he knew that. Beaten, downtrodden, never to recover. He might never leave that building.

As breakfast finished, Clifton rose with the other group at his table. He'd not mixed with them, didn't know any names; left to himself. That much he was grateful for.

A few of the men played a game of pool, some watched television. He headed to his cell; the doors were open during the day, allowing inmates to come and go as they pleased. He had not long reached his cell when a voice came from behind, Clifton turning to see the inmate now standing a pace inside the doorway.

"Are you Clifton Niles?" he repeated.

"Yes," Clifton said, the man stepping forward, face calm, but eyes wary.

"I've got a message for you," he began, a blade flashing from his pocket now, the man stepping in at speed, hand to the mouth of Clifton so he couldn't scream. As he said, "Don Zabala sends his regards," he drove the blade into Clifton's chest, twisting it then pulling it out, the wind going from Clifton. The attacker plunged the weapon into his stomach next, hand still to Clifton's mouth. His body fell backwards, the inmate lowering Clifton onto his bed, pulling the blankets over him.

Two prison guards would find Clifton Niles thirty minutes later and after raising the alarm, they pronounced him dead at the scene when the doctor arrived.

INTERNATIONAL BESTSELLING AUTHOR

TIM HEATH

THE BLACK DOLPHIN

THE HUNT / BOOK EIGHT

AUTHOR NOTES AND ACKNOWLEDGMENTS

When I planned *The Meltdown* (book six) I had wondered if that was the last book in the series, but by the time I finished writing it, I knew there were a few storylines that readers desperately wanted to know about. One of these was what happens to Alex––you'll be delighted to know that this gets covered in the next book in the series, *The Black Dolphin*.

However, I knew I had to write this book first.

The series will end with book nine, already written and coming out before the end of the year. The title for the ultimate book is *The Last Tsar*.

A question someone asked me during the editorial phase of this book was whether the prison was real. While I'll only put this information at the end of the next book (which is the more natural fit), I can confirm that the Black Dolphin prison is a real place, and all the practices and facts I've used in this book are real. I made nothing up! I will share with you at the back of the next book the various videos and links I researched that give a fascinating insight into the prison there in Russia!

During the first month of lockdown here in Estonia (March 2020), having completed this series in first draft form, I ventured to write by first stand-alone title since **The Song Birds,** which itself was a bit of an exception with nine titles written in this Hunt series. **The 26th Protocol** will be my 19th novel released when it finally comes out, which I don't expect to happen until 2021.

If you follow me anywhere you will hear about these in due course. My mailing list is also an excellent way of staying in touch.

As for this book, I once more have to thank my dedicated team who have taken the time to read it pre-publication and helped me to shape the book as much as possible. All mistakes that remain are entirely mine–– email me with anything you spot and I will correct it for future readers.

My faithful editor Elizabeth Knight has once again entertained me with her comments plus corrected my many mistakes. Every book she sees that I do a certain thing repeatedly that needs changing (always something different, I will add) and I didn't disappoint her this time either. Thank you, Elizabeth!

This is the first book for which I've taken complete creative control for the covers and I'm thrilled with that decision now. If you've not seen, all my covers have now been updated, some changed entirely.

I would like to thank my team of ART and BETA readers (a small but eagle-eyed bunch) for your help as always. I would like to thank especially Deborah Le Bihan for your quote and for emailing me during the process to say how much you loved this book and that it is your favourite in the series so far! That is always good to hear.

Finally, Rachel, my dear wife. Thank you for allowing me the space to do this. Thank you for your input at every stage and your support and belief in me. It means everything.

CHARACTER GLOSSARY

WHO'S WHO IN THE HUNT SERIES—AS OF THE START OF THIS BOOK

MI6 - Alex Tolbert, Anissa Edison, Sasha Barkov, Charlie Boon, Zoe Elliot, Gordon Peacock (head technician)

Svetlana Volkov––Acting President and former actress and founder of the Games

Radomir Pajari––elite Russian sniper and head of security for the Acting President

Nastya Pajari––wife of Rad
 - **Kostya & Olya**––Uncle & Aunt of Nastya

Anastasia Kaminski––The Belarusian former wife to Dmitry Kaminski. Had an affair with Alex Tolbert

Roman Ivanov––wealthy oligarch and long-time Host in the Games alongside **Timur Budny, Arseni Markovic, Vladimir Popov** and **Motya Utkin**

MAILING LIST

BECOME A SUPER-FAN!

Loved this book and want to hear when my newest ones are out? Like the idea of getting your hands on free novels of mine when I do a special promotion, or hearing about progress on the books I'm writing in your favourite series? Then become a Super-Fan!

My monthly emails are always fun, full of information and take-aways specifically related to my life as an author, and I only write when I have something to say (or to give-away).

VIP Readers' Group
    http://www.timheathbooks.com/books/super-fans

THE NOVELS BY TIM HEATH

Novels:

Cherry Picking

The Last Prophet

The Tablet

The Shadow Man

The Prey (The Hunt #1)

The Pride (The Hunt #2)

The Poison (The Hunt #3)

The Machine (The Hunt #4)

The Menace (The Hunt #5)

The Meltdown (The Hunt #6)

The Song Birds

The Acting President (The Hunt #7)

The Black Dolphin (The Hunt #8)

The Lost Tsar (The Hunt #9)

The 26th Protocol (Due out in 2021)

Short Story Collection:

Those Geese, They Lied; He's Dead

THE BOXSETS—TIM HEATH

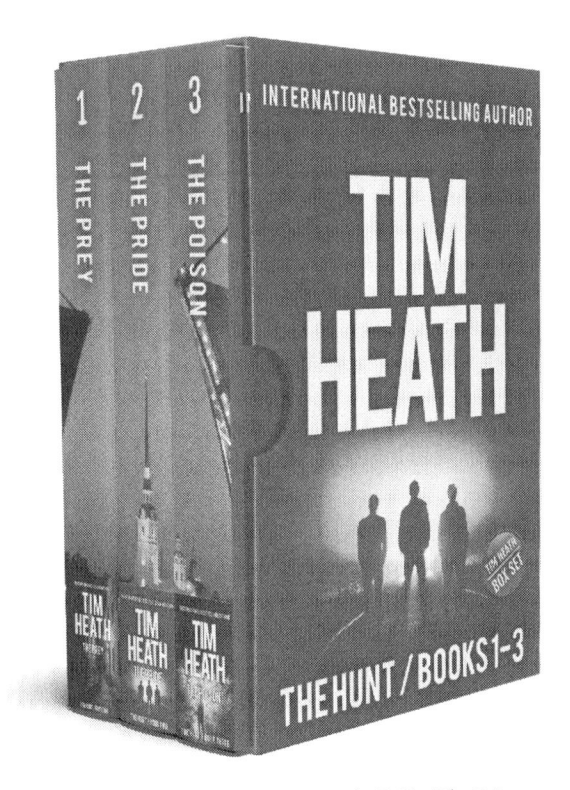

The Hunt Series (Books 1-3) - The Prey, The Pride, The Poison

The Hunt Series (Books 4-6) - The Machine, The Menace, The Meltdown

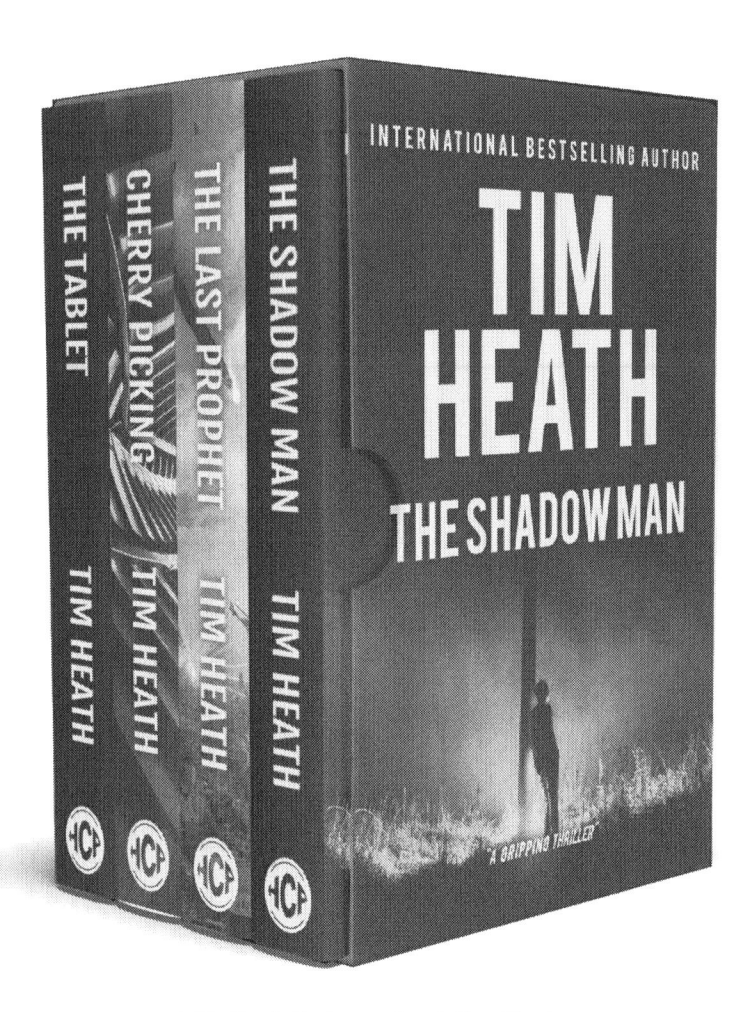

Tim Heath Thriller Collection—4 Stand-Alone Novels - Cherry Picking, The Last Prophet, The Tablet, The Shadow Man

THE BOXSETS—T H PAUL

PEN-NAME SERIES OF TIM HEATH

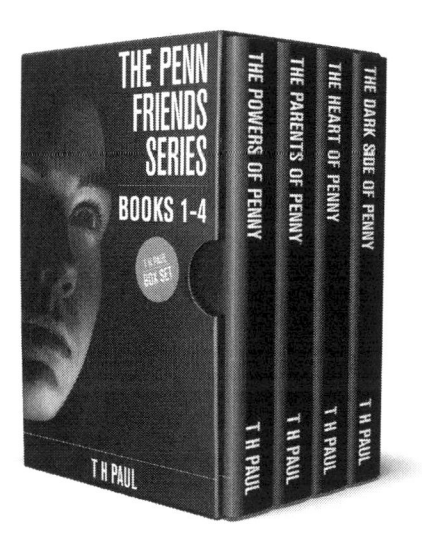

Penn Friends Series (Books 1-4) — Season One Volume One

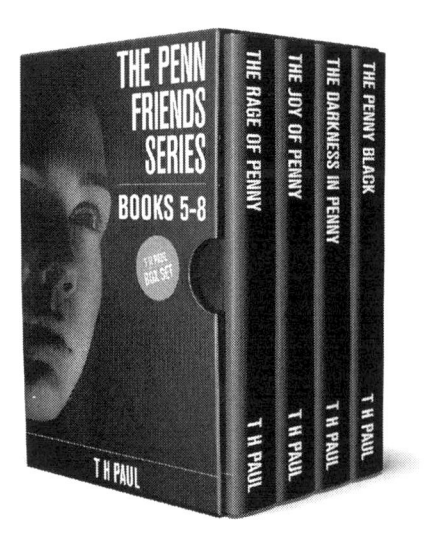

Penn Friends Series (Books 5-8) — Season One Volume Two

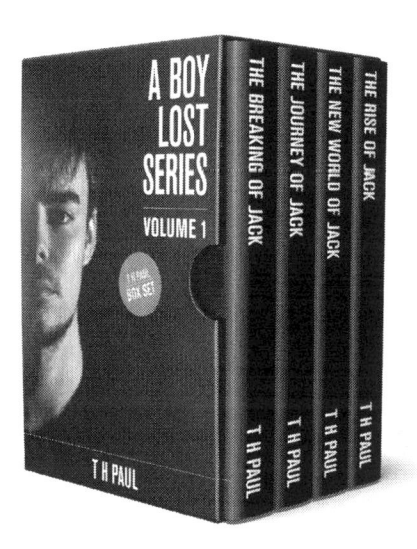

A Boy Lost Series (Books 1-4) — Season Two Volume One

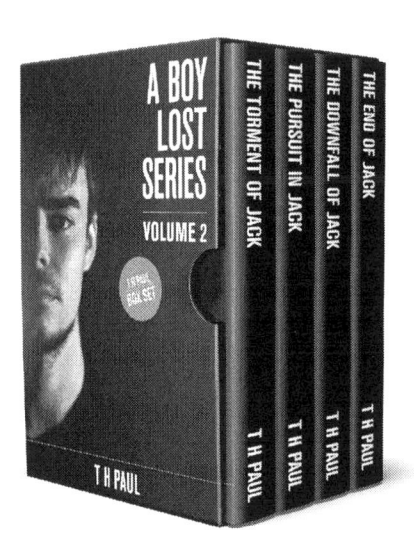

A Boy Lost Series (Books 5-8) — Season Two Volume Two

ABOUT THE AUTHOR

Tim has been married to his wife Rachel since 2001, and they have two daughters. He lives in Tallinn, Estonia, having moved there with his family in 2012 from St Petersburg, Russia, which they moved to in 2008. He is originally from Kent in England and lived for eight years in Cheshire, before moving abroad. As well as writing the novels that are already published (plus the one or two that are always in the process of being finished) Tim enjoys being outdoors, exploring Estonia, cooking and spending time with his family.

For more information:
www.timheathbooks.com
tim@timheathbooks.com

facebook.com/TimHeathAuthor
instagram.com/timheathauthor
amazon.com/author/timheath
bookbub.com/authors/tim-heath
twitter.com/TimHeathBooks
goodreads.com/TimHeath
youtube.com/TimHeath

Printed in Poland
by Amazon Fulfillment
Poland Sp. z o.o., Wrocław